I0733329

The Little Library

Kim Fielding

This is a work of fiction. Names, characters, places, and incidents are either the product of the author's imagination or are used fictitiously. Any resemblance to actual persons living or dead, business establishments, events, or locales is entirely coincidental. All person(s) depicted on the cover are model(s) used for illustrative purposes only.

The Little Library
Copyright © 2018 by Kim Fielding

Cover art: L.C. Chase, lcchase.com/design.htm
Editors: Sarah Lyons and Chris Muldoon
Layout: L.C. Chase, lcchase.com/design.htm

All rights reserved. No part of this book may be reproduced or transmitted in any form or by any means, electronic or mechanical, including photocopying, recording, or by any information storage and retrieval system without the written permission of the copyright owner, and where permitted by law. Reviewers may quote brief passages in a review.

First edition
March, 2018

ABOUT THE EBOOK YOU HAVE PURCHASED:
Thank you very much for purchasing this title. Your nonrefundable purchase legally allows you to replicate this file for your own personal reading only, on your own personal computer or device. Unlike paperback books, sharing ebooks is the same as stealing them. Please do not violate the author's copyright and harm their livelihood by sharing or distributing this book, in part or whole, for a fee or free, without the prior written permission of the copyright owner. Your honesty and support are appreciated.

The Little Library

Kim Fielding

*To my wonderful readers, who perhaps share my belief that
we can find much happiness in books.*

Table of Contents

# Chapter One

"**Dr.** Thompson," said the stern woman on Elliott's laptop screen, "you left what seemed to be a promising career at a research university and have spent the past two years teaching at a community college and online instead. And you moved from Washington State to somewhere in the middle of California?"

His heart thudding, Elliott kept his expression neutral as he nodded.

"What prompted this sudden and drastic change?" she asked.

Despite his churning stomach and the heat that rose to his cheeks, he managed to speak evenly. "There were personal reasons."

Up until this point, the job interview had seemed to be going well. They had covered his teaching philosophy and classroom leadership style. He'd talked about his particular research interests within the history field. But now, if he could judge from the expression on the search-committee member's face, Marge had googled him on the device she was trying to hide on her lap.

"Personal reasons?" she parroted, raising an eyebrow and ignoring a withering look from the committee chair.

While she smirked, Elliott loosened his tie, pulled it over his head, and tossed it off to the side. Then he unfastened the top button of his scratchy new dress shirt. Neither action made breathing any easier, but at least he didn't feel like such a huge idiot.

Elliott caught the committee chair's uneasy gaze. "There was a . . . scandal. Some legal issues. I was cleared eventually, but the university and I decided it was best if we parted ways. And now that the issue is far behind me, I'd really like to resume my academic career. Online teaching is okay, but I miss personal interactions with students and opportunities for research. I'm only thirty-six, and I have a lot of career years ahead of me."

"I see," said the chair. He picked up a pen, clicked it open, then clicked it closed again. He cleared his throat. "Well, we'll be concluding the rest of our Skype interviews this week, and then we'll be, um, contacting the finalists for on-campus interviews. Thanks for chatting with us today."

"Thank you. It's been a pleasure," Elliott lied. He didn't bother to say anything about hoping to hear back from them, because he knew he wouldn't.

When the Skype session ended, Elliott slammed his laptop shut with more force than wisdom and slumped in his chair. Fuck. Why had he ever thought this would work? At one point, he'd actually considered changing his name so his past would be less accessible to the Marges of the world. But his transcripts and diplomas would still say Elliott Thompson, and explaining the discrepancy would only raise more red flags.

His stomach made a sudden alarming flip. He lurched from his chair and stumbled to the bathroom, where he barely made it to the toilet before puking. Then he sat on the cold tile floor, feeling miserable. His parents and brother had been nagging him for months about seeing a therapist and maybe trying antianxiety meds. As if it were that easy. Elliott currently lacked insurance to pay for a therapist, and his settlement from the university stretched only so far. Besides, he didn't want to talk to anyone about what had happened, especially not a stranger.

It wasn't until he'd hauled himself upright and rinsed his mouth at the sink that Elliott remembered he had plans tonight—a date, in fact. His brother, Ladd, had insisted on calling it anything but. "It's not *romance*," Ladd had said. "It's simply dinner with me and Anna and her coworker Kyle."

"Who happens to be gay and single, just as I'm gay and single."

"Yeah, sure, there's that. But this is a no-pressure thing. Anna says Kyle has no expectations of sweeping you off your feet or being swept off his. We're just going to try out that new Italian place downtown."

Somehow Elliott had let himself be persuaded, maybe so Ladd would shut up for a while. It was true that Elliott's dating life had been almost nonexistent recently, but that was nothing new. He'd never been a social butterfly. And his actual sex life? Well, some decent porn, a few toys, and his right hand sufficed. Mostly. They certainly provided simpler options than the alternatives.

He made up his mind to text Ladd and cancel.

But by the time he made it to his phone in the living room, Elliott was feeling foolish. It *was* just dinner. He could handle it. He'd duck out as soon as the bill was paid, and then he'd be able to put off his meddling relatives for a few months at least.

What he ought to do was clear his mind with some exercise. And not with the weights he kept in the spare bedroom. Today's autumn weather was lovely, with just a hint of crispness in the air. He would go for a run, damn it.

It felt wonderful to shed the dress shirt and put on a T-shirt instead. Under the assumption that the hiring committee would see him only from the chest up, he was wearing jeans rather than slacks. After a moment's consideration about what clothes the weather called for, he changed to shorts. He and John used to run together—one of the few activities they'd done in public, in fact. Now as Elliott laced his shoes, he wondered whether John was allowed to jog in prison.

"Motherfucker," Elliott mumbled in a vain attempt to ward off the usual burst of emotional pain. Then he strapped his phone into an armband and headed outside.

He'd bought this little house mostly because he could afford it. Rental costs in the area tended to be high compared to mortgages, and Ladd had convinced him that home ownership was a good investment. Even if a job opportunity forced Elliott to move, property values were increasing so rapidly that he'd likely turn a profit on the sale. The house had been in bad shape, and he'd put a lot of sweat equity into making it habitable. It still had a lot of annoying quirks, and the to-do list daunted him, but the house had some other benefits in addition to a reasonable mortgage. A privacy fence and some trees edged the good-sized backyard, where he intended to plant herbs, vegetables, and citrus in the sunny spots. Even better, the house was situated along a greenbelt and walking path, with nothing on the other side of the path but an irrigation canal backed by fields and orchards. Having the walkway so nearby was handy, as was his relative lack of neighbors.

He passed a few of those neighbors as he strode quickly along the path. He saw a young woman pushing a baby stroller, an older couple ambling side by side, and three students running in their high school T-shirts. A middle-aged woman had two yappy dogs on leashes. A guy on a bicycle zoomed by; *nice ass*, Elliott noted. He exchanged nods with most people and *hellos* with a few, but nobody interrupted the *Radiolab* podcast he was listening to.

Maybe he should sell his place here in Modesto and buy a house in the Sierras. A one-room cabin with a little porch where he'd sit and be visited—like Snow fucking White—by deer and birds and squirrels and friendly bears. He would wear nothing but denim and flannel, he'd grow a beard halfway down his chest, and he would communicate with the outer world only twice a year, when he'd hike down the mountain for supplies.

Elliott was so caught up in this daydream—now analyzing whether he'd have to learn to ski—that he nearly collided with a man traveling in the other direction. He was a big man, taller than Elliott and solid. Muscular, yes, but also with a bit of a belly. His biceps stretched the sleeves of his T-shirt, and his thick thighs strained his sweatpants. A sturdy brace supported one knee. He had dark hair, dark eyes, and a dark mustache and beard, neatly trimmed. If he hadn't been frowning so fiercely, he would have been devastatingly handsome.

"Sorry," Elliott mumbled, dancing out of the way. He almost tripped over the man's cane.

The man smiled slightly. Sure enough, he was gorgeous. "Nah, my fault. Not really used to this fucking thing yet." He shook the cane as if he wanted to murder it.

"I should watch where I'm going."

"We can both practice our movement skills, I guess."

Elliott laughed politely, nodded once, and continued on his way. When he turned the corner near his house, his heart sank. The guy who lived across the street stood in Elliott's driveway, scowling at the walkway to the front door. Elliott had interacted with Mike Burgess only a handful of times since moving into the neighborhood two years ago. Once, Burgess had rung the doorbell to complain that Elliott's front lawn needed cutting. Another time, he'd bitched about the mail carrier, who didn't deliver early enough for Burgess's taste. When

Elliott was having some electrical work done in his garage, Burgess had come over to remind him he wasn't supposed to park his car on the street, even though the street dead-ended right past Elliott's house. Burgess was like one of those cranky old people who chased kids out of their front yard, except he probably wasn't any older than Elliott.

"Hi," Elliott said mildly when he was close enough, although he'd have preferred to just ignore him.

Burgess didn't bother with a greeting. "The CC&Rs prohibit signs in front yards," he said. "Except political advertisements, which can be displayed only for the seven days preceding an election."

Elliott wondered if the guy had the subdivision's covenants, codes, and restrictions tattooed on his ass. "I don't have any signs."

Burgess pointed in the general direction of the front door.

"That's not a sign," said Elliott. "It's a garden ornament." The tin rectangle depicting a curvaceous woman and purporting to advertise Dirty Hoe Garden Supply was a recent gift from his brother.

"It has words on it," Burgess insisted.

"Well, yeah. But it's decorative. It's a joke, right? Dirty hoe?"

Burgess shook his head. "It's a sign, and the CC&Rs prohibit it."

Elliott's head hurt. "Fine. I'll take it down. But this is stupid." Burgess stood there, hands on hips, until Elliott yanked the thin metal post from the soil and stalked inside. He slammed the door and locked it, then tossed the ornament aside, ignoring the dirt it left on the carpet. He'd put it somewhere in the backyard later.

Now as he stood in the entryway, he couldn't breathe. He was alone in the house, yet he could still hear Marge's triumphant interrogation and Burgess's demands. He could hear his former department chair's accusations, the snide comments of his former colleagues, the flat tones of police officers and lawyers. He could even hear John Davis, first pleading with him and then shouting. The voices were deafening. He wanted to cover his ears with his hands. No, he wanted to climb into bed, pull the covers over his head, and shut out the world.

His heart was beating too fast, and his lungs felt tight. His *skin* felt tight.

With his eyes squeezed shut, he counted slowly to ten, then back to zero. Out loud, like a crazy person. But it calmed him enough to function instead of curling into a fetal ball.

Elliott pulled his phone out of the armband and texted Ladd. *Canceling for tonight. Sorry. Just not up to it.* Then he turned off the volume and tossed the phone onto the couch.

He walked to his desk, sat down, and woke up his laptop. After a long time spent staring blankly at the screen, he found himself typing the one URL that universally soothed him. The webpage came up to tempt him with items from his wish list and Recommendations for You.

For the better part of an hour, he gazed at covers, perused blurbs, and skimmed reviews. He often took up the offer to Look Inside. Sometimes he rejected a book, sometimes he added it to his wish list, and sometimes he strayed off the page, following the "customers who bought this also bought" trail. But sometimes he clicked on Add to Cart. He watched the little orange number near the top right of his screen gradually tick upward. Each time he browsed a new book, and especially with every addition to his cart, the constriction around his lungs eased a bit more.

When his breathing had returned to normal, he clicked the yellow Place Your Order button. And then he buried his face in his hands and tried to hold himself together.

Chapter Two

Ladd dropped by a few days later and moved a pile of books off the couch so he could sit. "You've got a problem here, El."

Elliott was sitting in his armchair. "I'll build some more shelves," he said defensively.

"Wasn't what I meant. Although yeah, that's an issue too." He looked around doubtfully. "Where the hell are you going to put more shelves?"

He had a point. All the living room wall space was filled, and bookshelves crowded the master bedroom and the guest room. There was even one in the tiny dining room, although that was full of gardening guides and cookbooks, which seemed fair enough.

"I was thinking maybe the garage," Elliott said. That could work if he got a little shed for his garden tools, freeing up the second stall in the garage. His Honda didn't take up that much room.

"Jesus, El."

"They're books. Books are good."

"Didja ever hear of the Collyer brothers?" Ladd leaned back in his seat.

"No."

"They were these eccentric recluses in New York in . . . I don't know. The forties, I think. One of them was sick and the other one took care of him. They filled their house with books and other crap. Then one day someone reports a bad smell coming from the house. Cops show up and discover the sick one—only now he's dead. No sign of the older one, and people figure maybe he took off. But two weeks later they found him too, also dead, and not far from where his brother had been. Turns out he got buried when a bunch of their books and crap fell on him, and then his brother starved."

"That's a lovely story."

Ladd grinned. "Isn't it? If I ever have kids, I plan to tell it to them at bedtime."

"I'm not a hoarder. Nothing is going to bury me."

"Okay, maybe not. But do you really need all these books?"

"Yes." Elliott had considered converting to e-books, but he found the reality of paper soothing. He even liked the musty smell of the volumes he bought at used-book stores and thrift shops. And okay, yes, maybe he did have a lot of books. But there were certainly far worse addictions for a person to have.

Perhaps taking in Elliott's defensive posture, Ladd sighed. "I didn't come here to nag you about your literary obsession."

"What did you come to nag about, then?"

"You backed out of dinner the other night."

"Yeah. I'm sorry. It was shitty of me, okay?"

Ladd shrugged. "I'm not pissed off at you, man. I'm worried."

Fuck. They'd been leading up to this conversation for months. Part of Elliott wanted to yell and toss Ladd out the door. Elliott was a grown-ass man who didn't need other people digging into his business. Except . . . maybe he kind of *did* need that, considering what a mess he'd made of his life. And he knew Ladd loved him and wanted the best for him. Maybe Ladd—eleven months his senior—felt as if he owed Elliott some guidance, seeing as Elliott had given him tons of semi-wanted advice when they were younger. Elliott had been the more analytical brother.

"I know I'm fucking things up," Elliott said, not meeting Ladd's gaze. "I know I'm a disaster. You don't have to tell me."

"Not a disaster. Exactly. More of a fixer-upper."

"Great. I'm a mess. Which I'm well aware of, so you don't need to remind me."

"I didn't come over here to rub your face in it." Scowling, Ladd picked up a nearby book and scanned the cover. "*The Handmaid's Tale.* I've heard of this one. Didn't they make a movie of it or something?"

"I don't know. Probably."

With a pained expression, Ladd set the book aside. "I just don't think you're doing yourself any favors with the hermit act. I know you've had a rough time of things. It . . . it sucks, okay? But you lock yourself in here with nobody but yourself and you forget about the big picture."

"What is the big picture?" Elliott failed to keep the derision from his voice.

Ladd waved his arms in a wide arc. "Everything outside this house is the big picture. Life itself is the big picture. Like right now the trees up in the Sierras are starting to turn color. It'd be a great time to hit Calaveras for an easy hike." That was the good thing about Ladd—well, one of the good things. Sometimes his glass-is-half-fullness made Elliott want to strangle him, but most of the time, Elliott was grateful for his brother's forgiving and optimistic nature.

Elliott grunted, still unconvinced.

"And there's love. You're a great guy, El, and someone out there is going to be really lucky to meet you. Somebody who's not a manipulative fuck-head. If you don't want to believe in love, what about sex? Plain and simple sex, no strings attached. When's the last time you got laid?"

"None of your business. And fucking someone isn't going to fix everything."

Ladd hopped up from the couch and began to pace. "No shit. But it doesn't have to fix everything, does it? It just has to make you feel good. Get some of those good juices flowing in your brain for a while. Endorphins or whatever."

"And when the juices go away?"

"Then you find something else. You move on. You don't wall—" Ladd stopped himself and looked slightly abashed.

"Wallow. That's what you were going to say."

"It was a shitty word choice. I don't have a PhD, remember? I'm not the goddamn professor."

"Neither am I. Not anymore," Elliott said with a sigh.

"Well, word choice aside, the point stands." Ladd shook his head. "And self-pity's not a good look on you, bro."

Elliott couldn't argue with that; he knew Ladd was right. He *was* wallowing. He *was* moaning around, feeling sorry for himself. But stomping through the woods or swiping on Grindr wasn't going to help.

"Maybe I've seen my big picture and it looks like an Edvard Munch painting," he said. "Or Edward Hopper."

Ladd stopped pacing to squint at him. "Wasn't Hopper the guy who painted that grumpy-looking couple with the rake?"

"*American Gothic*? No, that was Grant Wood, and it was a pitchfork. I was thinking of Hopper's *Nighthawks*. It shows— Oh, what the hell difference does it make *what* it shows?" The problem with arguing with Ladd was that somehow Elliott always found himself sidetracked. Or going around in useless circles like a dog chasing its tail. "What do you want from me?" he asked after a long pause.

"Give me just a little bit, okay? Don't change your life. Just try *one* thing outside your comfort zone, just for a few hours."

"Like dinner with that Kyle guy?"

That earned him a grin. "If you want."

"He doesn't hate me already for canceling the other day?"

"I don't think so. I told you, that wasn't a date anyway."

Elliott closed his eyes briefly. "Fine. I'll go on a not-date with him; then you leave me alone."

"I am *never* going to leave you alone, Elliott. What's the point of being your brother if I can't annoy you?"

"But I get to annoy you back."

"Deal."

Two minutes after Ladd left, Elliott almost texted him to cancel. But that would be chickenshit. And next time Ladd might come with reinforcements—like Anna. So Elliott put the phone away and tried to occupy himself. Sitting down at his laptop, he logged in to the course management software.

He was teaching three online courses this semester, one on California history and two on ancient civilizations. His expertise was actually the twentieth-century Balkans, but such a class would appeal to very few students. Most Americans couldn't find the Balkans on a map and didn't care who'd been killing whom over there. California colleges always needed instructors for their large general ed courses. His specialty, an area that wasn't well studied in the United States, had been John's idea. He'd lured Elliott away from his initial academic dabblings in the American West. Elliott had been a dewy-eyed grad student, interested in human conflict in general, as if by studying it he might prevent it. And John Davis had been there to take Elliott under his wing. And into his bed.

So. He was left with California and everyone's old pals: Mesopotamia, Egypt, Greece, and Rome. He didn't have much original to say about them, but then, nobody was asking him for originality anyway. He just needed to make sure his syllabi matched his courses' learning objectives. Make sure the students could parrot back appropriate dates, rulers, place names. Make sure his retention and pass rates were reasonable and hope none of the students left him crappy evaluations. This was what his life had come down to.

"No self-pity," he said aloud as he clicked and brought up the latest batch of student assignments. At least he had a nice place to live and a job that helped cover the bills. At least he had family that cared about him. At least, unlike a goodly proportion of the sophomores in his California class, he knew that California did not become a state in 1776 nor was it originally settled by the Pilgrims.

By the time he'd finished grading the assignments, his shoulders felt stiff and his mood had darkened. He didn't like teaching online. It took away the joy of seeing that moment when a student finally got it, the fun of discussing issues that arose unexpectedly in the classroom, the pleasure of chatting informally with students after class or during office hours. He used to like getting to know his students as people—this one with the funny laugh and the hair that changed colors weekly, that one with the son who'd recently been diagnosed with autism. Now his students were nothing more than the college's unimaginative login names. Aperez84. Tsilviera51. And their online communications told him little about them personally, except that they had appalling grammar and punctuation.

"You need to get out of here," he told himself as he pushed away from the desk. He stood a few moments, considering whether to take his own advice, then headed to his bedroom. There he changed into exercise clothes and slipped on his armband.

He frowned at his front yard as he left the house. Without that silly little sign, the space looked as boring and cheerless as Mike Burgess's yard. Burgess had landscaped with water-wasting grass, a couple of big rocks, and those nondescript bushes apparently beloved by the subdivision's developers. A generic yard, a generic house. Just like Elliott's generic classes with generic students. It was as if the world were being slowly overtaken by robots and nobody cared enough to notice.

The greenbelt was nearly deserted this afternoon, probably due to temperatures that felt more like summer than fall. The fence lizards were happy, basking on the pavement and scurrying away from Elliott as he jogged. A mockingbird sang from atop a power line and, when Elliott passed by some crepe myrtles in bloom, a hummingbird buzzed him indignantly. Although Elliott wasn't running quickly today, the movement—and probably the change of scenery—helped lighten his mood a bit. It was really hard to stay mad at the world while dodging a pissed-off hummingbird.

He slowed his pace to a stroll, the better to extend his time outdoors. His spirits lifted even more when he recognized the man walking slowly in his direction. It was the handsome guy he'd collided with a couple of days before—the one with the cane and the knee brace—and today he wore shorts that showed off his powerful legs and a tank top that displayed the musculature of his shoulders and upper arms. He'd tied his hair into a tiny ponytail, but a few strands had escaped. And although his walking looked painful, his smile widened as he and Elliott neared each other.

"You had a run-in with El Diablo," said the man as he drew close.

"Who?"

"That bird. I think he's got a nest in one of those trees." His voice was deep, but the softness surprised Elliott again.

"Yeah. He's fierce."

"He's not scared of anyone. Last week I saw him chase away a crow, and he dive-bombs me every time I pass." The man chuckled. "You looked like you were doing some kind of dance."

"I didn't want him to . . . Well, I'm not sure what kind of damage he might inflict."

"Pointy beak. He could skewer your eye. Or worse. One of 'em took out my knee." He gestured at the bulky brace on his left leg.

"Shit! Seriously?"

The man threw back his head and laughed. "No! But it's kind of funny to picture, isn't it?"

Elliott imagined a tiny bird circling this large man like a miniature Sopwith Camel, and he laughed too. God, when had he last done that?

"Maybe next time I should bring something to defend myself with. A shield? Armor?"

"Yeah, sure. You go jogging around this neighborhood in chain mail and see how far you get before someone calls the cops."

"It's probably not the best thing to exercise in either," Elliott added.

The man mopped his forehead with the back of a hand. "Nope. You'll sweat and rust up, and then you'll be like the Tin Man, only with no Dorothy in sight." He shrugged. "Maybe I should carry an oilcan from now on. Just in case."

"I'd appreciate that."

Banter. That was what this was. He used to banter, now and then, with colleagues in the department copy room or before department meetings. They'd lightly tease one another about their coffee-drinking habits or the condition of their offices, and although he hadn't socialized with any of them outside of work, he'd considered them casual friends. Until the shit hit the fan, of course, and every one of them had turned away from him.

Elliott must have frowned, because the smile disappeared from the other man's face. "Well, you probably want to get back to running," he said.

Elliott didn't want that, not especially, but he nodded. "Enjoy your walk. Watch out for El Diablo."

"Will do."

And they continued on their way, each at his own speed.

Elliott jogged for another half mile before circling back home. By the time he reached his street, he was parched and overheated, daydreaming of a cold drink, a cold shower, and a nap under an air-conditioning vent. But he paused before he reached his porch. His front garden needed something, damn it. He'd planted lavender and geraniums, and they lit up the space in purple, pink, and orange. But they wouldn't bloom all winter.

An idea hit him and caused a sly grin.

Inside the house, he drank a tall glass of cool water and took a quick shower. But instead of napping, he grabbed a beer from the fridge and sat in front of his laptop. Like a horse who knew its way home, his browser faithfully took him straight to Amazon.

The words *rainbow flag* in the search box brought over two thousand results. After some consideration, he decided that two by three feet was bigger than he wanted, and he didn't want any of the variations, like the one with the California bear or the one with the Coexist symbols. No stars, and no words at all, because verbiage might technically violate the stupid no-sign rule. Just stripes from red to purple.

There. Twelve by eighteen, with an included metal stand. Fifteen bucks and free one-day shipping, because of course Elliott was a Prime member. Smiling, he added it to his shopping cart.

But before he could check out, he found himself scrolling down to Featured Recommendations. The website was suggesting he might also want an American flag or one with a smiling ghost, which he didn't. Yet there, next to the flags? Oh. An exploration of the plight of the white working class in the rust belt. A memoir by Oliver Sacks's partner. A novel about a maimed Civil War veteran.

Almost of its own accord, his finger clicked Add to Cart three more times and then, very quickly, Place Your Order.

That felt good. A release a little like an orgasm. Except when he looked around the living room and saw his overflowing shelves and the stacks on the furniture and even on the floor, shame washed over him in a bitter wave.

Ladd was right—Elliott was well on his way to becoming a Collyer brother. One of these days, he was going to end up buried under hardcovers, and nobody would notice until Mike Burgess went outside to snoop and caught the foul stench of death emanating from Elliott's sign-free house.

Fine. He'd make a pledge right now. "I, Elliott Samuel Thompson, solemnly swear to a book-buying moratorium, which shall last one year." There. The books he already owned would last him at least that long.

But then a thought hit him. "Textbooks are excepted from the moratorium. And, um, books I need for research." Which was a shitty cop-out because he could justify almost *anything* as research if he tried hard enough. Which he undoubtedly would.

He needed to find a different way to protect himself from a literary avalanche—and from his brother's badgering. Maybe it would help if he got rid of the books he'd already read. That would free up a lot of space. He could donate them to charity or to the library. He pictured the volumes as if they were puppies going to good homes all over Stanislaus County, their covers petted lovingly by their new owners. But what if nobody wanted his books? What if the volumes languished in the twenty-five-cent bin at a thrift store or, worse yet, got sent to the landfill? Just the idea made him shudder.

If he *had* been breeding dogs, he could investigate potential adopters, scoping out their home lives and suitability for his breed. He couldn't do that with books, though; once they left his hands, he had no control over them at all. Too bad he couldn't run his own library. Then he could lend his books to carefully selected patrons, a cultured few whom he could trust to not spill things on the jackets or dog-ear the pages.

As he sat at his desk, smiling at this ridiculous scenario, he suddenly remembered a trip he'd taken to San Francisco four years earlier. At the time, he'd still had his comfortable tenure-track job in Washington State. He and John had flown to San Francisco, ostensibly to attend a conference—and in fact, they'd each presented a paper. But they'd spent most of their visit far from the conference Marriott, holed up together in a funky little hotel near Lands End. It was the perfect getaway, with nobody at work questioning a thing. Colleagues went to conferences together all the time. But that wasn't the point right now.

Just down the hill from that hotel lay the ruins of the Sutro Baths, now part of the Golden Gate Recreational Area. Elliott and John had spent several happy hours wandering around the decaying concrete structures, walking through the old pedestrian tunnel, and watching the waves pound beneath Cliff House. As they'd cut back through the parking lot toward their hotel, Elliott had spotted a wooden box perched atop a post. The box was painted green and orange and had a slanted roof, a bit like a birdhouse, and a plexiglass front door. Instructions were in white hand lettering: *Free books. Take one now, leave one later.*

"What is this?" Elliott had asked, peering in through the plexiglass.

"A miniature neighborhood library."

"What?"

Eager to return to their room—or, more specifically, to the bed—John tugged at Elliott's arm. "C'mon, El."

But Elliott stood his ground and, after pulling his arm free, opened the door. The box contained four books: a thick historical novel set in medieval England, a children's chapter book about dragons, a spy thriller, and, fittingly, a well-worn travel guide to Northern California.

"Do you know anything about this library?" he asked.

John huffed and put his hands on his hips before answering. "It's a . . . I don't know. A movement? An organization. People build these things, stick them where they're accessible, and fill them with books. It works on the honor system." His sour expression reflected his opinion; John had never been much for trusting others. Maybe because he was such a sneaky shit himself, although Elliott hadn't yet come to that realization.

"So anyone can just take a book?"

"Yup. In theory, you either return it when you're done or replace it with one of your own."

"Huh." Elliott would have taken one of the books—probably the historical novel—but John grabbed him again and yanked harder, and Elliott had allowed himself to be towed away. He hadn't really minded. He'd been enjoying the stolen few days with John, one of the few opportunities he had to appear with John in public. Hell, they'd strolled through the city together, and as long as they were well away from the conference, they'd even held hands.

Now John was in prison, and Elliott sat in his living room gazing at the books that surrounded him. A miniature neighborhood library. That was just what he needed.

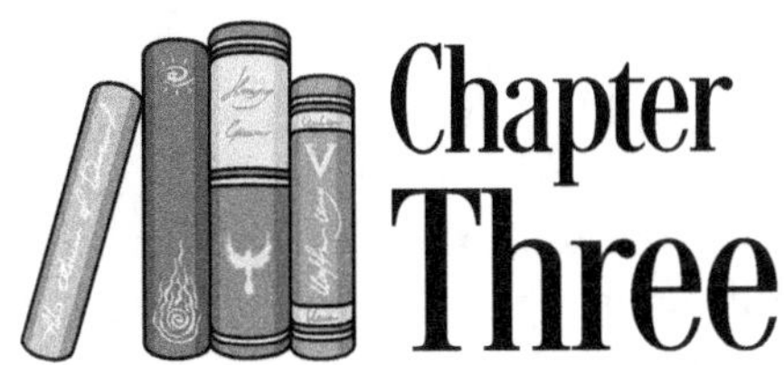

Chapter
Three

"We're building a what?"

Ladd had that expression again—the one Elliott had seen a lot lately. It meant Ladd was questioning his brother's sanity.

"A library."

Ladd bit his lip and rubbed his neck, clearly in search of an inoffensive way to suggest that psychiatric services might be in order.

But Elliott held him off with a raised hand. "A tiny library. Like this." He walked to the kitchen table and retrieved the photos he'd printed off the internet.

"Oh." Ladd studied the pictures. "Okay. Some of these are kind of adorable. Look! This one's a robot."

You could buy premade libraries or kits, but Elliott was relatively handy with a hammer and saw. Besides, this would give them the chance for some brotherly bonding time, which might help ease Ladd's fears.

"I think we'll start with something a little plainer, though." Elliott handed him the plans for the model he intended to make.

"Probably wise." Ladd looked over the construction details. "But why are we doing this?"

"It'll help me get rid of a little of my . . . excess."

Ladd cast a significant look at the books piled everywhere around them and then held up the plans. "This thing's gonna hold, what? Maybe twenty books max? That doesn't even make a tiny dent."

"It's a start, okay?"

After a pause, Ladd shrugged philosophically. "Fine. I guess anything's a help."

Elliott had prepared everything before Ladd arrived. He'd gone to the home improvement store and, when he returned with supplies, had parked the car in the driveway. He'd dragged his workbench into the middle of the garage so he and Ladd would have more space to maneuver. And he'd set out all the tools they'd need. That was satisfying in itself; he hadn't really used any of his tools since he and Ladd had completed the major house renovations.

With the White Stripes playing in the background, Elliott and Ladd soon settled into a comfortable routine. They were well practiced at this kind of thing, even if they hadn't worked together lately. When they were kids, they used to draft elaborate designs—miniature castles, gravity racers, space ships—and build them from plywood and scraps. Elliott had usually had the patience for the intricate finish painting, while Ladd had climbed their creations or rode them down the street to test their integrity. Multiple trips to the urgent care center hadn't stopped them. And when a grown-up Elliott bought a house that had been trashed by renters, Ladd had been happy to help him fix it up.

"So what's really the deal with this library?" Ladd penciled a line onto a board.

Elliott was trying to find the right size drill bit. "I told you. To get rid of—"

"Bullshit."

Fine. "I don't know. It just . . . seemed like something new, I guess. Something that wasn't just me feeling sorry for myself."

"I don't think you are, really. Feeling sorry for yourself, I mean. Hey, where's your router?"

Elliott pointed at a shelf. "If I'm not feeling sorry for myself, what am I doing?"

At first Ladd didn't answer. He fetched the router, plugged it into an extension cord, and set up the jig on the workbench. Then, tongue peeking slightly between his lips, he carefully cut a dado into the plywood. Holding the wood up, he blew away the bits of sawdust, inspected the groove, and nodded with satisfaction. "You're blaming yourself," he finally said.

"For what?"

"For not being perfect. For doing some dumb shit. El, I know you hate to admit it, but you are not some kind of . . . advanced being. You make mistakes sometimes. Welcome to humankind."

"I don't think I'm advanced." Elliott scowled.

"No, but you think that just because you're super smart, you can't do dumb shit. But you can. You do. Everybody does. I bet Einstein fucked things up too, now and then." He glanced up from the wood, which he'd set back on the workbench. "You gotta forgive yourself, man."

Elliott finally found the right drill bit and set the others aside. "Since when did you become a shrink?" he asked sourly.

"Since they got me teaching psychology this semester. Incidentally, you want amusement? Try discussing penis envy with thirty-five high school juniors."

"Ugh."

"No, it's fun."

It didn't take them much longer to assemble the library's main structure. They still needed to wait for the glue to dry before they could paint it, and in the meantime they would dig the hole for the support post. But first Elliott fetched a couple of bottles of beer. Ladd stood and drank his while Elliott cleaned up the debris from their project.

Just as Elliott was about to propose ordering pizza, the mail truck stopped at the end of the driveway and the driver got out, carrying a box. "Wish I could offer you some beer," Elliott said as the carrier handed over the box.

"Me too! I'm tired of the heat and ready for cooler weather for sure."

"Can I get you a bottle of water?"

Smiling, he shook his head. "No, thanks. I'm good." He walked back to his truck and drove away.

The box contained part of Elliott's purchase from the previous day—the flag and the metal stand. Ladd watched with amusement while Elliott unwrapped and assembled them. "Flag-waving now?"

"Just decorating." With Ladd trailing along behind, Elliott walked to the front of the house, considered for a moment, and then stuck the flag into the soft soil of the flower garden. It looked good. He turned to Ladd. "That asshole neighbor insisted I take down the Dirty Hoe sign you gave me."

"Why?"

"It violates some kind of stupid rule."

"Seriously? And the flag's okay?"

"It had better be." Elliott muttered threats about the ACLU under his breath.

They finally ordered and ate a pizza—washing it down with another beer—and then, with the sun still searingly warm, they fetched the posthole digger and began to excavate.

"I fucking hate hardpan," Ladd said when it was his turn.

"It hates us too." Despite wearing heavy gloves, Elliott had developed a blister on his palm. It stung when he flexed his hand.

Ladd paused, leaned the digger's handle against his leg, and peeled off his shirt, tossing it aside before returning to his task. When they were little kids, he'd been somewhat chubby, but the fat had turned to heavy muscle as he traveled through his teens. He'd ended up a high school sports star. Now, in addition to teaching whichever classes the principal threw his way, he coached the school football and baseball teams, tasks that kept him in excellent shape.

Always taller than Ladd, Elliott had been skinny up until college—the stereotypical string-bean nerd. He'd eventually taken up running with a bit of light weight-lifting on the side, but he remained lean. John used to say he liked Elliott's long, wiry body. But then, John had said a lot of things.

Ladd grunted as he worked the posthole digger. "Did I mention you're joining us for dinner next Saturday?"

"With that Kyle guy, I take it?"

"Yep. No excuses. We're going to that Cajun Vietnamese place."

"Seriously? You want me to eat a crab boil on a first date? First dates should never involve bibs and plastic gloves."

"That's kinky." Ladd flashed a grin. "And anyway, it's not a date, remember? It's a noncommittal social experience."

Elliott snorted and was going to tell Ladd exactly what he could do with his social experience, but then he spied someone turning the corner onto his block. It was that hot guy from the greenbelt, again wearing a tank top and slowly walking with his cane. Ladd didn't notice—he was too busy swearing at the resistant soil—but Elliott waved when the man drew closer.

"Hi," the guy said. He paused on the sidewalk nearby, his gaze traveling between Elliott and Ladd. He had an odd expression Elliott couldn't read. But he sounded pleasant enough when he chuckled and gestured at the hole in the lawn. "Digging for gold or bodies?"

"Neither." Elliott hoped. "At least I don't think so. Unless they built the subdivision on top of an old burial ground."

"*They're here*!" Ladd chimed in, using a spooky high-pitched voice.

They all laughed. "For your sake, I'll hope for gold," said the man. Then he gestured at the rainbow flag. "Are you installing a larger version of that?" He was smiling as if the notion made him happy.

Elliott shook his head. "Nope. At least not today. Hey, I'm Elliott Thompson, by the way. The big galoot over there is Ladd."

"Simon Odisho." He shook hands with Elliott, and Elliott pretended the contact neither hurt his blister nor made him feel a bit giddy. Ladd just waved a gloved hand. "I'll let you guys get back to your excavating," Simon said. Then he pointed at his knee. "I've got two miles to go on this thing today." After a few short pleasantries, he hobbled away.

"You can put your tongue back in your mouth," Ladd said. At least he had waited until Simon was out of earshot.

"I'm not—"

"You can't protest while you're still watching him, man."

With a twinge of regret, Elliott turned away. "He has a nice ass," he mumbled.

It wasn't until the next day, Sunday, that the paint was dry enough for Elliott to mount the library onto the post. He took a few minutes to critically examine the finished product. Nice. The design was simple, just a miniature house with a sloped roof, but most of it matched the burgundy of his front door, while the trim was the same beige as his house's exterior walls. The lettering on the roof and side was also beige, and he'd used stencils to get it perfect. *Mini Neighborhood Library. Take one, leave one.* Maybe he'd plant something around the base of the post—purple and white alyssum, perhaps. Late October was still a good time to get things in the ground.

Satisfied that the library was ready for occupancy, he went inside for the next task—the most important and the most difficult. It was time to choose which books to leave outside.

He'd actually been mulling over this topic since he decided to build the library, and he'd already come to a few decisions. No textbooks or academic books on obscure subjects nobody but him cared about. No books on cooking, gardening, or home improvement. He wanted to provide literature and quality nonfiction, not how-to. None of the yaoi books he'd squirreled away in his bedroom. He didn't want some little kid to pick one up, thinking it was an ordinary comic, and then be confused or horrified.

But even those criteria left him with hundreds of volumes to choose from. With a beer in hand to fortify himself, he began to peruse his shelves and stacks.

The first several choices were surprisingly easy. Two of them, both sci-fi, were titles he'd accidentally bought twice. Another was an omnibus collection of Mark Twain stories, most of which were duplicated in his other holdings. One book was a translation of Aeschylus's *Oresteia*, left over from his college days and never touched since. And one was the first in a series about vampire cowboys. He hadn't enjoyed it enough to read the next installment.

He set those five books aside and reckoned he still had space for ten more. But those presented a much bigger challenge. It was important to choose titles that might appeal to his neighbors, yet he wanted an interesting variation in genres. And it turned out that parting with each of his beloved books was a bit like giving away a favorite pet.

Okay. A couple of different volumes of *The Year's Best Fantasy and Horror*. He could spare those. Ivo Andric's fictional portrayal of Bosnian history was wonderful, but Elliott had read it three times, so it could go. One of Neil Gaiman's novels—yeah, that one was painful to give up, but Elliott could handle it, mostly because he thought everyone should enjoy Gaiman. And a couple of Gabriel García Márquez's books, holdovers from when Elliott had gone through a serious magical realism phase.

The rest should be nonfiction. After considerable hesitation, and then a repeated holding of books and returning them to the shelves, he settled on something by Oliver Sacks, a biography of Justice Blackmun, an exploration of the microclimates in an average house—that one had creeped him out a little—and a history of dogs.

Which left him with room for, he estimated, only one more.

As if of its own accord, his hand reached for a familiar volume. *Balkan Ghosts*. It wasn't the most recent edition, which had been published near the end of the messy wars that had torn Yugoslavia apart. Instead, it was the original version, written when blood was still wet on the ground. This book, its jacket a little tattered around the edges, had been a gift from a faculty member to his favorite graduate student, an inducement to settle on the Balkans as a dissertation topic. Nothing was inscribed inside the book, no personal note at all—John had been too careful for that—but Elliott still remembered the thrill when the handsome prof had handed it to him. Had chosen *him* to receive the gift.

Elliott left *Balkan Ghosts* on the shelf and pulled the book next to it, even though it was another novel. It was *The Cellist of Sarajevo*, and Elliott had bought it for himself. It could go into the library.

Darkness had fallen, giving him a slightly furtive sense as he filled the library. He stepped back and took a long look. Yes. Good.

But when he went back inside, he felt oddly empty and bereft.

Chapter Four

Elliott liked to keep to a schedule. Although he could have completed his tasks whenever he liked, doing them at particular times made him feel less as if he was falling apart. He started every morning with coffee and a light breakfast and, three times a week, a date with his weight machine. Then he showered before logging in to his work accounts and reading panicky, barely literate emails from students. *What chapters where we supossed to read for the test?* Or *I turned the assignment in on time but now Blackboard is saying i didnt hand it in.* He pointed them to the parts of the syllabus that answered their questions, and he dealt with their various technical issues, although sometimes he needed more coffee before he could be patient about it.

Having conquered the emails, he next made sure his courses were up-to-date. Sometimes he tinkered with PowerPoints and other materials, and occasionally he recorded a lecture for the students to download. He prepared exams and assignments, then graded the ones the students had already completed. This generally took him well past lunchtime, which he ate in front of his laptop.

Every Tuesday, he dutifully scanned for new job openings and submitted his materials to any he was remotely qualified for. He wasn't picky about geographical location or type of institution, which meant he'd sent his CV everywhere from Alaska to Florida, from tiny private colleges to huge state universities. The only places he avoided were the types of religious schools that were apt to object to his being gay; he wouldn't go into the closet no matter how desperate he became. So far, he'd advanced to the phone interview stage three times, but never beyond. He kept on trying, though.

During the hottest months, he'd run early in the morning to avoid being roasted alive, but at this time of year, he jogged in late afternoon instead. If he had energy when he was done, he spent some time doing yard work. He hadn't done much with the backyard aside from keeping the grass mowed and the weeds tamed, but he hoped to begin some more ambitious projects in the spring. A shaded patio, maybe, and a xeriscape garden.

Unless his teaching duties were heavy, Elliott spent the evenings reading in front of the TV. And then, if the spirit moved him, watching some porn.

It would have been an exciting and fulfilling life—if he were eighty years old.

This week he added one minor task to his daily schedule: he checked the mini library. He did that twice a day, in fact. Once in the morning, on the off-chance someone had wandered the neighborhood in the wee hours, frantic to find new reading material. And once before dinner, when he walked to the mailbox across the street. Each visit had found the library untouched, and Elliott's heart had sunk a little more.

But on Thursday, returning from the mailbox with some bills and a catalog in hand, he'd been delighted to discover gaps on the wooden shelf. One of the fantasy/horror collections was gone, as was the dog book and the Gaiman novel. But even better, a new volume was there. It was a well-worn paperback.

He set his mail on the grass so he could examine the new book. It turned out to be a romance. He grinned at the cover, which featured an extremely buff shirtless man in tight jeans and chaps, his face hidden behind the brim of a Stetson. Rounding up cattle without a shirt on was probably dangerous—too much risk for sunburn, rope injuries, and the like. The model was very pretty, though.

With a sigh, Elliott returned the book to the shelf and shut the plexiglass door. He was tickled that someone had discovered the library and had gotten into the spirit enough to contribute a book of their own. He was not happy, though, that his biggest sexual thrill of the week involved ogling a fake cowboy on a paperback.

"His name's probably Brock Steele," Elliott said as he gathered his mail. "Or Rex Remington. He's a gruff billionaire who reveals his tender heart when he tames mustangs. And his love interest is Lark

Starr. She is a wild hellion who secretly wants to get married, have babies, and hold Tupperware parties. While wearing jewel-studded ball gowns, her chestnut mane tumbling over her bare shoulders."

Elliott looked around guiltily, but there were no neighbors to hear his blathering.

Inside the house, he tossed the mail onto the kitchen counter. Then he poked around inside the fridge and through the cupboard, trying to decide what to make for dinner. But instead of finding creative new ways with chicken breasts and pasta, he found himself thinking about that romance novel. It bothered him. Not because he had anything against the genre—every reader deserved to find his or her own joy—but because of that damned half-naked rancher and the no-doubt-clichéd relationship he eventually built with the beautiful but headstrong young woman. Did anyone in real life have love stories like that? Nobody he knew, that was for sure. Ladd and Anna had met in college when they sat next to each other in American Government. And Elliott and John . . . Well, nobody was going to write a romance about that shit.

But. People had written books about the diversity of love, hadn't they? And some of those stories were sitting on his shelves right now.

Temporarily abandoning his meal plans, Elliott strode into the living room. With barely any hesitation, he pulled two volumes: Paul Monette's memoir and *Maurice*. Then he trotted outside and slipped them into the empty spaces on the shelf. He'd made sure to put *Maurice* next to the cowboy, just because.

"There," he said as he closed the door. "Maybe Brock Steele will discover that he really prefers men, so he'll dump Lark and leave for the English countryside instead. Lark, on the other hand, is going to take a closer look at the local Tupperware representative, Scarlet St. Bouvais, and they'll end up running a lesbian dude ranch."

Elliott smiled as he went inside to rustle up some dinner.

By Friday afternoon, *Maurice* was gone, along with the Western romance and *A Hundred Years of Solitude*. Elliott grinned, imagining a Merchant and Ivory film starring a gay couple who lived near a cowboy who spoke only in Latin and was busily decoding prophetic manuscripts. Oscar material for sure.

Three new books had appeared: a volume in the Harry Potter series, a different paperback romance—this one with a half-naked man in a kilt—and a guide to photographing nature. Another interesting combination. He speculated on which of his neighbors had taken his books and who had left theirs. It could be anyone, though. A lot of people used his street on their way to the greenbelt. He spent the rest of the day feeling more optimistic than he had in ages, simply because his library was proving a modest success.

But by the time he woke up on Saturday, his mood had sailed toward gloomier shores. The library had nothing to do with it. His impending dinner obligation was the culprit. He liked Anna and enjoyed spending time with her and Ladd, and he was sure Kyle was a great guy. But he just didn't want this, even if it was officially a not-date. Meeting a new person, trying to make himself seem interesting and likable—those undertakings terrified him. Like bungee jumping off Mount Everest in the nude.

"Get a grip," he told himself as he choked down some breakfast. But he had trouble following his own advice.

Instead of relaxing or doing some housecleaning, which were his usual Saturday morning tasks, he decided to take his daily jog early. Maybe the exercise would help clear his head. He ran farther than usual, heading out past the edge of town and past dairies and orchards, the leaves still clinging to the almond trees as if they weren't ready to admit that fall had arrived.

Elliott had mixed feelings about the change of seasons. For almost all of his life, autumn had meant the beginning of a new school year. Whether he had been a student or professor, that meant the promise of new classes, new people to interact with. Sure, by mid-April he was always counting the days until summer, just like everyone else. But in October, the optimism of the academic year was still bright.

Not anymore, though. Now autumn reminded him of his failure, of the things he'd lost, and of his fruitless struggle to regain a sense of self-worth.

Wow, this run was really doing wonders to lift his spirits.

When he returned to the greenbelt, he encountered an inordinate number of bicyclists. Some were serious about the sport, wearing bright-colored spandex and riding expensive bikes. But others were more casual—some teen boys swerving erratically, a couple of families with kids tucked into bike trailers or using training wheels, a young woman with a fluffy white dog in her front basket. What they all had in common was a tendency to come up from behind him and zoom past unexpectedly, startling him even when he turned down the volume of his music.

He'd almost decided to move a block south, where he'd be able to travel the sidewalk in relative peace, when he caught sight of a familiar figure. Simon Odisho was moving slowly his way, his cane measuring each careful pace. The bicyclists didn't seem to rattle him—he just ignored them and they went around.

Simon waved at Elliott and, when Elliott came nearer, greeted him with a wide grin. "Hey there!" Simon called.

Smiling back, Elliott came to a halt beside him. "How come the bicyclists don't run you over?"

Simon rubbed his belly. "I'm too big. It'd be like colliding with a squishy mountain."

That led Elliott's brain places it shouldn't be. Places where he was the one doing the colliding, and where he and Simon were wearing a lot less clothing. He smiled wanly and shifted his footing.

"I should let you get back to your run," said Simon.

"I'm almost done with it anyway."

"And I'm just starting out. God, there are snails that make better time than I do."

"But you're exercising, right? Isn't that the main point?"

Simon scowled. "I guess. Although I think my PT is just looking for ways to torment me when he can't get his hands on me."

"PT?"

"Physical therapist. This guy's got a place off Orangeburg, over near the hospital. It's like a cross between a gym and a torture chamber. I totally recommend it if you want to suffer."

"I'll keep that in mind." And maybe, Elliott chided himself silently, he should remember he wasn't the only person in the world with problems. The thing with John had fucked him over, but at least he was physically intact.

They stood there a moment longer. Simon looked ready to say something else, but then a woman on a ten-speed came bearing down on them as if she were in the Tour de France, and she rang her bell imperiously. Simon hobbled out of her way, while Elliott gave him an awkward wave and resumed his run.

The Vietnamese crawfish place was a favorite of Anna's, so Elliott had met her and Ladd there several times before. As usual, he was there first, so he staked out a table underneath a tableau of plastic seafood and ordered a Thai iced tea, although he really wanted something stronger.

Anna and Ladd arrived five minutes later, and Elliott knew right away that he was in trouble. Anna tried to smile at him, but her face looked tight, and Ladd's cheeks were florid. Great. Apparently they were mid-argument.

Elliott seized on the opportunity even before they sat down. "If you want to cancel—"

"No!" Anna snapped. Then she took her chair, and her voice softened. "Kyle'll be here in a few minutes."

"But you look—"

"Seriously pissed at your stubborn-ass brother? Yep. But I'll get over it."

Elliott looked to Ladd, who shrugged. "It's domestic argument number 5B. Don't worry about it."

Elliott understood, although his relationship with John had been quite different, mostly because they'd rarely spent domestic time together. They'd lived several miles apart—John in a Craftsman bungalow and Elliott in an apartment—and busy schedules meant they saved most of their furtive meetings for weekends and vacations. When they did have time together, they had sex. And talked about campus gossip and their research. They squabbled frequently too, but they'd had only one big fight, when Elliott said he was tired of sneaking around and insisted they make their relationship public, and John had shouted that doing so would end both their careers. True enough, and so Elliott had given in and they'd kept everything hush-hush. But then their careers had crashed and burned anyway.

Maybe it was good Kyle arrived just then, derailing Elliott's pitiful thought train. Kyle was a few years older than him, Elliott guessed, and a little on the short side, with close-cropped sandy curls and a trim body. He was handsome in a bland sort of way, wearing jeans and a navy-blue button-down. He greeted Anna and Ladd and shook Elliott's hand, then took the empty chair beside him.

"Sorry I'm running late. I lost track of time."

Elliott analyzed that statement. Did it mean Kyle didn't really care about the not-date, or was he trying to minimize its apparent importance? And how about that handshake? Had it been too short or too long? Was the amount of eye contact sufficient? Had Kyle looked disappointed when he caught sight of Elliott?

Elliott cleared his throat. "No problem. And I'm sorry I had to cancel last time." He didn't elaborate because he had no idea what excuse—if any—Anna had given. Maybe *My brother-in-law is a chickenshit weasel.*

A round of mildly awkward small talk ensued while everyone perused the menu and then ordered. Kyle asked for a beer. Elliott couldn't help but wonder whether it was to help him relax or to take the edge off his disappointment.

"So, um, you and Anna work together?" Elliott figured that seemed like a safe enough topic.

Kyle seized on it. "We do! I was an escrow officer in the Bay Area, but I moved to Modesto a few months ago. Anna's been wonderfully patient with me while I learn the ropes here."

She'd been glaring at Ladd, but she broke that off in order to nod.

So then they talked about title insurance. Which was important, Elliott had to admit, and was possibly fascinating for those in the business. Not so much for him. Still, he tried to ask questions, and Kyle gamely tried to answer, and the whole time Ladd and Anna flashed them brittle smiles between exchanges of dirty looks.

The entire situation was ridiculous. Elliott pictured himself speaking with complete honesty. *Come on, guys. None of us is gonna get laid tonight. By the looks of things, either Anna or Ladd is going to end up sleeping on the couch, and Kyle and I have no chemistry at all.* Not that there was anything wrong with Kyle. He was, as advertised, a nice guy, but he didn't seem to have much in common with Elliott apart from being a gay man in Modesto. He didn't read much, he liked to spend his free time dirt-biking or watching soccer on TV, and he didn't make Elliott's heart go pitter-pat. Elliott didn't seem to do much for him either.

But everyone was civil, and the crab boils tasted great. So there was that, and at the end of the meal, Kyle insisted on paying for everyone. "Next time it can be on you," he said to Elliott in a polite fiction.

"Sure. Great."

Out in the parking lot, Anna and Ladd beat a hasty retreat, no doubt eager to get home and begin the next eight rounds. Elliott wasn't sure which of them he was rooting for. Their departure left him and Kyle standing beside their cars, watching traffic zoom by on McHenry.

"That's, um, a fun store." Elliott pointed at the building next door.

"I've never been there. Comic books?" Kyle sounded doubtful.

"Yeah. I used to hang out there when I was a kid. It's cool that they still exist."

"Sure." Kyle scratched under one ear. "Look, about tonight—"

"I am *so* sorry." Elliott wasn't sure what he was apologizing for— his quarreling relatives or his unexciting self.

Kyle gently grasped Elliott's upper arm. "Don't. That was . . . Well, it was super awkward. But you tried, I can tell. A for effort, Professor."

"But F for execution."

"I have the feeling you weren't too wild about the matchmaking to begin with."

"No offense. Nothing at all to do with you. It's just . . . I don't think I have my head together very well right now."

Kyle nodded. "Been there, done that." The corners of his eyes crinkled when he smiled. "Do you want to talk about it over coffee? Nothing romantic, I promise. I'm just willing to lend a friendly ear."

Elliott was going to refuse, but it was still early evening, and it wasn't as if he had to be anywhere the next morning. Or any morning, for that matter. He'd kept everything bottled up inside for over two years. Maybe some venting would help. "You don't want to hear me whine."

"I do. I don't know a lot of people around here, and I'm badly in need of gossip and small talk. Indulge me?"

They ended up driving separately and meeting at a coffeehouse downtown. The place was crowded on a Saturday night, and an awful guitarist was moaning something tuneless inside, so Elliott and Kyle took a table outside instead. The night air almost felt like autumn.

Kyle had ordered some kind of complicated mocha thing with a caravan-load of spices, but Elliott opted for a plain old Americano. He wrapped his hands around the oversize ceramic mug and wondered if he should have gone home instead. It was too late to bail now.

"Do you like living in Modesto?" he asked. "It's not exactly San Francisco."

"Not exactly. But I lived in Hayward actually and hardly ever made it into the city. Modesto's not bad, I guess. It's a hell of a lot cheaper to live here, that's for sure. How about you?"

"I grew up here. Escaped for several years. But like you said, it's affordable."

Kyle sipped his drink, then licked a bit of whipped cream from his lip, but unfortunately it wasn't sexy. Not Kyle's fault. Elliott just wasn't in the mood. Kyle probably hadn't intended it to be sexy anyway.

"What brought you back?" Kyle asked. "Family?"

"Not really. It's just Ladd and Anna here now. Our parents moved to Vermont a few years back."

"Vermont?" Kyle chuckled. "Were they trying to get as far away as possible?"

"I think so. And they wanted snow. I guess they got that."

"I guess so. Why did you come back?"

Elliott drank coffee while he considered how to answer. What version of the sordid tale did he want to share? He finally settled on a moderate account—neither too skimpy nor too detailed. "I had a really messy breakup," he began.

Kyle winced. "Ugh. I'm sorry to hear that."

"Thanks. My own damned fault—I knew better going in. There were practically neon lights flashing *Don't do it, idiot! Run far away!* But I ignored them. I got involved with— Hell. I started fucking around with one of my profs while I was in grad school."

"Oh."

"Yeah." Elliott wished he was drinking something stronger than caffeine. "So right around the time I got my degree, he became dean at another university. And when a tenure-track line opened up, he urged me to apply. Gave me a glowing recommendation. They hired me." Elliott liked to think he would have gotten the job anyway—he *was* qualified for it—but he'd never know, and that doubt was like acid eating away his insides.

"Did the other people there know the two of you were—"

"Fucking? Nope. Not a soul, not even after I was settled into the job. Our being a couple wasn't against the rules. If we'd been honest about it from the start, nobody would have cared. Academics maneuver jobs for their significant others all the time. But he was buried pretty deeply in the closet. We kept our mouths shut." His coffee tasted bitter; he should have added more sugar.

"Doesn't sound like it was destined to turn out well," Kyle said mildly.

"Are you kidding? It was a train wreck in slow motion. But then it got even worse. Money started mysteriously disappearing from various university accounts."

"Shit!"

Elliott drained his cup and nodded. "Yep. Shit is right. Turns out John was embezzling. Had been for years. And when they investigated, well, all the dirty laundry got dragged out of that closet."

"Including you."

"I didn't know anything about the money, but it took a long time to convince the powers that be. And then nobody there trusted me anymore. Can't blame them—I'd been lying by omission since my interview."

"What happened to John?"

"Prison." Elliott's stiff smile held no humor.

Kyle nodded but didn't say anything right away. He stared into the murky depths of his coffee cup, clearly gathering his thoughts. Then he looked up with a small grin. "I can see why you might not be eager to step into something new."

"Yeah. Look, you're—"

"It's fine," Kyle said, holding up his hand. "It really is. My ego isn't bruised, and I don't think you're a jerk. But can I give you some free advice?"

"Sure." Why not? Weren't escrow officers renowned for their relationship counseling?

"Not everyone out there is John. Get yourself in a good place first, but don't feel too afraid to open yourself up again."

He was so earnest that a little of Elliott's cynicism faded. "Voice of experience?"

"Yep. I had two serious boyfriends who cheated on me. Two. I was actually engaged to the second one, and we were in the middle of wedding plans. Made me feel like such a chump. But I'd hate to miss out on the possibility of something real just because there are assholes in the world. I guess I'm a glass-half-full kinda guy." He lifted his mocha in a little salute before chugging the rest.

They ended up getting refills and chatting for another hour. Some of the talk was about dastardly exes, but not all. Kyle described a recent vacation in Hawaii, and Elliott found himself admitting he'd really like to write a book. The companionship was . . . nice. They parted with a brief hug and a promise to get together again soon—as friends. And on the drive home, Elliott realized that a little of the ice inside his heart had melted. Not much, but it was a good start. It looked as though he might owe Anna and Ladd a thank-you.

After parking in his garage, he checked the library on a whim. Two more books gone, including the Monette memoir. He jogged inside and chose replacements almost immediately—an omnibus of gay literature and Mary Renault's *The Charioteer*. He felt almost buoyant after placing them in the box, especially when he realized he hadn't ordered any new books for a week.

Maybe he had room for some hope after all.

Chapter
Five

Elliott's spirits stayed remarkably light during the following week. He knew it was ridiculous to be happy just because of a few borrowed books, but logic didn't matter. Evidence that others were enjoying his reading material—and getting into the spirit by adding their own—warmed his heart. It also made him look at his neighbors with fresh eyes, wondering which households currently harbored which volumes.

His curiosity was especially sharp about the gay-themed books. He'd been slightly hesitant to include them in the first place—Modesto was a relatively conservative place, at least by California standards. But those books were important. Important to him, important to the world. He wasn't about to censor himself. Besides, he'd figured the titles might help a homophobe or two see the light.

Every gay-themed book he'd put out had disappeared within a day. Some had been returned, while others remained out in the wild, replaced—at least temporarily—with thrillers. James Patterson, mainly. Elliott wasn't a huge fan, but to each his own. At least they were books.

After considerable thought, probably when he should have been doing something more productive, Elliott concluded that one particular person was borrowing the books by Edmund White, James Baldwin, Gore Vidal, and the rest. Someone, obviously, with an interest in LGBT themes, although Elliott's collection was mostly lacking in the L, B, and T parts. Not only did this mean he couldn't fully assess the mystery person's curiosity, but it showed Elliott's own literary net wasn't cast very widely. He got as far as logging in to Amazon and surfing to the transgender nonfiction category before he remembered he was supposed to be on a book-buying moratorium. With a pang of regret, he closed the laptop.

He wandered to the couch and sprawled comfortably, trying to imagine his mystery reader. He decided to assume the person was male, although he knew that wasn't necessarily a safe assumption. How old was he? Not a kid. Some of the books were pretty heavy reading, so the person was probably an older teen at the least. And was he gay or just wanting to learn more?

Elliott sat up quickly. "This is stupid. I need to get a real life . . . and stop talking to myself."

He needed a change of scene—something more than his familiar neighborhood. After slipping into shoes, he grabbed his phone, wallet, and keys and headed for the garage.

At first, he drove without a particular goal or destination in mind. He didn't have any errands to run, and the Modesto area wasn't known for its intriguing scenery. After filling his gas tank, he hopped onto the freeway, and eventually he headed west.

He stopped for lunch in Dublin, at a strip mall where an assortment of restaurants would have allowed him to eat his way across Asia. After wavering between Korean fried chicken and Taiwanese noodles, he ended up opting for Afghani instead and happily munched his way through lamb qorma and rice. He hadn't thought to grab a book when he left the house—very unusual for him—so he couldn't read while he ate. Instead, he allowed his mind to wander, pulling it back when it meandered into dangerous territory such as jobs, his future, or John.

Happy to be going against the heavier Friday afternoon traffic, at least for the time being, Elliott continued west. His car seemed to have chosen a route—238 to 880, then over the long San Mateo Bridge, where the gray waves lapped beneath him and San Francisco gleamed in the distance like a mirage.

He didn't go to San Francisco, though. Instead, he continued southwest on Highway 92, where traffic got more congested as he snaked his way over the hills. He emerged in Half Moon Bay, a coastal community he hadn't visited in years. The road was lined with elaborate pumpkin farms, the type with hay mazes, petting zoos, and haunted houses. The farm parking lots were stuffed with SUVs as families prepared for the coming holiday.

Elliott drove past all the activity, turned north on Highway 1, and then pulled into the lot at the first beach he came to. Predictably, the air was chillier than in Modesto, but Elliott checked the trunk of his car and was delighted to discover a warm if somewhat tatty blanket—a holdover from a trip over the Sierras. He liked to be prepared in case of emergencies. And, really, this was an emergency of sorts—a personal crisis, at least a very small one. He'd driven all this way, after all, because he needed to somehow change his life.

Only a handful of people were on the beach. Elliott sat on the sand with the blanket around his shoulders and a large chunk of driftwood as a backrest, gazing out at the pounding surf. It was almost like meditating. His mind remained blissfully clear, with some crying gulls and a gamboling dog the biggest distractions. The passage of time ceased to matter until finally the horizon turned shades of brilliant orange and the sun sank into the ocean. Even then he remained, thankful for a cloudless night so he could watch the sparkling stars. Modesto wasn't a good place for stargazing—too overcast in winter and smoggy over the summer. Here, though, he felt as if the entire universe was open for his inspection and admiration.

Eventually, he grew cold even with the blanket. And he had to pee. He stood, brushed the sand from his clothing, and trudged to the car.

He decided he couldn't quite face returning home—not yet. So even though he didn't have a change of clothes with him—didn't even have a toothbrush—he checked into a modest little chain hotel just up the highway. He hadn't eaten dinner, but he peeled off his clothing, climbed into bed, and was asleep almost at once.

During the drive home the following morning, Elliott made two dumb decisions. He wasn't sure exactly when the resolutions hit him. Maybe when he began the rise over the Altamont, the rounded hills still brown from the summer drought. Maybe it was as he drove by a flock of sheep on the outskirts of Tracy, or when a line of semis crawled in front of him on the turnoff to Highway 99. In any case, by the time he turned into his driveway, his resolution had hardened, even though he'd chided himself for his stupidity.

"*Viva la idiotez*," he murmured as he got out of his car.

Before he could shut the garage door, he saw Mike Burgess hurrying over. Lovely.

"Hi, Mike." Elliott stood at the entrance to the garage.

Mike didn't bother with pleasantries. "What's that?" he demanded, pointing at the library.

"A mini neighborhood library."

"A what?"

"Pretty self-explanatory, Mike. I put books in there, people can borrow them. Or replace them with their own. Help yourself."

Judging from Mike's sour expression, he wouldn't be reading Elliott's copy of *The House of Spirits* anytime soon. "You can't have that here," he said. "The CC&Rs—"

"Don't forbid it. I checked. The city says it's A-OK too." That was a small stretch of the truth. Elliott hadn't bothered to call anyone at city hall to check on the legality of tiny libraries. But he had looked at an online directory and discovered that several other mini libraries existed in his part of town. One of them had been there since 2012, which did tend to suggest the police chief wasn't going to be sending a SWAT team to demolish Elliott's small effort.

Mike pouted. "It's stupid. There's a perfectly good library downtown. A *real* one."

"Sure. When's the last time you were there?" Elliott received only a scowl in reply. "Thought so. Ditto with pretty much everyone else. This is just a fun little thing. It encourages literacy and education and . . . neighborhood solidarity." He'd made that last part up, but it sounded legit.

For a moment Mike seemed at a loss, his gaze shifting around quickly. Then his face brightened, and he pointed triumphantly. "Well, you can't have *that*!"

"Geraniums?" Elliott was in the mood to be deliberately obtuse.

"The sign."

"There is no sign."

With a small growling noise, Mike stomped up the walkway until he reached the flag. He jabbed his finger like a weapon. "This."

"That is a flag, not a sign. A small, tasteful flag. The CC&Rs don't say a word about flags."

"It's political."

"Not especially. Even if it was, there's nothing to prohibit it. Several of our neighbors fly American flags. That guy a block away has one that's bigger than my living room. Are you going to tell me a US flag isn't political?"

"It's patriotic," Mike said but didn't sound entirely convinced.

They could have continued this pointless argument for much longer, but Elliott wasn't in the mood. Besides, he was on a mission. He had stupid plans to make.

Deliberately keeping his voice soft and his expression mild, he said, "Look, Mike. We're neighbors, and I really want us to get along. I'm sorry if you don't agree with some of my front yard decisions, but they really don't affect you. So I'll tell you what. You stop complaining about my flag and library, and I won't ask any questions about whether you followed proper procedures before you built that tool shed thing."

When Mike blushed and averted his gaze, Elliott knew he'd scored a victory. People in this subdivision were supposed to get approval from their neighbors before erecting permanent additions or structures. Mike's tool shed had already existed when Elliott moved in, so it was possible Mike had collected permissions, but his guilty expression confirmed that he had not.

"Fine," Mike grumbled, still not meeting Elliott's eyes. "But I better not see a lot of cars driving or parking on our street on account of your library. And no . . . political activity." He waved vaguely in the direction of the flag.

"We'll schedule the Pride march for somewhere else," Elliott deadpanned.

"Good." With no indication that he realized Elliott was joking, Mike stalked away.

Elliott took off his shoes as soon as he was inside the house, but he had sand in his clothing and hair, plus a grungy sensation caused by not brushing his teeth since the previous morning. So he shed his clothes in the laundry room and walked naked to the bathroom.

Standing under the warm shower, he decided it was as good a time as any to think about one of his new resolutions: to have sex.

Not that he'd been celibate since returning to California. Two or three times a year, he rented a hotel room somewhere in the Bay Area and, thanks to the wonders of modern technology, found a hookup nearby. That was fine. An hour or two of fucking, and then he and the other man went home. Itch scratched.

Only, he'd realized during the past twenty-four hours that he needed more than that. He needed . . . God. He wasn't sure. *Touch*. Not simply the quick and purposeful kind aimed at getting him and his partner off efficiently. He needed hugs and soft caresses. Familiar pats. Playful tickles. Tender strokes.

As these thoughts wandered through his mind, his hands wandered his body, mimicking the contact he craved. But while playing with one's own body could certainly be fun, it didn't fulfill his requirements. That would take someone else. Not just a handy stranger, but a . . . companion? Someone who knew him. Elliott wasn't asking for love and devotion, just someone who cared.

He was half-hard by the time he got out of the shower, and he took extra care with the towel, rubbing himself more thoroughly than was necessary just to dry off. Still naked and now fully erect, he padded to his bed and arranged himself comfortably on the mattress and pillow. He didn't bother to fetch his laptop from the next room or even get his phone. Porn wasn't necessary today because he could easily imagine everything.

His partner, this mystery man, would splay himself over Elliott's body, holding him in place with his weight, making Elliott feel . . . not trapped, but . . . secured. The man would stare into Elliott's eyes, the intensity of his gaze proving that, for the moment, he had no interests other than what they were doing together. Proving that Elliott was currently the center of his universe.

And this man? He'd be the center of Elliott's universe too. Past mistakes forgotten, future choices irrelevant. They'd have each other for the *now*; and for the now, that would be all they wanted.

Elliott rolled his nipples between finger and thumb until the sensation became almost too much. Then he closed his eyes and ghosted his fingertips across the lids, over his cheeks, around his lips. If he allowed his concentration to slip just a little, he could almost imagine they were someone else's fingers, a bridge to another man's nerves and blood. Those fingertips, no longer exactly his own, traced the history of Elliott's life as writ upon his skin. The tiny lines at the corners of his eyes, the stubble on his unshaved cheeks and chin, the lean muscles he worked so hard to maintain, the bones caging his heart, the tiny scar just behind one hip—the result of one of those childhood indiscretions with a homemade wheeled vehicle. His cock, now straining, begged for the thumb that teased the tip before running the length of the shaft.

Soon he was moaning and gasping, his balls pulled tight, his toes curled, his fist flying. Deep in his fantasy, his hand was both another man's stroking Elliott, and Elliott's stroking another man, a duality that defied logic but was just enough to . . .

There. Like that.

Elliott came with a noisy exhalation. Even then, while his skin continued to tingle and buzz, he smoothed his palm—his imaginary lover's palm—over his belly and chest, marking himself with his own spend.

He lay still as his overheated body cooled.

There was a flaw in his illusion, one he'd been aware of even as he chased his orgasm. His imaginary lover was really nothing but a hand. He'd had no face, no voice, no name. Elliott wasn't about to feel guilty for that—nothing wrong with a bit of unreality while he was getting himself off. Lots of people entertained sex daydreams they would never want to replicate in real life. But now that his climax was past and his dick was soft, he was left with the original puzzle: how to find a real-life lover.

The answer didn't burst into his thoughts with fanfare and confetti. In fact, it had been there in his consciousness for some time, patiently waiting to be acknowledged.

Kyle.

Elliott didn't have a crush on him and wasn't eager to get into bed with him. They didn't really have that much in common. But he'd been fun to hang out with. Elliott could imagine inviting him over for dinner, watching a movie on TV together. Maybe it wasn't such a big step from that to cuddling. To making out. To having sex and falling asleep in each other's arms.

Okay, none of those ideas especially inspired Elliott. But hell, he'd just jerked off. He might feel differently if it had been a while since he'd come.

Elliott wasn't a complete asshole—he acknowledged that thus far he'd factored only himself into the equation. What about Kyle's wants and needs? Well, Kyle seemed to enjoy Elliott's company—if not, he wouldn't have invited him to coffee. So there was that. Kyle was single, new to town, probably past the age where hanging out in bars and hoping to pick someone up sounded attractive. Plus this was Modesto, which was hardly renowned for its swinging gay scene. It was hardly renowned for its swinging *anything* scene.

What if Elliott proposed a friends-with-benefits arrangement? He and Kyle could get together now and then for company and sex. No strings attached, no expectations. Kyle would be free to sleep with other men if he wanted to and even search for his One True Love, if that was what floated his boat. If Kyle got sick of Elliott or tired of their deal, Elliott would step away immediately, no hard feelings. If that happened, Elliott wouldn't feel like his heart had been torn from his chest, because there was no emotional connection. It would be a . . . Well, they used to have marriages of convenience. This would be a small equivalent of that.

Energized by having decided on a course of action, Elliott got out of bed, wiped himself clean with a washcloth, and got dressed. He'd call Kyle the next day, invite him somewhere for a drink, and lay out his plan. Yes, it was a weak plan, foolish and perhaps even a bit pathetic, but at least it was something. It was like building a tiny library—inconsequential in the grand scheme of things but better than sitting on his ass and bemoaning his fate.

Elliott hadn't eaten since the Afghani lunch the previous day. Food wasn't a priority when he had things to strategize. But now his empty stomach growled, so he took the time to make a hearty meal of corn chowder, chili-lime chicken, and rice and beans. While he ate, he read a few chapters of a book about Magellan's travels, a choice that seemed to fit Elliott's recent, if unplanned, trip to the ocean.

Afterward, he washed up and moved into the living room to contemplate his other scheme. Sitting in his favorite armchair in the silent, dimly lit room, he felt a little Machiavellian. He was a miniature mastermind! That was a comforting idea, considering he'd taken so little agency over his own life.

Aside from finding someone to get up close and personal with, the other decision he'd made on the drive home was to find out who was borrowing his gay-themed books. Unlike the first plan, this one wasn't out of personal need. Really, it was nothing more than gnawing curiosity, but since so few of his desires had been met in recent years, he felt justified in indulging himself in this regard.

Okay. How best to spy on his innocent neighbors?

He could install a camera somewhere, either a security camera outside or a more conventional one indoors. The big window in his living room offered a perfect view of the library. But either option would require him to watch possibly hours of footage to find his man—or woman. Besides, recording library visitors felt sneaky.

"I'm going to have to do this in person." The concept appealed to him, actually. It made him feel very James Bond. But it would require some preparation because currently a low bookcase squatted beneath that window.

It took him over an hour to unshelve all the books, wrestle the empty case to the only free wall space he could think of—in the guest bathroom—and put all the books back. Then he dragged his dining room table into the vacated spot under the window. It wasn't a big table and he rarely used it, preferring to eat and do a good chunk of his work at the kitchen table instead. Finally, he carried over one of the dining room chairs.

"Done!" He stood, hands on hips, inspecting his work with a degree of satisfaction. Yes, it was an unorthodox location for a table, but it would make a good place to slave over his laptop while keeping an eye on the front yard. It wasn't *totally* weird. Lots of people preferred to work with a view. Elliott would keep the curtains open so he'd be fully visible to anyone who glanced at his house. That way he wasn't being sneaky and underhanded.

He hadn't gone for a run that day, but between the drive home, the scheming, and the furniture rearranging, he let himself off the hook. He set up his computer in the new workspace, and before booting it up, he strolled outside for a quick library survey. That way if someone came along and took a book, Elliott would easily know which book it was.

Satisfied his undercover efforts were fully in place, Elliott sat down in front of the window and turned on his laptop.

A few pedestrians strolled by, and a couple of people wheeled past on bikes, but none of them stopped. Nobody stopped at all, except for a fluffy white dog with a pink collar, who paused to sniff at the library pole until her person tugged her onward.

Elliott did get a lot of assignment grading accomplished, and he commented on the online discussion boards for all three of his classes. Which was a good thing, because a considerable subset of his ancient civ students were engaged in a discussion about whether King Tut's curse was real and whether mummies—the horror-movie type—were actually a subspecies of zombies. Elliott set them back on course. Then he answered emails, most of which were straightforward. One young woman, however, was apparently in the midst of an identity crisis and had sent him a string of emails, each asking confusing questions about which classes she should take for her major. If Elliott counted correctly, she had changed her major four times within two days.

There was an email from the chair of one of the departments Elliott taught for, asking whether he was interested in three online classes in the spring: another two sections of California history, plus one on twentieth-century Europe. Elliott responded with an enthusiastic yes. He'd even get a chance to talk about the Balkans in the European class.

Just as he clicked Send, movement caught his attention. A thin lady with curly gray hair and a purple tracksuit was approaching his property, two paperbacks in hand. He watched as she surveyed the library for a minute or two before pulling out a volume; he couldn't tell which one. She put her own two inside and closed the plexiglass. Then she looked over at the house—straight at Elliott.

He froze, a look of guilty terror no doubt clear on his face. But the lady smiled at him and waved. After a brief hesitation, he waved back. She pointed at him, pointed at the library, and gave a theatrical thumbs-up. After another wave, she was off toward the greenbelt, Elliott's book clutched under one arm.

Elliott waited fifteen minutes—sheer torture—and finally decided the coast was clear. He walked outside, wondering whether he looked as sneaky as he felt. He was trying for casual while he checked the library.

Ah. So that had been his romance fan. The lady had left one book about a farm girl in love with a shirtless, buff lycanthrope and one about a nurse who fell for a shirtless, buff, tattooed fallen angel. She'd taken a biography of a KGB undercover agent. Interesting, but not what Elliott was looking for. Still, even if his mystery wasn't yet solved, he was pleased to learn that he'd made someone happy with his library. What with all his assignments, testing, and grading, he didn't often do things that delighted other people.

Dusk was falling, the temperatures beginning to drop and the moon becoming bright above his head. It was unlikely his library would have more visitors until tomorrow. Parts of the greenbelt were poorly lit, so few people used it at night.

Elliott returned to his table by the window. He'd have a light late dinner of the leftover soup, and then he'd turn in early and watch a movie—maybe two—while tucked in bed. Tomorrow he would wake up early and look for new job postings.

He shut down the laptop and started closing the drapes. But before his view was entirely obscured, someone approached from the direction of the greenbelt. The romance lady? No. As the figure came closer, Elliott saw that this person was larger, moving slower—and carrying a cane.

While Elliott watched furtively, Simon Odisho hobbled to the library and stopped. Simon spent several minutes removing books, examining them, and returning them. He finally settled on one, which he replaced with a paperback he took from his hoodie pocket. He continued on his way without ever glancing toward Elliott.

This time, Elliott waited so long that full darkness arrived. The only street light was at the end of the block, so he used the flashlight app on his phone to investigate the library's contents. The new book made him smile—it was Neil Gaiman's most recent, and Elliott hadn't read it yet. Before he could decide whether it was kosher to borrow from his own library, he realized which book was gone. It was one of the nonfiction choices, a history of gay activists before Stonewall.

It seemed Elliott's gay-themed book fan was Simon Odisho.

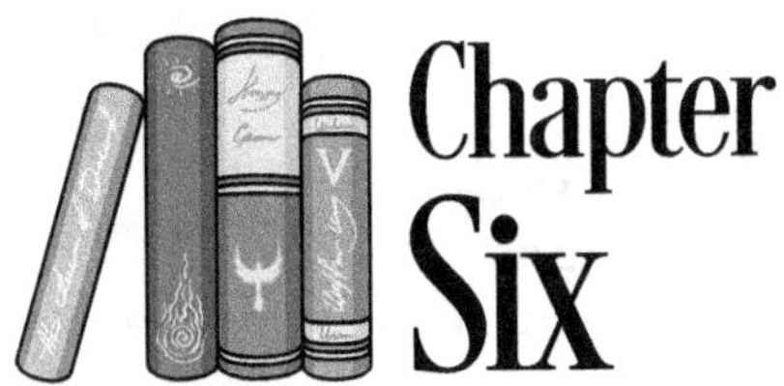

Chapter Six

I t didn't mean Simon Odisho was gay. He might simply be interested in LGBT issues, which was cool. Or maybe he had a friend or relative who was gay, and Simon was bringing them the books. That was perfectly great too.

Even if Simon *was* gay, what difference did that make to Elliott? The question ran through Elliott's head as he lay in bed that night, and it finally forced him to give up on the movie. No matter how many times he asked it, his speculation would inevitably turn to related matters. Was Simon single? Was he out of Elliott's league? What exactly *was* Elliott's league? Would Simon be fun to hang out with? Would he think Elliott was fun to hang out with? What did he look like naked? Did he want to know what Elliott looked like naked?

Jesus Christ.

Elliott gave up on sleep and tried to read, but his mind was too far away from the printed page.

He ended up jerking off again. It had been years since he'd indulged more than once in a single day, yet here he was with his hand down his underwear. This time, though, he didn't imagine that the hand belonged to somebody else. This time he did watch porn, because otherwise he kept picturing Simon, and that was all kinds of creepy. If he happened to pick a video in which one of the guys had a dark beard and a generous build? Coincidence.

The next morning he woke up later than intended, and he felt groggy and out of sorts. But he forced himself to go for a run—no sign of Simon along the route—then showered and set out to accomplish things. He found a new job listing and sent off an application immediately, despite the position being in Alaska. He could buy a parka, learn to snowshoe, and take up salmon fishing or whatever Alaskans did for fun. With those long winter nights, Alaska was probably a great place to get a lot of reading in.

He scuttled—at least for now—his plans to propose friendship with benefits to Kyle.

He considered moving the table back into the dining room, but then it occurred to him he liked looking outside while he worked. The view wasn't much, but it was diverting to watch the birds hop and flutter around. One mockingbird in particular seemed fond of the tall evergreen across the street. He'd sit at the top and sing away, undeterred even when jays scolded him.

"Bachelor life, huh?" Elliott commented. "I feel you, bud."

The day went by more or less as usual. Two people used the library—a teenage girl and a middle-aged woman. Neither of them noticed Elliott in the window, and he didn't bother to see which books they took and what they deposited.

Then Simon showed up.

He came from the greenbelt. Today his hair was down, the locks glossy in the sun, and he wore jeans and a rust-colored long-sleeved T-shirt. Although Elliott knew better, he sat by the window, watching as Simon browsed the library. Until the inevitable happened—Simon glanced over and saw him.

To Elliott's credit, he didn't freeze this time. Instead he waved, fervently hoping he looked casual and friendly. Simon waved back. Good. But then instead of choosing a book, Simon walked toward the front door, and Elliott's stomach did its best to tie itself into a knot.

"I am an idiot," Elliott growled. Despite his nerves, he forced his feet to walk him to the door, forced his hand to undo the lock, forced his mouth into what he prayed was more a smile than a grimace.

"Hi," Simon said.

"Hey."

Wow. An entire word.

Simon squinted and rubbed his ear. "I, um, just wanted to thank you. For the . . ." He waved at the library.

Miraculously not swallowing his tongue, Elliott nodded. "Have you been using it?"

"Yeah. Quite a bit. I might be one of your most frequent borrowers, actually. It's a really cool idea."

"Well, I didn't invent it myself."

"Still." Now Simon rubbed his beard. "Um, I wanted to ask you . . . Are you the one who picks out the books to include? Or does your boyfriend?"

Confused, Elliott blurted, "My boyfriend's in prison."

Simon actually moved back a step. "Prison? Shit! I mean, I'm sorry. He seemed like a good guy. Not that I really knew him or anything, but I'm usually a pretty good judge of people's character."

"He's a complete asshole." Elliott's sluggish brain struggled to keep up. "But . . . wait. When did you meet him?"

"When you guys were digging the hole?" Simon pointed at the library.

Comprehension dawned, and a slightly hysterical laugh escaped Elliott's throat. "That was my brother."

"Oh! Jesus, I'm sorry. I just assumed . . ."

Simon looked mortified, an emotion Elliott could empathize with. Somehow that calmed him down and cleared his head. "It's fine," he said. "I can understand. We don't look much alike, and I am literally flying the rainbow flag."

"And your brother's not in prison, right?"

"No, that would be my boyfriend. Ex-boyfriend, more accurately."

His embarrassment apparently receding, Simon grinned. "And he's a complete asshole."

"He truly is."

Simon nodded and moved his gaze to the side. "Look, I didn't actually come here to be nosy about your personal life, believe it or not. I really just wanted to say thanks for the books."

Maybe it was something in Simon's expression, which was hesitant—perhaps even shy. Or maybe it was that Elliott was lonely and Simon was, well, incredibly hot. Maybe it was just gratifying to have a neighbor who wasn't a jerk like Mike Burgess. Whatever the cause, Elliott deviated from his usual careful script. "Want to come in? I've got beer in the fridge."

Simon replied without hesitation. "Thanks! Sounds great."

Inside Elliott's house, Simon somehow seemed more real, as if stepping over the threshold had worked an enchantment on him. Elliott fought desperately to keep his nerves calm. *Just a neighbor stopping by for a friendly chat. For God's sake, chill.* His internal pep talk was not as successful as he'd have liked.

He led the way to the living room, where, thankfully, Simon didn't seem to think a table in front of the window was weird. "Have a seat," Elliott said. "Kona IPA okay?"

"Sure. Whatever." Simon collapsed onto the couch ungracefully, grunting a bit in the process. He leaned his cane against the end of the couch and, wincing, massaged his thigh above the knee brace.

Naturally Elliott wanted to ask him about the knee. It might not even be a terribly intrusive question, considering Simon had—accidentally—gotten Elliott to blab about John. But maybe it was best to wait a bit. So Elliott grabbed a couple of bottles from the fridge, popped the caps, and brought them to the living room, handing one to Simon before taking a seat in the armchair.

Simon tried a swallow. "Hmm. Good stuff. Never had this brand before. It's from Hawaii?"

"I guess. I buy it at Raley's."

"Well, Hawaii's kinda far to travel for a cold one. Unless you're really into it."

Simon looked especially handsome when he laughed. His eyes squinted almost closed, and his teeth flashed white amid his dark beard. His laughter was warm and rumbly, wrapping around Elliott like a soft blanket.

"So you must live nearby." Elliott hoped it didn't sound like a feeble pickup line.

"Yeah. Two blocks. You're on my walking route. I'm up to a whopping two miles. Whoopee."

"Do you, uh, mind my asking?" Elliott waved his bottle in the general direction of Simon's knee.

"Nah. It's not exactly a state secret. My doctor likes to rattle off all kinds of fancy names for what I did to myself, but basically I got in a fight with the wrong guy and fucked my knee up royally."

"A fight?" The last time Elliott had been in a physical confrontation with anyone was eleventh grade, when Richie Pyle called him a faggot one too many times. Of course, Elliott had been scrawny and uncoordinated, so while Richie had gotten a bloody nose, Elliott had ended up with two black eyes, a loose tooth, and a three-day school suspension. But the fight also meant Ladd found out Richie had been tormenting Elliott—a problem Elliott hadn't previously mentioned to anyone. Ladd and a couple of his football team buddies cornered Richie and described what they'd do to him if he didn't back off. Elliott's dignity might not have survived entirely intact, but at least he never heard a peep from Richie again.

But Simon was nodding, bringing Elliott back to the here and now. "Yeah. It was my own fault. I was talking to this dude, and he was pretty worked up, but I thought he was calming down. Then all of a sudden, bam! He pulls out a gun." He mimicked a shooting motion.

"Do you do that kind of thing often?" Elliott asked worriedly. He really had let a virtual stranger into his house.

"Used to." Simon snorted. "I was a cop."

"Oh! Um, was?"

Asking and receiving permission, Simon propped his foot on the coffee table and sighed. "Yeah. I've been out on temporary disability. I could go back once I'm healed up, but I don't know . . . I guess my heart's not really in it. I only ever did it because it paid okay and I couldn't think of anything else I wanted to be when I grew up."

Elliott was trying *very* hard not to fall into a porn fantasy of Simon in a police uniform. "Time for a career change, then?"

"I guess so, but I haven't decided what. My parents want me to work at the family restaurant when I can stay on my feet for a full shift, but I did enough of that when I was a kid." He shrugged. "I'm still considering my options."

"I can understand that." And somehow, with Simon's friendly, nonjudgmental attention, Elliott ended up spilling the whole ugly John story, complete with admissions of his own idiocy and current lack of career-related promise. By the time he was done, he and Simon had polished off their second beers, and Elliott was feeling somewhat aghast.

"Shit. I'm sorry. You didn't ask for my life story, and I didn't mean to dump on you."

"No, it's totally cool. It's too bad your ex is in prison in another state—otherwise we could have introduced him to the guy who screwed up my leg. They could have been buddies."

"Is he in prison too?"

"Jail for now. The DA's piled a shitload of charges on him. He'll plead it out, but since he's a frequent flyer, he'll still get a good five years of vacation with the Department of Corrections."

"That's good."

Simon didn't look especially pleased. "I guess. It won't help him any—he'll be an even bigger mess when he gets out. Won't help my knee either." Then he brightened. "But you and I are sort of in the same boat, right? Life fucked us over and we're not sure where to go next."

Elliott hadn't thought about it that way, but now that Simon had mentioned it, the similarity was somehow encouraging. Misery loves company, perhaps.

"Do you want another beer?" Elliott asked.

Although Simon shook his head, he didn't seem in any hurry to get up from the couch. Instead he looked around, as if noticing his surroundings for the first time. "You have a lot of books."

"Um, yeah. I sort of have a problem, I guess."

"I've *seen* problems, and believe me, this ain't one."

"Well, I'm running out of room for them. I've got shelves everywhere, and they're all full. My brother says one day I'll be buried alive under toppled stacks of them."

Simon grinned. "That would be an interesting way to go. Is that why you built the mini library?"

"Mostly."

"Well, then I'm glad you're an addict." Simon's expression grew suddenly serious. "I've been reading some of your books."

"That's the idea."

"The, uh, ones about gay people." He leaned forward to set the empty bottle on the table near his foot. Then he chewed on his lip briefly. "Can I ask you something really personal?"

"I just told you the sob story that's my life. Go right ahead." Despite his glib answer, Elliott braced himself for what was to come.

"Does your family know you're gay?"

Elliott wasn't sure what he'd expected, but it hadn't been that. "Yep. I told Ladd when I was fourteen. I came out to my parents later, in college."

"And they're cool with it?"

"Sure." Well, that required a bit of explanation. "Ladd was always fine with it. My parents, they took some time to get used to the idea. They were uncomfortable with it at first. I think Mom kept hoping I'd change my mind, and Dad didn't want to talk about it at all. But they came around eventually."

"That's nice." Simon looked thoughtful as he rolled his shirt hem between two thick fingers. Then, in a voice so soft Elliott could barely hear it, he added, "My parents don't know."

Shit. "You don't think they'd handle it well?"

Simon barked a laugh. "No. My parents are immigrants. Assyrian. They've been here for decades, and in a lot of ways they've assimilated, but at heart they're still old country. Conservative. Religious. And I'm their only kid too."

"I'm sorry," Elliott said with sincerity. "It sucks not to have family support. Were you out at work?"

"No. No way. I know it's 2017, but we're in the Central Valley and they're cops and . . . Just no. Hell, I didn't really admit it to myself until a couple of years ago. I sure as hell haven't talked about it with anyone. Until you." He glanced at Elliott, then looked away.

The knot returned to Elliott's stomach, and he wasn't even sure why. Maybe because he rarely discussed anything this important with anyone, let alone with a sexy man he barely knew. It was like entering into an emotional minefield where one false step might not only destroy this budding friendship, but also—more importantly— damage Simon. Simon had been damaged enough already.

"Is that why you've been borrowing my books?" Elliott asked after a brief pause.

"Yeah. It's like . . . there's this whole culture and history that I don't know anything about, but maybe I'm supposed to be a part of it."

Elliott was peeling the label from his empty bottle, a bad habit that used to make John yell. "I think it's good to learn those things," Elliott said carefully. "Obviously, since I'm a historian. But also I think everyone should feel free to make his own space. To create his life in a way that feels comfortable to *him* instead of trying to fit a mold. Crap. I'm lecturing. Sorry."

Simon grinned. "I don't mind. It's an occupational hazard, huh?"

"I guess I miss having an actual classroom full of students who have to pay attention to me if they want a decent grade."

"I like paying attention to you. You don't even need to give me a grade."

Was Simon flirting? Elliott had always been bad at judging that sort of thing, which was probably one reason he had such a poor relationship scorecard. If the other guy was in a gay bar or using an app, well, at least then Elliott could be pretty certain what the agenda was. Or if the guy was a professor who closed his office door one day while Elliott was inside, crouched next to Elliott's chair, and said, "We work well together. I bet we'd fuck well together too." But otherwise? Elliott was at a loss.

"I'm glad you came over," he said, playing it safe.

"Me too."

They looked at each other and smiled slightly, neither saying anything.

Grow a pair, Professor Thompson.

Elliott took a deep breath. "This, um . . . Shit. I'm probably getting this all wrong. I'm probably embarrassing myself and being an idiot. But would you be interested in going out with me sometime? On a date?" He braced himself for rejection.

Simon's answering smile spread ear to ear—and it wasn't mocking. "Seriously? Me?"

"If you're interested."

Simon waggled his thick eyebrows. "I'm interested."

Jesus. Relief washed over Elliott, and his lungs started functioning properly again. He gave a warm smile as he got up.

"Let me get us another beer. To celebrate."

Chapter Seven

Over the following several days, Elliott had to keep reminding himself he was thirty-six, not fifteen. Grown men were supposed to be more confident in their relationship-building skills. They were supposed to go forth and conquer with charm and wit. They were not supposed to dither around the house, wishing someone could pass Simon a note reading *Do you like like Elliott?* With *yes* and *no* checkboxes.

But in high school, Elliott hadn't attempted to date anyone. There had been a few out gay kids, but they were way cooler than Elliott, who was still hesitating at the threshold of his closet. He might have daydreamed about Cesar Guzman, who wore a fauxhawk and had the world's dreamiest eyes, but Cesar had never looked twice at Elliott.

Elliott *had* dated in college, but rarely, and mostly guys from the campus LGBT club or, on a couple of occasions, friends of a friend. Then in grad school he'd met John.

So he'd never really gotten the hang of this whole relationship business, which explained why he spent the week mired in self-doubt.

Okay, yes, Simon clearly liked him well enough to hang out and have a few beers, exposing a bit of his soul in the process. Simon had agreed to a date readily enough. But given what he'd said about his history, he probably didn't have many gay friends. So maybe he was simply viewing this as a chance for friendly social interaction—possibly with some sex thrown in.

Wait. Wasn't that exactly what Elliott had just told himself he wanted with Kyle? He'd been satisfied with that idea, pleased with himself for coming up with it, even. But friends with benefits didn't sound so satisfying now that Simon was in the picture, however tentatively . . . Shit. Elliott needed to grow up and get his head straight.

He needed to get some sleep too. But instead he'd spent every night tossing and turning in bed, mummy-wrapping himself in the bedding while he agonized over Simon. Over what Simon thought of him and what would happen on their date and oh God would they have sex and then what would happen the morning after . . .

Elliott agonized during the days too. He ran a lot and was both disappointed and relieved he didn't see Simon. He tried to do his work, but the students' answers seemed more nonsensical than ever, the misspellings and twisted grammar spinning around on his screen until nothing made sense at all.

Somehow he and Simon had agreed that Saturday would be their date night. Elliott wasn't sure why—he didn't work a traditional schedule and Simon wasn't working at all, so they could have gone out any night. Yet on Saturday night, there Elliott was, parking in front of Simon's address. The house was in the same subdivision as Elliott's, but Simon had a two-story model. It was too dark to see much of his front yard, but elaborate landscaping didn't appear to be his priority. Of course, his knee injury likely meant he couldn't do much in the way of gardening even if he wanted to.

Simon must have been watching through a window, because he came out his front door before Elliott had a chance to turn off the engine. Hurrying as fast as his bum leg and cane likely allowed, Simon grinned as he approached Elliott's car.

"Hi," he said when he dropped into the passenger's seat. He balanced the cane over his lap. "The inside of my house looks like an EPA Superfund site. I don't want you to see it."

"A little mess wouldn't traumatize me."

"Big mess. Superfund, Elliott. I saw your place, remember?"

Elliott snorted. "Books everywhere."

"Yeah, but they're neat. Orderly. My house . . . Nope. And that's just the downstairs. I haven't been going upstairs hardly at all since I fucked up my knee. For all I know, it's become a wildlife habitat."

"Pigeons? Mice?" Elliott grinned.

"Elk. Bears. Mountain lions. Could be anything."

Simon was belted in by then, so Elliott backed out of the driveway. "Housecleaning isn't your favorite chore?"

"No. When I lived with my parents, my mom wouldn't let me do any of it. She has these old-fashioned ideas about gender roles, and I wasn't about to argue with her. I mean, what kind of kid demands to be allowed to vacuum and dust? I did make a stab at learning basic skills when I got my own place, but with the knee, I've let things slide big-time." He sighed. "Now it's like I don't even know where to start."

"You could hire a housecleaning service. Not permanently, necessarily, but they could come in and get your place back in shape." Elliott was glad they were having this conversation. In part because it reminded him that Simon was as human as he was. And in part because it provided a welcome distraction from Simon's close physical presence: his tidy beard, his nicely tamed hair, and the light scent of a woodsy cologne. He was dressed simply—in jeans, a white button-down, and a brown leather jacket. And God, he looked good.

"You don't think housecleaners would run screaming from my mess?" Simon asked.

"Well, I haven't seen it, so I can't judge. But I bet the experienced ones have seen a lot."

"Yeah, probably. I once had a call where this guy had been squatting in an empty house. He'd OD'd but nobody was around to notice, and it was summer. No electricity in the house, so no AC, and by the time we got there, he'd just kind of melted into the couch. It was—" Simon stopped abruptly. "Shit. Sorry. This isn't really a good first-date discussion, is it?"

Elliott laughed. "I think it's a little unorthodox, but that's okay."

"My point is that some poor souls had to clean that house. I should find out who and hire them. At least I don't have any corpses in my place."

"Just wildlife."

"Yeah. Just that."

Elliott and Simon lived in the northeast corner of town, which meant there was no particularly great way to get downtown. Elliott took Standiford to McHenry before heading south, which was direct but heavy with traffic. "I bet this is a lot easier to do with lights and sirens," he commented.

"Yeah, except you have no idea how fucking oblivious a lot of drivers are, even with sirens blaring. Sometimes I needed to get somewhere fast, right? I used to wish I had one of those monster trucks and could just run right over the roofs of the assholes who didn't get out of my way. Like this one time— Crap. I'm sorry."

"For what?"

"Shop talk. You probably don't want to hear it."

They were stopped at a light, so Elliott glanced at Simon. "Why wouldn't I?"

Simon didn't answer right away. "I don't know. You're a college professor. Cop stuff must seem . . . stupid. All I have is an associate degree."

Genuinely puzzled, Elliott shook his head. "Cop stuff's interesting. Think of how many TV shows and movies are made about police. A lot more than they make about history professors, that's for sure. Even when I had a tenure-track job, well, it wasn't Hollywood material. My big excitement was when I got an article published or caught a student plagiarizing."

"Cops spend a lot more time doing paperwork than doing high-speed chases or slapping cuffs on bad guys."

"Professors do almost nothing but paperwork. But we rarely get shot at."

They'd reached downtown by then, and they were silent as they neared the restaurant. One of the nice things about living in Modesto was that parking was easy, even on a Saturday night. Elliott found a spot only a block from their destination.

The specific restaurant had been Elliott's suggestion. It was only a few months old, and he'd never been there before, but Anna had recently raved about it. Simon had been agreeable. "As long as we don't go to my parents' kebab place, anywhere is fine," he'd said with a smile.

As they walked into Il Piatto, Elliott hoped it wasn't too pretentious for a first date. The restaurant was small, the décor elegant but very simple. No trace remained of the antique store that had been the previous resident of this storefront. Now there were brick walls, unadorned wood floors, and slightly artsy light fixtures, including the colored glass pendant lampshades above each table. Wine bottles in wood-and-steel racks lined most of the back wall.

A cute young guy with sleeve tattoos greeted Elliott and Simon when they walked in, then led them to the only empty table, which was near the front window. He handed them menus—typewritten, with the day's date at the top—and a wine list.

"Nice," Simon said after the host left.

"Is it okay?"

"Yeah, it's great. I wonder what the kitchen looks like. My parents' place was a dump when they bought it. I was just a little kid, but I remember. They've sunk a lot of money into it over the years, and now the kitchen is . . ." He smoothed his beard. "You don't care."

"Sure I do."

"Why? Are you planning a culinary career now?" Simon looked stricken and added quickly, "Not that you should. You're a great prof, and I'm sure you'll find a good job soon, somewhere they won't give a shit about your asshole ex." He looked at the table and, when no drink mysteriously appeared, searched for a waiter.

Elliott wished he had a drink too.

Fortunately, the waiter appeared within seconds. He was a blonder version of the host, with surfer-dude hair, a shell necklace, and more tattoos. "Hey," he said. "I'm Zach and I'm gonna take care of you tonight. Something to drink? We've got a couple of killer brews on tap if you're more into that than the vino."

Elliott and Simon glanced at each other. "Just water for me," Elliott said, feeling unbearably prim. Simon ordered a beer. Then Zach gave a five-minute speech about the menu, including the provenance of all the meats and most of the veggies. Apparently, Il Piatto's theme was small plates, which meant customers were expected to order several items apiece. Simon asked a few questions, but Elliott mostly just nodded.

"Do you know what you're going to have?" asked Simon after Zach went away.

"Not a clue." Honestly, Elliott hadn't made much sense of what Zach had been saying, not because it'd been complicated but because it'd been a whole lot of words. And Simon was sitting right *there* across the table, his tongue sometimes darting out as he'd listened to the details.

They both stared at the menus for what felt like a century, but Elliott was too distracted to read his. "Everything sounds good," he finally said to excuse his indecision.

"Yeah. I can order for us both if you want. Not that you can't do it yourself, and I'm not such a huge expert or anything—just an ex-cop who used to make kebabs and stuff—but I have some ideas. Or we can go with whatever you want. Or just order separately." He mashed his lips together and looked away, but his fingers tapped on the table.

"You can order. That'd be great."

Simon stared at the menu with a degree of concentration usually reserved for students taking final exams, while Elliott played with his napkin and wondered whether Simon could tell how much he was sweating. Simon probably could; he was a police officer, after all, trained to notice things. What else was he noticing? Did he think Elliott was a crappy driver? Was he pleased Elliott was abstaining from alcohol since he was driving? Or did Simon think it was just a ruse to fool him into believing Elliott was a good guy?

Elliott was relieved when Zach arrived with their drinks. Simon rattled off several dishes, glancing at Elliott as if for confirmation. Elliott nodded, although none of those food words were making any sense to him tonight. For all he knew, Simon had ordered pickled sheep eyeballs with sriracha sauce.

"Was that too much?" Simon asked as soon as Zach was gone. "I kind of ordered a lot."

Elliott smiled at him. "No, it was fine."

"Good. I get hungry when I'm—" Simon patted his belly. "I get hungry a lot, actually. As you can tell."

Elliott had no idea how to respond to that. He liked Simon's substantial body—liked it a lot—but he wasn't about to blurt that out. So instead he nodded like an idiot and reached for his water. Which he promptly knocked over, sending a flood of icy liquid over the paper tablecloth and onto his lap.

"Shit!" Elliott jumped up, sending his chair scooting back against the one behind him. The woman sitting there made a startled noise, but Elliott was too busy dabbing a napkin frantically and ineffectually over his crotch to deal with her.

Simon jumped up too and managed not to ram his chair into anyone. But he must have put too much weight on his bad leg, because he yelped, swore, and staggered back into his seat.

As everyone in the restaurant watched, Zach, the host, and a pretty waitress rushed over with handfuls of towels. While the waitress and host dealt with the puddle on the floor and the disaster on the table, Zach tried to wipe some of the water off Elliott, who grabbed the towel and did it himself. The worst part was that Zach kept apologizing, as if the spill was somehow his fault.

Eventually the flood was absorbed, the tableware replaced, and Elliott seated on his newly dried chair. Zach brought him a fresh glass of water.

"Maybe I should have a lid," Elliott said. "Or a sippy cup." His lap was still wet and cold, but there wasn't anything he could do except spread a napkin over it.

"Hey, it's no biggie, man. People do it all the time."

Elliott doubted that. But he smiled, first at Zach and then, when Zach was gone, at Simon. "Are you okay? Your leg's all right?"

Simon grimaced. "Yeah. I forget about the fucker sometimes. Sorry I wasn't much help during your emergency."

"I don't think it was quite 911-worthy." Although judging from the glares of the lady he'd played bumper chairs with, he'd come close to being assaulted.

"Not quite," Simon agreed, then took a long drink of his beer, which had survived all the upset. Elliott drank his water—using two hands to hold the glass—and they stared at each other.

Simon began to tap on the table again. The rhythm seemed as if it might be a tune, but Elliott couldn't identify it. "I'm not good with music," he blurted.

Simon blinked. "What?"

"Music. I can't sing or play any instruments, and I never really pay much attention to it. And John said I had bad taste."

"Me and two of my cousins had a band when I was in high school. We sucked. I played, like, three chords."

Elliott wondered what Simon had been like in high school. A lot cooler than Elliott, that was a given. "I was on the debate team," Elliott admitted.

"Did you win?"

"Sometimes."

"I couldn't do that. Speaking in front of people freaks me out. In college, I had to do an oral presentation for one of my classes, and I got so nervous I had to go barf in the bathroom first. But then I was *still* nervous. I was afraid I was going to piss myself in front of the entire class."

"I'd think—you know, policeman—you'd kind of have to be good at public speaking."

Simon shrugged. "Not really. If I'm in uniform? With a badge and a gun? People sort of have to listen to me, so it's not as bad. Jesus, I don't know how you do it."

"Do what?"

"Teach. You have to talk in front of people all the time. When you're teaching in person, I mean, and not online. Not that there's anything wrong with teaching online but . . . Christ." He wiped his forehead and took another drink.

"When I'm teaching a class, people sort of have to listen to me," Elliott pointed out with a grin. "If they want to pass, anyway."

Zach brought them bread and butter—placing the dishes closer to Simon, which was probably safer—and told them their first plates would be arriving soon. But the loaf wasn't sliced the whole way through, and when Elliott went to tear off a piece, he wrenched a little too hard and sent a chunk of crust flying. At least he didn't hit the lady behind him.

He managed to butter his bread without incident.

"See?" He held up the slice. "I'm capable of eating and drinking without mayhem."

Simon laughed. Unfortunately, he'd just taken a big bite of bread, and now he started to choke. Elliott looked on, alarmed, and wondered if he should try the Heimlich maneuver. But then Simon swigged his beer and washed the bread down.

"Sorry. I'm not very good in a crisis," Elliott muttered.

A man and woman in their forties sat at the next table, both of them smartly dressed. Maybe on their way to a show at the Gallo Center after their meal. They were speaking softly, smiling a lot, and laughing. When Zach refilled their wineglasses, the couple clinked them together in a toast. Married? Maybe. They certainly seemed happy with each other.

Zach brought Simon another beer and refilled Elliott's water. Then he returned with his arms laden with dishes, which he arrayed over the tabletop, naming each one as he set it down. "Enjoy your meal!" he said. "I'll be back to check on you in a few minutes."

Simon and Elliott eyed the assortment of food. There was a lot of it. Enough to feed them, the twinkly couple next to them, the angry lady behind Elliott, plus her friend. "I ordered way too much," Simon said mournfully.

"We can taste everything and bring the leftovers home." Wait. Did that sound weird, as if they lived together, or at least as if Elliott was imagining them living together? Moving with extreme care, he took a few forkfuls from the nearest dishes and transferred them to his own plate. Nothing resembled sheep eyeballs.

Simon was hesitating, fork in hand. "Um . . . Shit. I've never done this before. Well, I've eaten before. Obviously. That's not what I meant. But I've never done this before, and I'm not sure how it's supposed to work."

"How what's supposed to work?"

Simon sighed. "A date."

"You've . . . never been on a date?"

"No, I have." As Elliott watched, Simon chose several dishes—seemingly at random—moved samples to his plate, and ate them steadily. His plate emptied almost at once, and he refilled it.

Elliott hadn't yet eaten anything but the bread. He nibbled at his food. Pasta with squash in it. Tiny meatballs that tasted like lamb. A salad with cranberries and goat cheese. Some kind of mushy potato thing with green speckles. It was all probably delicious, but he was too focused on Simon to notice.

And Simon continued to shovel food into his mouth as if he hadn't eaten for days. Not that he was rude about it; his table manners were perfect, and he kept asking Elliott if it was okay to take more. He just ate a lot. After a while, Elliott settled back and watched. It was entertaining, both for the quantity consumed but also because Simon was so nice to look at. His mouth was generous, as if it was meant to be used often and with enthusiasm, and his brown eyes were as soft as suede. He was good with his hands too, wielding cutlery and glassware with a surprising amount of grace.

Zach came by a couple of times to check on them and refill Elliott's glass. On the third visit, the dishes were all empty. "Can I get you anything else?"

Elliott would have said no, but Simon was still toying absently with his fork. "How about dessert?" Elliott said.

Il Piatto had three options that night: chocolate cake, tiramisu, and a poached pear thing. Elliott ordered one of each, plus espresso. If Zach felt judgmental, he hid it behind an easy grin. Probably looking forward to a hefty tip.

"I can't believe I ate all that," Simon said after Zach zoomed away.

"It was all really good."

"Yeah. But Jesus. It was a lot. Um . . . I have no idea how to ask this without being completely awkward . . ."

Although that introduction made Elliott nervous, he forced a smile. "My pants are still wet. I don't think *you* have to worry about being awkward."

Simon scratched his beard. "Yeah, well, I can sure as hell try." He huffed out a breath. "Who's supposed to pay for dinner? I mean, we could go dutch, and that's fine, but I don't know if maybe it's weird for a first date. Or I can pay for everything—I'm totally cool with that especially since I ate about ten times as much as you. And you drove. But maybe that would offend you? I don't know."

"It's a date."

"Right. But . . . I've never done this with a guy. Just girls. So I don't know if the rules are the same."

While Simon was blushing, Elliott felt himself pale. "Um . . . never?"

"No."

"So you're . . . uh . . . inexperienced?" Elliott had never been anyone's first, and he had no desire to be. Way too much responsibility.

"Oh, I've fucked men," Simon said. Loudly. Which not only caught the attention of the couple at the next table but was also overheard by Zach as he approached with their desserts. He dropped the plates, which landed with a tremendous clatter on the floor. And he didn't even scramble to pick up the mess—he was too busy holding his knees and laughing hysterically.

Simon hid his face in his hands.

Eventually Zach and his colleagues cleaned up the mess, and Zach delivered replacement desserts as he tried very hard to keep a straight face.

"Oh God," Simon said. Then he picked up his fork and gobbled half of the tiramisu. He reached for the chocolate cake next. "I am so sorry."

Elliott hadn't been particularly embarrassed by the scene—his own thing with the water had probably exhausted his mortification points for the evening. So he just grinned and shrugged, then snagged a bite of the pear. It was good, but watching Simon scarf it down was more enjoyable than eating it himself. He imagined kissing Simon right now. His mouth would taste so sweet.

As Simon was swallowing, an epiphany hit Elliott—one that should have occurred to him much earlier. Simon—handsome ex-cop Simon—was nervous. About Elliott. About their date. And somehow that realization relaxed him. He no longer felt like such a fool for all the lost sleep and panicky running he'd experienced over the week.

"I'm really honored to be your first male date," Elliott finally said. "Thank you."

"I'm such a moron."

"You're not. And dinner tonight is completely on me because I'm the one who asked you out—and because I'd really like to pay."

"Even though I ate enough for an army?"

"Especially because of that," Elliott replied with a smile.

"I eat when I'm nervous. Hell, I eat all the time. But extra then."

"And I spill things."

That made Simon chuckle, which was a good thing. "But you've dated men before. The ex, at least."

"Sure. Although to be honest, he didn't want us to be seen together in public, so we hardly ever went out. Anyway, how about if we stop worrying about what we're supposed to do on a date and just . . . let things happen?"

Simon cocked his head a bit. "Complete with spills and gorging?"

"Yes."

"Okay. But I still want to polish off that tiramisu."

Elliott gestured at the plate. "By all means."

Simon ate more slowly now, which was fine. Elliott didn't feel hurried. The couple next to them paid and stood up, then flashed grins in Elliott and Simon's direction before leaving. They'd had a memorable meal, at least.

"Do you want to explain the no-dating thing?" Elliott asked.

"Not much to explain, really. Like I told you before, I didn't realize I was gay until a couple of years ago. I mean . . . I knew, but I didn't *know* know. Like this one time I had a really bad toothache, and I sort of acted like if I pretended it wasn't there, it would go away. It didn't. I ended up needing a root canal."

"I'm the root canal?" Elliott stared into his empty espresso cup.

"No! Jesus, I didn't mean it that way. It was just a lot easier for me not to be gay, so I kind of went with that for a while. Until I couldn't anymore. Then I hooked up with some guys, but that was just sex."

"Apps?"

Simon snorted a laugh. "Sometimes. Or this bar in Oakland. It's a dive, but at least none of the guys there are real picky."

Although Elliott wondered why Simon thought a lack of standards was necessary for him to be found desirable, he didn't ask. Another question was more important. "So what made you decide to go out with me?"

"The trouble with my leg, it's given me a lot of time to mull things over. All those hours sitting around in hospitals and shit. I'm not like you, Prof—never was much of a thinker. But with nothing much else to do, I decided I didn't really want to be a cop anymore. And . . . I decided that pretending I wasn't gay maybe wasn't as easy as I thought."

Elliott nodded. He knew a life crisis could lead to a lot of introspection and reexamining of priorities.

"Then I found your books," Simon continued. "And I'd never read anything like them before. Got me thinking about who I am in a new way. 'Cause it's not just the sex, right? I haven't gotten laid since I got shot, but that doesn't make me any straighter. I could be a monk but I'd still be gay."

"So . . . you're getting to know yourself."

"Exactly!"

Elliott knew this was an excellent idea. Since ancient Egyptian times, philosophers have said *Know thyself*. And Elliott was firmly convinced that unless a person was comfortable and confident in his own self-identity, he'd never have a meaningful relationship with anyone else. But that led to sticky questions. What did Simon want from him? Mentoring? Was Simon even attracted to him?

Maybe asking him would be best. Clear the air. Avoid misunderstandings. Elliott opened his mouth, but before he could find a tactful way to word the question, someone tapped on the outside of their window. Elliott didn't recognize the man, but Simon blanched. "Shit."

"Someone you know?"

"My cousin." Simon glanced around quickly, as if searching for an escape route, but his cousin was already walking to the front door. The restaurant's back door wasn't visible; it was probably around the corner, past the bathrooms.

"Do you want me—" Elliott began.

Simon shook his head. "Too late. But thanks."

The cousin bore a close resemblance to Simon, but he wasn't as sexy. He was thinner and a few years younger. He wore jeans and, beneath an unzipped hoodie, a T-shirt emblazoned with the logo for Pita Palace. His confident strides brought him quickly to their table, where he clapped a hand on Simon's shoulder. "Hey, Si! What're you doing here? Scoping out the competition?"

Simon looked as if he might have swallowed his tongue. "I'm having dinner with a friend," he managed to choke out. "We just finished, actually."

The cousin raised his eyebrows and turned to Elliott with his hand held out. "Hi, I'm Ashur Odisho. Si's cousin."

Elliott shook his hand. "Elliott Thompson."

"Are you one of Si's cop buddies?"

"No." Elliott wanted to laugh at the idea of anyone mistaking him for a cop. "I'm a history professor."

"Not Si's usual crowd." Ashur turned to Simon. "How come you didn't eat at the Palace?"

"Because maybe once in a while I feel like eating something different."

"But we haven't seen you around in a while. Are you trying to avoid us or something?"

"We're just having a nice dinner."

Ashur looked back and forth between Simon and Elliott, the gears obviously turning in his brain. But Elliott maintained a poker face and Simon didn't say a word, and finally Ashur grunted. "Okay. I guess I'll let you get back to it." He patted Simon again, exchanged a final brief pleasantry with Elliott, and left.

Simon was still pale. "Fuck," he groaned.

"Is he going to out you to your parents?"

"I don't know. I mean . . . there's nothing really to out. We're having dinner together, not fucking on the table. But they'll speculate."

Elliott wanted to offer his sympathy but was afraid that would only make things worse. "I should have picked a less visible restaurant."

"Not your fault. I should have known one of my relatives would walk by. The Palace is only a few blocks away, and my family members pop up everywhere. Like dandelions. Or maybe thistles." Although Simon attempted a smile, he was clearly miserable.

Zach brought the bill a few moments later, but Elliott noted all of the desserts and a few of the other dishes were missing. He waved at the bill. "You left a bunch of stuff off."

"Comped it, dude. 'Cause I'm really sorry about dropping everything. That was, like, really unprofessional of me."

Soon afterward, Elliott and Simon walked to the car. It was a short walk, yet Elliott half expected something to explode in front of them or the sidewalk to collapse into an enormous sinkhole. Or maybe another Odisho would pop out from behind some bushes. But no disasters befell them. The car even started right away, and traffic on the way home was light. Simon and Elliott remained silent for the short drive.

Then they were in Simon's driveway, still not speaking but with the engine humming smoothly. "Thanks for the date," Simon finally said, his voice quiet yet rumbly.

"Not all dates are like that." Thank God.

"Well, it was interesting. Good food." Simon placed his hand on Elliott's thigh. "Good company."

Oh no. That one little bit of contact—that broad palm and those wide fingers lying heavy on his jeans—was enough to send Elliott's libido into emergency overdrive. His heart sped, his throat constricted, his face flushed, and his dick woke up and remembered how it used to have fun. Elliott froze, unsure what to do next.

But then Simon shifted in his seat and leaned toward Elliott, and Elliott leaned toward him, and despite the interloping emergency brake and Simon's cane, they kissed.

It was a surprisingly good kiss, considering it was their first. As predicted, Simon tasted delicious, and his warm, plush lips and soft beard felt wonderful against Elliott's skin. Simon tightened his grip on Elliott's leg slightly while Elliott reached over and grasped one of Simon's strong shoulders.

"That was nice," Simon said when they moved apart. He briefly traced his finger along Elliott's cheek and then across Elliott's lips—a touch perhaps even more erotic than the kiss.

"Yes."

Elliott wanted a lot more kisses like that, hopefully accompanied by lots of bare skin. Reality intruded, however, as it had the unfortunate tendency to do. "What do you want from me?" Elliott whispered. He wasn't demanding, but he needed to know.

Simon sighed. "I don't know. You're . . . you're something special. But you saw me tonight. I'm a goddamn mess, and I don't mean the leg."

"I don't think you're a mess. Or if you are, well, I'm an even bigger one."

"It's not a contest," Simon said with a gentle smile.

Trying to block the arousal still coursing through his body, Elliott shook his head. "I spent a lot of years . . . skulking with John. I totally understand that you're not comfortable being out, but I can't skulk anymore."

"I get it. Fuck, that wouldn't be fair to you at all. But I don't know if I have the balls . . ."

"You need to be comfortable with what you're doing." Elliott wasn't really as charitable and understanding as he sounded. He simply realized from hard experience that if his partner had doubts about the relationship, the entire enterprise was doomed. Better not to drag them both through the agony, especially since Simon—unlike John—was a genuinely nice human being.

"I'm still gonna read your books, okay?"

"Good. And if you want to stop by, I'm almost always home. I've got a lot more books inside."

"I know."

They kissed again, but this time it was just a quick peck on the lips. Elliott watched as Simon hobbled up the driveway. Simon turned to wave before he closed the door, and Elliott waved back.

At home, Elliott changed out of his still-damp jeans and into sweats and a T-shirt, and he seriously considered going for a run. But although his appetite hadn't matched Simon's, he'd had a lot of water. He'd probably end up getting only a few blocks before he'd have to pee. He booted up his laptop instead, intending to check on his students. Somehow, though, he found himself browsing that familiar website, scrolling though the Recommended for You sections. The algorithms were on point tonight, sending him a slew of tempting titles. He added a half-dozen books to his shopping cart.

Just as his cursor hovered over the Place Your Order button, the doorbell rang.

Chapter Eight

Simon stood on Elliott's porch wearing the same clothing as earlier in the night but with messier hair and a cloud of tiny moths wheeling and dipping around his head. He carried a paper grocery bag.

"Hi," he said when Elliott opened the door. He smiled and then looked away.

"Hi." Elliott tried to keep his expression neutral, but he suspected some of his surprise leaked through.

"Am I disturbing you?"

"No," Elliott said. Well, yes, but not by showing up unannounced—that part was actually lovely. When it came right down to it, Simon had been haunting Elliott since they'd met.

"I came to apologize."

"For what?" Before Simon could answer, Elliott waved his hand. "Want to come in?" The moths were annoying, and Elliott had the impression Simon's leg hurt when he stood still.

Simon entered but stopped in the little entryway. "Here." He held out the bag. "Peace offering."

"I didn't realize we were at war." Elliott took the bag, which proved to contain a six-pack of Heineken bottles.

"Not war. Just . . . Shit."

Simon looked utterly exhausted and defeated, and Elliott wished he could gather him in his arms before leading him to bed. Not for sex—although that wouldn't be awful either—but mainly for a good, long rest. Hell, Elliott could use one of those too.

Instead, they walked into the living room where Simon collapsed onto the couch. "Right back," Elliott said. He fetched a bottle opener from the kitchen, using that minute or so to try to compose himself. He wasn't sure why Simon felt the need to apologize, and that meant he couldn't prepare himself to react. Not for the first time, he wished life came with a playbook or—even better—a script. Extemporizing was hard.

Back in the living room, he uncapped two bottles, leaving the others in the bag on the floor. Instead of his usual armchair, he chose the couch, allowing a wide no-man's-land between him and Simon. Not that it helped much. Simon was still within reach, big and handsome and tempting. Somehow more real than anything else in the house.

"I'm a mess," Simon said after swallowing some beer.

"Yeah, we went over that already. Neither of us is a model of functionality at the moment."

"I hate being like this."

"Oh, not me. I love being a basket case."

Simon rolled his eyes as skillfully as a teenager. "I've always tried to keep myself . . . together. Do what's expected. Not make waves."

"That sounds safe," Elliott said thoughtfully. "But doesn't that mean your life remains small?"

"Yeah. One of my criminal justice profs used to go on about how most CJ policy is a balance between safety and freedom. More of one means less of the other. She must've told us that a dozen times. Now I'm thinking that it applies to more than just law enforcement strategies, you know?"

Although he had no idea where Simon was heading with this conversation, Elliott gave a small smile. "I bet she'd be happy to know you remember her lectures."

"Maybe I should write her an email. You think she'd give me a helpful lecture on my personal life too?"

"*That* was a quagmire I studiously avoided. I'd help my students with their studies and with deciding what to be when they grew up, but no way was I going to play Ann Landers." He'd kept a box of tissues in his office, though. For the kids facing unexpected pregnancies, deaths in the family, mental health crises, and all the other difficult predicaments young people faced. Because Elliott was open about being gay—even if not about his partner—quite a few students came to him for help in dealing with their sexuality. Mostly he referred those students to the counseling center or LGBT resource center, but he gave them a little pep talk too: his version of It Gets Better.

When Simon was momentarily silent, Elliott tried not to fidget. He was happy to follow along on Simon's tangents, but it was clear Simon hadn't come over to talk about his college days. His actual intentions remained opaque, which made Elliott nervous. Yet Elliott didn't want to rush him.

Simon drained a good portion of his bottle in one long go. "Another of my profs, his mantra was how important clear and consistent communication is for police. 'If you don't tell people what you want them to do, they can't do it.'"

"Sounds like good advice."

"Yeah. But I'm not really following it, am I? That's why I came here—to tell you I'm sorry. I haven't been at all clear with you. I'm not trying to be an asshole, I promise."

"Maybe you haven't been clear because you're not sure what you want. There's a lot of that going around." Elliott raised his bottle in a mock toast before taking a swig. The beer was cold, its slightly sour bitterness calming to his nerves.

"How about if I tell you what I do know?"

Elliott wasn't sure he wanted to hear this, but he nodded. "Sounds good."

Before speaking, Simon drained his beer, then took a second one with a grateful nod. Instead of drinking it, he twisted it gently between his palms. His good leg jiggled as he bobbed his foot, and he scrunched his face like a man expecting a blow. "I want you," he said softly. "Have since the first time I saw you. Do you remember? You were out running."

"I remember."

"Yeah, well, you look really good when you run. You look really good all of the time." Simon gave a crooked grin.

"I noticed you too."

Simon patted his stomach. "I'm hard to miss."

"You keep acting like there's something wrong with how you look." Elliott shook his head. "Believe me, there is not."

"Yeah?" Simon appeared shyly pleased.

"Yeah."

"Okay then. So we're clear on that—I want to get into your pants and you're not disgusted by that idea."

Elliott felt the polar opposite of disgust. Even those words—*get into your pants*—made his skin heat and his brain leap to places involving a lot of nudity.

Simon wasn't finished, however. "It's not only how you look. You . . . Your head turns me on. You're one of the smartest people I've met, but you're not stuffy about it. You're funny. You're good just to hang out with."

That was new. John used to tell Elliott how sexy he was, a refrain repeated by some of Elliott's hookups. But none of them seemed all that interested in him except in bed. Even John fancied his role as Elliott's mentor more than his role as a friend.

"Thank you," Elliott said.

"I want to have sex with you. I want to simply spend time with you. I want to hear about all your books and the stuff you teach and . . . everything. I want to know you. Um, assuming you want to know me too."

Although these words made Elliott slightly giddy, he kept his hand steady as he reached over and set it on Simon's good knee. "I do."

Simon's breath came out in a shudder. "It's like you said—you don't deserve to be forced to skulk. I'm shitty at that kind of thing anyway. But I don't think I'm ready to do the big reveal to Mom and Dad."

"They really don't know you're gay?"

"They . . . It's like Don't Ask, Don't Tell, family style. I'm careful about what I say, and they skip around the subject. I think avoiding difficult issues is an Odisho trait."

"Plus you don't want to alienate them."

Simon shook his head slowly. "I love them. They have faults, but so do I. We all do. I don't want to hurt them."

It was a difficult situation, one filled with potential for heartbreak and disappointment, and it wasn't Simon's fault he was stuck in the middle of it. Elliott appreciated his honesty. They didn't really know each other that well, but already Simon seemed more trustworthy than John.

As Simon toyed with his bottle, Elliott stood and slowly paced the living room. He held his beer in one hand but didn't drink it.

Simon silently let him move from place to place. Sometimes Elliott stroked a book cover or even picked up a volume, but he didn't register any of the printed words. Far too much going on in his head. When he returned to the couch, he broached the no-man's-land, sitting close enough to feel Simon's body heat.

"How about if we take this slowly?" Elliott offered. "See if there really is an us. There's no point in straining things with your family if you and I . . ."

"Fizzle out?"

"Yeah."

"You're willing to do that? Take me on a trial basis even if I can't be open about us yet?"

Elliott considered those questions carefully. God knew he didn't want to make another monumental mistake. But choosing Simon—even on a limited basis—didn't feel like a mistake. It felt right, as if some gear in his heart was finally clicking into place.

"I'd like to try us out," Elliott answered.

A kiss seemed an obvious way to seal the deal. It should have been awkward, with each of them still clutching a Heineken. In fact, Simon's cane, which had been propped against the couch, toppled to the floor. But none of that mattered when their lips made contact, when Simon's beard bristled against Elliott's cheek, when Elliott buried his fingers in the hair at Simon's nape.

Breathless, they put the bottles on an end table so they'd have both hands free. That turned out to be a good decision, since it meant they could stroke at will. Elliott wasn't sure which he liked more—being the groper or the gropee—and Simon seemed equally enthusiastic about his roles. Simon's hands were big, his fingers broad and hot on Elliott's skin.

As they made out, they slowly repositioned their bodies so eventually Elliott lay flat on the couch, Simon fully blanketing him. Simon was beautifully heavy and solid. Almost larger than life, he reminded Elliott of a Hellenistic statue of a mighty deity, except Simon wasn't cold marble or unyielding bronze. He was soft flesh and hot blood, and he writhed and moaned in an entirely lively and lifelike way.

Elliott managed to squeeze his hands under Simon's waistbands and grab palmfuls of his firm ass. Simon couldn't quite return the favor, but he cupped Elliott's face, which was also very nice. Meanwhile, they pressed their groins together. Even through several layers of clothing, Elliott felt Simon's hard cock against his own. For the first time since college, Elliott was in very real danger of coming in his pants.

Suddenly Simon went still and then propped himself on his elbows above Elliott. His face was flushed, his hair hanging down in a soft curtain. "Are we supposed to be doing this?"

"Supposed to?"

"First date?"

Elliott tried to clear his head. "I don't think it counts as a first date anymore. I dropped you off, and then you came over later."

Simon's laugh made Elliott's body vibrate. "Fair enough. What about the 'going slow' part?"

"Oh. That." It had seemed like a good idea at the time, but now that Simon was on top of him . . . Okay. It was probably still a good idea.

Shifting carefully, Simon moved off Elliott. They ended up seated next to each other, this time with their thighs pressed together. Elliott's sweats were embarrassingly tented. But then, he was probably more physically comfortable than Simon, who sported an impressive bulge in his jeans. "I didn't want to stop," Simon said. "Just so you know."

"Me either."

"But we probably should, huh?"

Should. It was a heavy word, crammed with meaning, open to a wide variety of interpretations. "I think," Elliott said after a moment of contemplation, "I want us to forget about what we think we ought to be doing. Forget about whatever arbitrary rules we think might apply. I want us to do . . . what we want. What's best for us." He gave Simon's beard a quick pet. "Let's be selfish, okay?"

"Throw out the rules, huh? I'm usually pretty good about following rules."

"Cop."

Simon chuckled. "Yeah, but even before that. I was one of those kids who practically broke out in hives just thinking about disobeying adults." He allowed himself to topple to the side so his head rested on Elliott's shoulder.

"Are you going to have a rash now? I have allergy meds."

"No. I think I can handle it." Simon gently rubbed Elliott's leg. "You know something I really want to do?"

"What?"

"Sleep with you. And I don't mean that as a euphemism. I want to snuggle up with you in bed and fall asleep listening to you breathe, and I want to wake up in the morning and see you all bleary-eyed. Is that weird?"

Elliott's response came out slightly choked because, God, he wanted that too. "No." He settled his hand atop Simon's, trapping it on his thigh. "Do you want to sleep over tonight?"

"Yes. But I won't."

"Why not?"

"C'mon, Prof. If we go to bed together, what are the odds we won't screw?"

"I'm not a statistician," Elliott said.

"Me either. But the odds are pretty close to zero, don't you think?"

Elliott sighed. "Yeah."

"And maybe . . . sometimes gratification is bigger when it's delayed, you know?"

"More wisdom from your professors?"

A grin flashed across Simon's face. "Yeah. I took a psych class once." Then his expression turned serious. "I want this—us—to be great. Not just good. So let's hold off a little."

"Okay."

They sat silently for a minute or two, Simon seeming as unwilling as Elliott to break contact. Then Simon shifted. "Tomorrow's Sunday. That means a big family dinner, and I don't know whether Ashur's had a chance to rat us out yet. I better get some good sleep, just in case. What are your plans?"

"Dunno. I have stuff to grade. I usually skip my run on Sundays and do some weights instead."

"Hmm." Simon rubbed a palm over his mouth as he thought. "Are you free Friday? I'd suggest earlier, but I've got a mess of doctor appointments and PT this week."

"Friday's good." Elliott's pulse quickened at the thought of a future with Simon, even if it was only a very near future.

"Good. I have an idea. Second date with very little chance of relatives interrupting. I'll pick you up Friday morning at eight. Dress for outdoors."

"Yeah? What will we do?"

Simon winked at him. "Surprise."

It had been a long time since anyone had surprised Elliott—pleasantly, at least. John's embezzlement and subsequent imprisonment had certainly been unexpected.

Their plans settled, Simon collected his cane, stood, and drank the last of his beer. With Elliott trailing, he walked to the door. Elliott thought Simon was favoring his bad leg more than usual. "Want a ride home?" he offered.

"No, thanks. Walking is good for me, remember? And I guess I believe it now, since that's how I met you."

Elliott nodded and smiled, then reached for the doorknob. He stopped as a thought occurred to him. "Hang on." He raced into the bedroom, grabbed a volume from one of the bookshelves, and hurried back. "Borrow this one," he said, handing it to Simon.

"*The Massive Book of Gay Erotica*?" Simon hefted the book and leered. "It's, um, big. Impressive. Are you trying to give me ideas, Professor?"

"I thought you had those ideas already. This is just nourishing them."

Simon leaned forward and kissed Elliott's cheek. "I think I'll enjoy this book a lot. See you Friday."

After Simon was gone, Elliott put the rest of the beers in the fridge, then rinsed the empty bottles and dumped them in the recycling bin. He'd intended to complete his interrupted shopping but found he was no longer in the mood. Instead, he shut the laptop down and wandered into his bedroom, where he stood staring for a long time at the new gap on the bookshelf. Then, smiling, he got ready for bed.

Chapter Nine

One of Elliott's students plagiarized on an assignment. That would have been bad enough, but he'd copied and pasted directly from Wikipedia, which was both lazy and insulting. Elliott gave him a zero on the assignment and sent an email explaining why and promising direr consequences should there be a repeat performance. That was on Monday. On Tuesday, the student emailed back, claiming he shouldn't have been given a zero because he only stole a couple of sentences. He also demanded to know how many other students had received failing grades for plagiarism. *Everybody does it*, the kid claimed.

The university probably frowned on instructors telling students they were entitled idiots who were bound for failure unless they woke up and grew up. So Elliott decided to wait a day or two before responding. He spent a lot of time wording that email in his head, though—complete with expletives and accusations about the student's ancestry and intelligence.

On Wednesday afternoon, shortly after he returned from a run and just before he sat down to write the actual email, Elliott's doorbell rang. A little girl with a backpack stood on his porch with a smiling woman—her mother, probably—slightly behind her.

"Thin Mints?" Elliott asked, although the girl wasn't wearing a uniform.

The girl looked confused, but her mother laughed and shook her head. "Sorry, no. That's at the end of winter. But we'll be glad to come back then and sell you as many boxes as you want."

"Sounds like a plan to me. What can I help you ladies with?"

After a quick glance back at her mother, the girl took a step closer. "I think your library is really cool."

Maybe praise from a nine-year-old shouldn't matter so much, but Elliott felt warm and fuzzy. "Thank you."

"I borrowed a book about constellations. It's really good."

That volume had been contributed by a neighbor—maybe even Simon. But Elliott decided lightning wouldn't strike him dead if he took the credit. "I'm glad. I always wanted to know about the stars."

"Yeah, you can find all these shapes and stuff. And there's stories about them too. Like one of them, she was this Greek princess. Andromeda."

Elliott nodded and wondered how much of Andromeda's story the girl had learned. Had she reached the part where Andromeda got chained to the rock as sacrifice to a sea monster?

But his visitor had other priorities. She shrugged out of her backpack and unzipped it. "I was thinking maybe you should have some books for kids too. 'Cause you don't, not really, but kids should be reading a lot. Mom says probably you don't have any children, so I brought some of my old books if you want to use them. They're chapter books, but they're not very hard ones. They're too easy for me." She dug out a stack of thin, well-read paperbacks.

"I hope this is all right," said the girl's mother. "It's your library, after all, and—"

"No, I think it's a great idea. I'd be happy to include them."

The little girl beamed and handed them over. "These were some of my favorites. Kids will like them," she assured him.

"I bet they will. Want to help me put them in the library?"

She seemed to like that idea. The three of them marched in a little parade to the public sidewalk, Elliott opened the plexiglass door with more ceremony than strictly necessary, and she carefully slid the books into the open space. "You can read them too," she said. "Junie B. Jones is really funny."

"I'll have to give them a try. Now, are you still working on the constellations book or do you want to start a new one?"

"I'm *almost* done with it." She looked at her mother as if for permission. Her mother nodded.

After a moment's consideration, Elliott pulled a book about California geography from the shelf. "This one has a lot of big words, but maybe you can look them up in a dictionary."

"I love dictionaries!" the girl exclaimed as she took the book. "I even sleep with one."

"She does," her mother confirmed.

Elliott grinned. "Perfect, then."

The girl plopped down cross-legged in the grass and began to pore over the book's pages. Elliott closed the library and walked the few steps to the woman. "Really, thank you both," he said. "It's great to include some children's books."

"Well, I'm just tickled you've decided to build this. It's such a fun idea! You've included some interesting choices too. I'm reading one of your books about the Great Stink right now."

"Makes you grateful for modern plumbing, doesn't it?"

"It certainly does!" She turned to her daughter. "Come on, Melanie. You have gymnastics today."

Melanie got to her feet, picked up her backpack, and started down the sidewalk, all as she continued to read. Her mother shook her head fondly. "I think I'd better shepherd her home."

"Thanks again for the books. You guys come back anytime."

"We definitely will."

Elliott went back inside to email the plagiarizing student and found he was able to be remarkably civil about it. He didn't include a single swear word.

Elliott was not a nervous wreck Thursday evening. For one thing, he now knew that Simon was attracted to him—he had, in fact, felt physical evidence of that attraction. Realizing another man found him sexy went a long way toward calming him. More than that, though, Simon apparently found him interesting. And despite personal complications, he wanted to try something more meaningful than a simple roll in the hay. That was gratifying as hell.

So Elliott spent Thursday night working on a journal manuscript he'd abandoned two years earlier. And then he read some Neil Gaiman, went to bed early, and fell asleep surprisingly quickly.

Okay, maybe he was slightly jumpy Friday morning. If he'd had time, he would have gone for a run. But instead, he took a shower and dressed in jeans, a long-sleeved Henley, and a plaid flannel shirt. "You look like you're trying Paul Bunyan drag," he muttered as he laced his boots. But he didn't change. He brewed himself a cup of coffee and leaned against the kitchen counter, sipping and waiting for the clock to move.

Simon arrived at eight on the dot. He wore a gray hoodie with the Pita Palace logo, and he looked delicious enough to eat.

"It's a little chilly this morning," he said from the front porch. "Fall's finally here."

"Should I bring anything?"

"Just you."

Simon drove a big extended-cab pickup, the kind featured in advertisements with men wearing construction gear or cowboy hats. He seemed slightly embarrassed by it. "Sometimes Mom and Dad do events. The Assyrian festival, stuff like that. They sell kebabs, shawarma, dolma . . . So I end up hauling a trailer with the grill and all their supplies."

"It's a very manly truck."

"I don't have plastic testicles hanging from the trailer hitch."

"That's a shame. But, hey, Christmas will be here soon. Maybe Santa will bring you a pair."

They climbed into the cab, Simon with some difficulty due to the knee. The inside of the truck smelled like a heady mixture of honey and Simon's cologne. He tossed his cane into the back seat, then pointed to the paper bag on the center console. "Breakfast? It's my mom's baklava. Best you've ever had."

As Simon pulled out of the driveway, Elliott took a piece of pastry, more out of politeness than hunger. It was delicious, however. "You're right." He brushed crumbs off his chest. "Best ever."

"My grandma's recipe. It's top secret, but she gave it to Mom as a wedding present. Mom says she'll pass it down to me when I get married." He cut his eyes quickly to Elliott, then back to the street in front of him.

Elliott waited a couple of minutes, then cleared his throat. "Did your parents, um, mention . . ."

"No. Ashur can't keep his big mouth shut, though, so either Mom and Dad are playing it cool or Ashur had bigger gossip to worry about.

I hear his sister's pregnant and she's not married. That ought to keep everyone busy for a little while."

"Does it outrank you being gay, on the scale of family catastrophes?"

"I doubt it," Simon replied with a sigh.

He headed north instead of west toward the freeway. With the radio playing eighties hair bands, they turned east in Riverbank and followed the river all the way to Oakdale and beyond.

"We're heading for the hills?" Elliott finally asked. He was eating his third piece of baklava.

"Yep. You don't mind, do you?"

"Not at all."

"I was originally thinking about going to Calaveras Big Trees. There's some nice little hikes there, but the damned leg's not quite up to it yet." Simon scowled, then shrugged. "I guess I should be grateful it's my left knee. If it was my right, I'd have a hell of a time driving."

"That was a very considerate bad guy."

"I'll send him a thank-you note."

They chatted lightly as they drove through rounded hills, the grass still withered by summer, and then past cattle lounging under oak trees or strolling past chunks of volcanic rock. The road grew twistier, but traffic was light and they made good time. Simon took them past the few blocks of Jamestown—Ladd had loved the railroad park there when he was a boy—and then into downtown Sonora, where touristy shops and restaurants lined the main drag. Past that, the highway climbed more sharply, and the trees' autumn colors blazed between the dark green of the conifers. Elliott smelled wood smoke and pine.

A few miles outside of Sonora, Simon took a turnoff to the right. "We're going to Columbia?" Elliott asked with a grin.

"Is that okay?"

"It's more than okay. God, I haven't been in years." As a kid, he used to beg his parents to drive there on weekends. Once a gold rush boomtown, Columbia was now a state park with many of the original buildings either restored or replicated. He'd loved stomping on the wooden sidewalks, pretending he was a prospector who'd just struck it rich, and climbing on the boulders left over from the town's hydraulic mining operations. Sometimes he and Ladd had wheedled their parents into a stagecoach ride or a try at panning for gold.

After a short journey down a narrow road, Simon pulled into a gravel parking lot behind the City Hotel. It wasn't yet ten o'clock, and the parking lot held only a few other cars, but when Elliott climbed out of the truck, he heard children's voices. "Field trip," he said.

"Yeah. We came here in fourth grade."

"Us too. And we also went to Sacramento for the gold rush museum and Sutter's Fort."

Due to the uneven ground, Simon leaned more heavily than usual on his cane as they walked toward the main drag. "I don't remember going to Sacramento, just here. Maybe you had a better grade school than me."

Columbia's paved Main Street ran past a few blocks of old brick-and-wood storefronts, with trees sporting autumn leaves as gold as the mother lode. Side streets led to a scattering of small houses. The ground dropped off at one end of town, leading to the boulders and gold-panning operation Elliott remembered from his childhood, while in the other direction, a hill rose toward the old schoolhouse and cemetery. As Elliott had guessed, schoolchildren swarmed everywhere, clutching bottles of sarsaparilla and candy sticks and jostling to watch the blacksmith work.

"Do you mind if we eat first?" Simon asked.

Due to the baklava, Elliott wasn't hungry, but he nodded agreeably. As it turned out, their breakfast options were limited to a single restaurant, a place with plank floors and the aroma of frying bacon. Their waitress wore a long gingham dress, her gray hair in a long ponytail.

"Coffee, boys?" she asked as she handed them laminated menus. They both said yes.

While Simon perused the offerings, Elliott looked around. The restaurant was surprisingly busy. A large group of men in orange construction vests occupied several tables, and other seats were taken by people who appeared to be locals, chatting with one another across the room. A few were dressed as if they worked ranches.

"Hoppin' place," Simon observed, putting his menu down. "Are you sure this is okay with you?"

"It's a great idea. I'm glad you thought of it."

Simon grinned widely. "I wanted to get out of town, you know?"

"To where there's less chance of running into cousins?" Elliott regretted the question as soon as it left his mouth. He reached over to pat Simon's arm. "Sorry. I didn't mean that as a dig."

"It's okay. As far as I know, I have no relatives in Tuolumne County, which is a good thing. I wanted to be outdoors, but somewhere I could handle." He sighed. "I used to be pretty ripped. I didn't run as much as you do, but I spent a lot of time in the gym. Now I hobble and I eat."

"But you're moving. Anyway, I told you. I like you just as you are." Elliott threw in a leer for good measure.

The waitress took their orders—some kind of elaborate skillet thing for Simon, a fruit cup for Elliott—and refilled their coffees. They sat without talking, but that was fine. There was a lovely solidity to Simon that meant he didn't always need to fill space with conversation. He could simply smile across the glossy pine table, and that was enough to make Elliott feel content.

When the food arrived, Elliott shook his head slightly. The portions were enormous. But Simon finished everything on his plate except two pieces of toast, which Elliott ate. Simon insisted on paying since this date was his treat. "You boys have a good day," the waitress said before giving them a wink Elliott didn't know how to interpret.

More kids had arrived while they were eating, each little group accompanied by a harried-looking chaperone. Loud crashes and cheers came from the gold-rush-era bowling alley, while a large group clustered around a costumed older woman who was telling ghost stories. Simon and Elliott strolled slowly, pausing now and then to scrutinize an exhibit or peruse a store. Simon left the candy store with a hefty chunk of peanut butter fudge, which he broke off in small bits as they walked.

Kids were having a great time tossing feed to the chickens in the large coop at one end of the storefronts, and Elliott found himself smiling at the spectacle.

"Do you like children?" Simon asked, leaning against the weathered boards of the adjacent shack.

"I guess. Never thought about it much." That was not entirely true. When he was in college, he'd imagined becoming a father someday.

He'd even thought about which books he'd buy for his hypothetical offspring. *Goodnight Moon* would be the first. But then he'd fallen in with John, and their twisted little version of domestic bliss clearly had no space for kids.

"My mom is desperate for grandchildren," Simon said. "She makes do with my cousins' kids, but I don't think that's enough for her."

"What are your thoughts on the matter?"

Simon chuckled. "I think I need to finish growing up first." But he was smiling at the field trip kids, and Elliott could picture him joking around with a son or daughter or folding himself into a tiny plastic chair for a student-teacher conference.

"Want to visit the schoolhouse and cemetery?" Simon gestured in that direction with his cane.

Elliott vaguely remembered that the route, although short, was steep. "Will you make it okay?"

Simon shot him a scowl. "If I can't, you can leave me to the bears and coyotes."

As it turned out, he had a good bit of difficulty with the uphill road. He grunted a lot but didn't complain, and Elliott didn't mind taking it slow. He wondered what it would be like to live in one of the little houses they passed—isolated yet beset by tourists. They didn't see any bears or coyotes, although a placid deer stood next to a lawn-statue doppelganger and gazed at them as they passed. The juxtaposition struck Elliott as unbearably funny, and he laughed so hard that he had as much difficulty with the walk as Simon.

The old hilltop schoolhouse was a two-story brick structure surrounded by green lawn. Simon carefully lowered himself to the grass, his bad leg in front of him at a somewhat awkward angle. He squinted up at Elliott. "You're gonna have to help me stand."

"Don't worry. I won't leave you to the bears and coyotes." Elliott sat next to him.

"Maybe it's the scavengers I should be worried about. Turkey vultures."

Elliott patted Simon's good knee. "You seem pretty lively to me."

"I'm thinking pretty lively thoughts with you here next to me. You look extra good outdoors. The sun catches the colors in your eyes."

Elliott blushed. No lover had ever complimented his eyes, which were an ordinary blue gray. He leaned back on his hands and looked up at the sky.

"What do you think it was like to live here in the 1850s?" Simon asked.

That was a line of inquiry Elliott could address with comfort. "Hard. Really hard. People died from disease, accidents, violence, drugs and booze." He gestured toward the nearby cemetery. "The dates on those headstones show a lot of young deaths."

"No way I'd do that to myself just in hopes of striking it rich. I'd rather be poor and safe."

"I don't know that they were all after money. I think some of them probably wanted adventure, fresh opportunities. They could reinvent themselves when they came here."

Simon plucked a tiny weed out of the grass and played with it, spinning the stem between thumb and forefinger. "Were some of them running away from something?"

"Yeah, probably."

A jay landed nearby and eyed them speculatively. When neither of them did anything interesting or produced any food, it pecked at the ground a few times, cawed in derision, and flapped away. But it didn't go far, landing on an oak tree branch near the reconstructed outhouse.

"Man, it must've been really hard to be gay back then," Simon said.

"In Columbia? Maybe not as hard as you think."

"Really?"

Elliott sat upright, brushing the debris from his palms. "Nobody would have been suspicious of two men sharing a house. Lots of men lived in close proximity with their mining buddies. And there weren't many women around, so perhaps folks were understanding if men turned to each other for company instead."

"That's . . . kind of cool. I never thought about it like that. Do you have a book about it? I'd love to read it."

"About homosexuality in the gold rush?" Elliott shook his head. "I've seen the subject mentioned here and there, but I don't think much has been published about it."

"Maybe you oughtta write that book, then, Prof."

"My specialty is the Balkans." But even as he said that, Elliott found himself intrigued by Simon's suggestion. Before John led him elsewhere, Elliott had been interested in studying minority groups in the state's early history. Here in Northern California, Elliott would have a good chance of discovering whatever original sources existed on the topic. There were a couple of archives on LGBT history in San Francisco, which might be a good place to start.

Except he was just an adjunct instructor of online courses now, and such people didn't begin original research projects.

Elliott helped Simon stand, and they held hands a moment longer than necessary. They might even have kissed if a gaggle of fourth graders hadn't appeared a few minutes earlier, accompanied by a droning teacher. Elliott didn't want an audience and doubted Simon did either.

They walked slowly around the schoolhouse and down the hill a bit, then through the gates of the Columbia Cemetery. It was a large graveyard, founded in the 1850s but still in use. Some of the headstones were shiny and new, with flowers and trinkets from still-living family members in front of them. Others were worn and covered by lichen. Nobody remembered the people buried under those stones.

Elliott paused to run a hand along a marker for a Mary Azevedo. According to her headstone, she'd immigrated from Portugal and died in 1879 at age 31—most likely in childbirth, because an unnamed baby boy was buried with her.

"The cemetery is like a book," he said softly. "It tells stories."

Simon leaned against a nearby tree, looking solemn. Next to him was the headstone of a New Hampshire native who'd drowned in 1858, age 28, and was memorialized in granite by his twin brother. A low fence with fancy metalwork—now badly rusted—surrounded that grave. Elliott wondered where the longer-surviving twin had eventually been laid to rest.

"I didn't much like history in school," Simon said. "It was all, 'Who won this war?' and 'What was the name of that president?' Boring. But those books I've been borrowing from you? They're like novels, only true."

Still stroking the old granite, Elliott nodded. "You want to know something? I think right here in this cemetery is where I decided to be a historian. Because it wasn't just a bunch of dead guys with dates to memorize—it was real places and real people. I can almost see Mary Azevedo, can't you?"

He pictured dark hair, a careworn face that looked older than her age, brown eyes that had seen a multitude of wonders and sorrows. She would have worn a dress similar to their waitress's, and she probably had several children before the one who died with her. Hard work would have roughened her hands. She would have been well acquainted with hunger and hardship, but perhaps she'd known joy as well. Maybe she was happy in the hope of her children growing up in this young country, surrounded by the promise of endless riches.

Simon walked over and cupped Elliott's cheek in one hand. His eyes were as soft and warm as melted chocolate. "You can see her for me," he rumbled. He looked as if that was a wondrous thing.

Elliott stepped back. If he hadn't, he'd have been in very real danger of jumping Simon's bones right there among the mortal remains of a century and a half of Columbians. Maybe some of them would posthumously approve, but the park rangers and the school chaperones probably wouldn't.

They strolled the cemetery for a long time, crunching the fallen leaves underfoot and pausing to read the inscriptions. Time hadn't altered Elliott's fascination with the place. He wanted to know every person interred, wanted to find the bits of their existence that had been buried under the decades and bring them once more to light. And Simon apparently wanted to hear about them. He asked a lot of questions, clearly fascinated by Elliott's impromptu lessons on the history of the region.

Although Simon appeared willing to keep going, Elliott eventually saw the lines of pain deepen around his eyes. "I'm thirsty," Elliott announced. "Want to try out that saloon?"

Walking down the hill was harder on Simon than going up. By the time they reached the level ground of Main Street, Elliott was honestly worrying whether Simon would make it. Luckily, the saloon was at the closer end of town and there were plenty of vacant tables.

Simon collapsed onto a chair with a loud groan. "I'm sorry."

"Don't be."

"I try not to whine—most of the time. I could've ended up way worse. Or dead."

Elliott shuddered at the idea. What if he'd never met Simon? His life would be so much poorer. "You can whine all you want. And I'll buy you a drink. What'll it be?"

Simon's mouth quirked into a grin. "Sarsaparilla, pardner. I'm driving."

Elliott wandered to the bar, where the bartender proved to be laid-back and friendly. He poured Simon's drink with a good deal of panache before filling a glass mug with beer. "You want something to eat?" Elliott called to Simon. "They have pizza."

"No, thanks. I'm good."

They sat contentedly with their drinks, looking at the old photos on the wall. This place had been in business for over a century and a half and had undoubtedly seen some lively times. This afternoon it was quiet, however, with a couple of locals sitting at the bar and a quartet of retirees in one corner. The bartender brought over a basket of peanuts and encouraged Simon and Elliott to throw the shells on the floor.

Simon dug into the snack but was hesitant to toss the shells. "My mother would murder me for throwing garbage on the floor."

"Your mother doesn't work here." Elliott took the debris from Simon and let it drop.

"I still feel guilty. I've swept too many restaurant floors, I guess."

"When did you start working at the Pita Palace?"

"Jesus, I don't know. Mom and Dad opened it when I was a preschooler, and I think I spent more waking hours there than at home. Even when I was really little, I'd help out. I remember stacking endless plastic cups after they came out of the dishwasher." The softness in his expression suggested these were fond memories, not resentful recollections of forced child labor. "Did you work when you were a kid?"

"Not like that. My father was a supervisor at the glass factory, and my mom worked as a dental receptionist. No place for a child in either spot. Ladd knew how to hustle up money—he'd mow lawns and stuff like that. All I ever did was pet sit."

For some reason, that answer delighted Simon. "Pet sit?"

"Sure. Neighbors would go away, and I'd take care of their dogs and cats. One family had a boa constrictor." That had been a short and easy gig—he just checked on the snake daily and refilled its water.

"I didn't take you as an animal lover."

Elliott scowled. "I love animals. Do you think I'm some kind of ogre or something?"

"You don't have any pets," Simon pointed out. "At least as far as I've seen. I guess you could have a fish tank hidden away somewhere."

"I don't." Elliott cracked a peanut, but Simon, grinning, snatched the meat away before Elliott could pop it into his mouth. "Ladd used to be allergic to anything with fur, and my mom said fish die too much. Reptiles were out since they eat live food—Mom put her foot down about that."

"Your mom doesn't live with you," Simon said, clearly pleased to throw Elliott's gentle gibe back at him.

Actually, Elliott wasn't sure why he'd never adopted a pet. Sure, it would have been a challenge in college and grad school, when he'd moved often from one apartment to another. But why not afterward? Maybe because nothing in his life had felt permanent, either with John or in the aftermath.

"I might get a dog someday," Elliott said. "When I'm more . . . settled."

The retirees noisily gathered their belongings and left. When the bartender came over to clear their table, he brought Elliott and Simon more peanuts.

"I guess you don't mind if we hang out here awhile, huh?" Simon asked.

"I can spare the table. Anyway, that's what saloons are for." He sauntered away with a bit more ass swagger than was strictly called for, leaving Elliott to wonder if the bartender had tagged him and Simon as a couple. Simon wouldn't have tripped Elliott's gaydar. Actually, neither did the bartender. Maybe Elliott's gaydar was defective.

"So this weekend I have family stuff," Simon said. "And Christ, it feels like I spend the whole week with doctors and PT. But I have some time free. Can we plan a third date, or is it too early?"

Elliott leaned closer and dropped his voice. "Not too early. I want more of you."

It was gratifying to watch Simon's cheeks color and his throat work. He even licked his lips—not like he was trying to be sexy, although that was very much the effect. "Ditto. So when can we get together?"

"You name the day and time. I'm wide open. I'll plan the itinerary, but it's going to be hard to top today."

Despite Simon's smile, he seemed a bit troubled by something. So Elliott added a proviso. "Don't worry. I'll find us somewhere uninfested by your relatives."

Still frowning, Simon waved the comment away. "El, what do you do all week?"

The nicknamed distracted Elliott enough that it took him a moment to respond. "Um, I have my classes. I run. I read—obviously. Sometimes I putter in the garden or do a little housework. Why?"

"You do all those things by yourself, right? Even the classes— you're not talking live to the students."

"I'm not a recluse." Elliott remembered Ladd comparing him to the Collyer brothers. "I interact with human beings on a regular basis."

Simon lifted his eyebrows and tilted his head. "Really?"

After John's arrest, Elliott had spent an unfortunate amount of time being interrogated by police officers who were convinced he'd played a part in the embezzlement. He wished he had his lawyer at his side again. "Ladd. And my sister-in-law, Anna."

"And?"

"Sometimes I hook up with a guy. *Did* hook up. I haven't since I met you."

That got him a quick flash of a smile before Simon put his cop face back on. "And?"

"Not long ago, I had dinner and coffee with Anna's coworker, Kyle. Also before I met you."

"Once. Okay. And?"

"I see people during my run on the greenbelt path."

Simon raised his eyebrows slightly.

Elliott tried not to wilt as he rummaged in his mind for other examples. The disastrous Skype interview? Mike Burgess and his endless complaints? The literary Girl Scout and her mother? "I go shopping," was what he finally came up with, and he knew exactly how pathetic that sounded.

Simon wasn't looking at him with pity, which was good. Pity would have damaged Elliott. But Simon did look worried, and that was bad enough. "Have you always closed yourself up so much?" he asked.

If they had been gold-rush prospectors, a question like that never would have arisen in conversation—Elliott was quite sure of that. Nineteenth-century miners drank heavily, got into gunfights, and often wasted away from consumption, but they were *not* in touch with their feelings. He envied them. But Simon was silently unrelenting, and Elliott finally sighed. "More or less," he admitted as he pulverized a peanut shell.

"Do you *want* that?"

"What do you mean?"

"I'm wondering whether you're a major introvert—which is totally fine—or if there's something else going on."

Elliott shot him a sour look. "Maybe you should be a psychotherapist instead of a cop."

"Maybe I should," Simon replied easily. "Or maybe I should mind my own goddamn business."

A big part of Elliott wanted to say that was a wonderful idea. Another part considered ordering a second beer—or maybe something stronger. Then the door opened and five young women strolled in, talking loudly. They all wore high heels and a lot of makeup, with their hair carefully styled, although they were dressed in jeans and casual blouses. They took a table next to the one the retirees had vacated and began a lively discussion about what kind of alcohol to order.

"Bachelorette party," Simon offered quietly.

"Really? Here?"

"Sure. They're going to have a dinner at the City Hotel tonight and spend the night there, and one of them will get married here tomorrow. She'll be in a traditional white dress, but I bet the groom will wear a cowboy hat. They may ride off in the stagecoach after they exchange vows."

Elliott squinted at the women. "Which one is the bride?"

"The one in the red shirt."

How Simon could deduce that, Elliott had no idea. "I see you can tell a story with a little base material too."

"I have attended ten thousand weddings."

"Ten thousand? You're sure of that?"

Simon laughed. "More or less. Most of them have been in a church with the reception at the Assyrian center in Turlock, but they've had themes. And I can tell a bachelorette party when I see one."

"Okay. But where's the groom and his pals?"

"Dunno." Simon dropped a couple of shells on the floor and looked guilty about it. "Getting drunk somewhere else. Is there somewhere else in Columbia to get drunk?"

Elliott thought for a moment. "There used to be a Mexican place."

"There you go. The boys are throwing back shots of tequila."

Simon was every bit as bright as John. And there was something so *easy* about Simon. From the very first, everything with John had been complicated, one of those games with a rulebook as thick as a Bible. With John, Elliott had to consider every move, worry about the implications and consequences, wonder how John would take it. Even though the budding relationship with Simon was still amorphous and uncertain, Elliott felt free to act without strategizing first.

"I'm a snail," Elliott said.

Simon gave a somewhat startled blink.

"You know those really big ones that get in the garden and eat all your seedlings? That's me."

"Um, okay. I don't have any seedlings. Sometimes I accidentally step on one of those snails when I go to fetch the mail. Then I feel bad."

"Yeah. I've done that too. Yuck." Elliott shuddered. "Nobody's stepped on me yet, but I'm one of those snails."

"You run pretty fast for a snail."

Elliott drank the last of his beer and set the empty glass down with a slight thud. "So the analogy's not perfect. Bear with me." He received a nod from Simon and then continued. "I've always been, well, not quite a loner, but not the life of the party either. I spent a lot of time studying. Reading. When I was a kid, I mostly tagged along with Ladd and his friends."

"You guys are pretty close, huh?"

"He's eleven months older than me. We didn't have a lot of choice." Their parents had never divulged whether the spacing had been intentional or an accident. In either case, two babies so close together must have scared them off, because they never had been interested in adding more to the family.

"Are snails loners?" Simon asked.

"No idea. Historian, not a biologist. Anyway, when I paired up with John, my social life really narrowed. I was busy with grad school and then my job—earning tenure is tough—but also John . . . The secrecy got in the way." Because Elliott couldn't tell anyone about his relationship, he couldn't open up enough to form a true friendship. Damn it, how the hell had he thought that was all right?

Simon wasn't pressing him to hurry up with the tale. Instead, he shelled a nut and handed it over. "Do snails like peanuts?"

"I guess." Elliott popped it into his mouth, taking a moment to savor the saltiness. Ah, saltiness. That had been his original point. He traced a fingertip along the scarred wooden table—slowly, like a snail. "As long as I was with John, I crawled along. But then that whole fuckup happened and . . . and it was like a snail confronting salt. I protected the vulnerable parts of me by tucking myself into my shell. And I haven't come out since."

"But you have." Simon laid his hand alongside Elliott's, their fingers not quite touching. "You built your library. You asked me out. And you came here with me today."

"God, I'm really glad I did."

Simon's smile was brighter than a shining gold ingot and twice as precious. "Me too." Then rapidly changing gears, Simon clapped his hands and said, "Hey, how about some ice cream?"

They stayed in Columbia for several hours more, not doing much except strolling, people watching, and eating. Elliott bought several volumes in the small, crowded bookshop. Both of them tried candle dipping, but the results did not turn out well, much to the amusement of some schoolkids. The students marched back to their buses, and as the daylight waned, the shops closed. Elliott and Simon had an early dinner at the Mexican place. No groom's party was in evidence, but Simon opined that they were all at the City Hotel, eating chicken and prime rib with the wedding couple's families.

Even after their stomachs were full from an excellent chicken mole, Elliott and Simon were in no hurry to get home. They walked to a little grassy area near the old city jail and sat across from each other at a picnic table. With music and faint voices wafting from the saloon, they tipped back their heads and looked at the stars. They didn't have to talk; they could just *be*. During that snippet of time, Elliott had the epiphany that sometimes people's injuries made them whole again.

"This feels right," Simon whispered, stealing Elliott's thoughts. His warm, strong hands grasped Elliott's.

"Yes."

"We could spend the night. The wedding party might have City Hotel booked, but there's always the Fallon."

"I overheard one of the guides today. She said both hotels are haunted."

"I ain't afraid of no ghosts." Simon smiled and squeezed Elliott's hands.

"I didn't bring any condoms."

Simon scrunched up his face. "Me either. I wasn't planning a seduction."

The nearest grocery or convenience store was several miles away in Sonora. Making a run there and back just so they could have sex felt tawdry somehow. So Elliott squeezed back. "Another time, all right?" He promised himself that whatever he planned for the third date, he'd make sure to have supplies handy. Just in case.

It was nice to drive back together in the dark with few other cars on the road. Sometimes Simon hummed along with the radio. Sometimes one of them rested a hand on the other's thigh. As far as Elliott was concerned, they could have passed Modesto and kept on going forever, and he wouldn't have complained.

But eventually they were in his driveway, the porch light just barely illuminating the little rainbow flag. Simon kept the engine running but shifted into Park and, as if for good measure, engaged the emergency brake.

"Thank you," Elliott said. "I think this was the best date I've ever been on."

"I like that you don't need fancy things. I had a really good day too."

The kiss began sweet and tender, just a delicate brushing of lips and the exchange of warm breaths. It soon grew more demanding, until Simon tilted Elliott's head back and nibbled and suckled on his neck, beard bristles sharp against tender skin. Elliott was at an off angle and couldn't find anything to do with his hands, so he clenched them into tight fists and moaned.

"You're not a snail," Simon said breathlessly. "You're . . . you're . . . Shit. I don't think I can do analogies. No, wait. I got it." He sat up straighter. "I've met people who could use drugs now and then for years and it was no big deal. They could take or leave it. Get high and then walk away. And I've met others who tried just one hit, one dose, and *bang*! They ended up so hooked that all the clinics in the world couldn't clean them up for good. You're like that to me, I think."

"I'm methamphetamine? I think I'd rather be a mollusk."

"You're Elliott Thompson, and you're under my skin. We're going to make this work. Somehow."

Elliott kissed him once more before heading inside, hoping some of Simon's optimism would be contagious.

Chapter
Ten

"Hello? Is this Elliott Thompson?"

Elliott had just returned from a run on Monday morning when his phone began to ring. He turned off the music before answering and stood sweating and panting on his front porch, the phone in his slippery palm. "Yes."

"Hi, this is Ginny Holmes. I'm chair of the history search committee at Nebraska State University. Is now a good time?"

Hoping his heavy breathing didn't sound too odd, Elliott wiped his forehead with his free hand. "Yeah, sure. Sorry. I was just jogging."

She sounded genuinely amused when she laughed. "The joys of cell phones, I guess. None of us ever has a moment's peace. I'll make this short. The committee is impressed with your application, and we'd like to conduct a phone interview. Are you free at ten Central Time on Wednesday morning?"

Ten Central would be eight Pacific Time. That was doable. He was free anytime except Thursday afternoon, when he'd be having a third date with Simon. "Yes, of course. Thank you."

"Perfect. Is this a good number to reach you?"

"Yes. You don't do Skype?"

Another laugh. "Our university's hiring practices are inscribed in stone and haven't been changed in decades. We consider ourselves lucky we're allowed to use telephones. Don't worry, though. Other than that, we've mostly progressed into the twenty-first century."

"From a historian's point of view, that's almost a shame."

"Good point. Maybe I'll suggest at the next department meeting that we give up our laptops in favor of papyrus scrolls."

"Is there much papyrus in Nebraska?" He hoped he wasn't taking the banter too far.

"Oh, sure. Fourth biggest crop after corn, soy, and milo. I'll be looking forward to chatting with you Wednesday morning, Dr. Thompson."

"Me too. Thanks."

As he ended the call and entered his house, he reminded himself not to get too excited. He'd had phone interviews before and knew there'd be nothing beyond that. At some point the search committee would google him, and then they'd move on. Also, Nebraska. But it was a good university and a tenure-track position, and beggars could not be choosers.

After showering and a light breakfast, Elliott sat down with a cup of coffee and his laptop and spent several hours researching NSU's history program. They had a Center for Central European Studies, which was undoubtedly why they were interested in him, but they also had strong offerings in human migrations and the Great Plains. Elliott could probably teach a course or two in those areas, if need be. The pay scales at NSU weren't great, and he wasn't at all sure he'd be thrilled to live so far from what he considered civilization. Were there gay bars in Broken Bow? On the other hand, the cost of living was low. For the price of his house in Modesto, he could buy three similarly sized homes there.

But, shit, what about Simon?

Elliott pushed away that thought as being doubly irrelevant. He'd never get an offer from NSU, and his fling with Simon was going to be short-lived. Fuck. Now he didn't even know which disaster to hope for.

On Tuesday morning, two things occurred to Elliott. One was that Halloween was just over a week away, and the other was that he hadn't decided what to do with Simon on Thursday. The Halloween problem had an easy solution. He simply went online and ordered a bunch of monster-themed bookmarks and pencils and a huge bag of plastic spider rings. He wasn't morally opposed to giving out candy, but he hated having the leftovers around, and in his experience, most kids got pretty jazzed over the trinkets.

He turned his thoughts to date planning. Thursday felt important, in part because Columbia had been such a fun excursion and also because it was their third date. That was a level of commitment he'd rarely achieved, and of course Simon never had. The usual suspects—dinner, movie, drinks—seemed trite. But anything involving too much physical movement was beyond Simon's abilities right now. There was a time element involved too, because Simon had an appointment Friday afternoon. So Elliott couldn't plan anything really wild like a surprise getaway to Catalina Island.

God, he sucked at this. No wonder his love life was a mess. Finally, out of sheer desperation, he texted Ladd. *Need advice. Can I come over tonight?*

The reply came almost immediately, even though Ladd was probably in class. *You're asking for advice? Is the world ending?*

Elliott sent him the flipping-off emoji.

He waited until after dinner to drive over to Ladd and Anna's house. He could have eaten with them—Ladd extended an invitation—but he decided Tuesday tacos and Ladd's homemade guac shouldn't be sullied by the awkwardness of dating advice.

His brother and sister-in-law lived not far from downtown, in a little bungalow that was nearly a century old. Unlike Elliott's house, theirs had almost no yard, and sketchy people tended to wander the neighborhood now and then. But their place had character, which his tract home lacked. They had built-in bookcases, arched doorways, and leaded glass windows, and the old hardwood floors creaked pleasantly underfoot.

They didn't start with small talk. Ladd and Anna curled up on the couch next to each other, each with a cup of tea, while Elliott sat in a leather armchair and clutched a glass of water. "I have a phone interview tomorrow," he said. "Nebraska State."

"Hey, that's great!" Ladd said. "Congrats!"

But the more observant Anna poked Ladd right before she said, "You don't look all that thrilled, El."

"Not optimistic. There are complications. That's sort of the part I need advice for."

Anna and Ladd both leaned forward eagerly. Great. They obviously expected that the *Elliott Rips Open His Chest Show* would be wonderful entertainment.

"I've started dating this guy," he began.

Ladd interrupted. "You're gay? Oh God! Not that!" He pressed a hand over his heart and fluttered his eyes at the ceiling.

Anna poked him again, harder this time, and Elliott smiled his thanks at her. "Not Kyle, I take it?" she asked.

"No. I like him. He's nice. Not to sound clichéd or anything, but there's no chemistry there."

She nodded. "He said almost the exact same thing about you."

Elliott could live with that. "Ladd, do you remember that neighbor we met when we were installing my library?"

Apparently a big, sexy man had less impact on Ladd's straight-boy brain than on Elliott's gay one, because Ladd looked puzzled. "Um . . . yeah? He had a crutch, right?"

"A cane. His name's Simon." Elliott gave them a quick biography, along with a summary of their first two dates. He downplayed the series of catastrophes at the restaurant, though.

"Wow, Columbia!" Anna enthused. "That's the perfect place for him to take you! Good catch, El!"

"Yeah, except he'll probably be the big one who got away."

Ladd pointed at Elliott. "That's awfully pessimistic, dude."

So then Elliott explained Simon's issues with his family, which made Ladd and Anna shake their heads.

"I'm lucky to have you guys," Elliott said. "And Mom and Dad, even though they're so far away. Simon's really tight with his parents, and I don't think he wants to strain that."

"This isn't another John situation, is it?" Ladd looked angry. "Because you don't deserve that shit, and you know it."

"No. It's . . . different. We're going to reach a decision point, Simon and I. Either he's going to determine that staying with me is something he wants to do, in which case he's going to come out to his people. Or he's going to decide I'm not worth it, and—"

"And he'd be a complete idiot," Anna interjected. "Don't you get a say in this too?"

"Nobody puts Elly in the corner," Ladd said and narrowly avoided a third poke from his wife.

Ignoring his brother, Elliott nodded at Anna. "Sure I do. But no way am I going to force him to make a choice he might regret later. I can be patient. It's not like I have much else going on. Besides, I think he's worth it."

Ladd yawned widely before giving an apologetic shrug. "Sorry. We had football practice at six thirty this morning."

"You having a good season?"

"Hey. No getting out of advice-receiving by shifting the conversation to football. What is it you want us to tell you? Whether you should go for it with this Simon guy?"

A car engine gunned loudly outside, making Elliott twitch. His nerves were as ragged as usual. "No. Something more concrete. I need ideas for where I could take him on Thursday."

While Ladd looked clueless, Anna smiled widely. "Criteria?"

"Um, somewhere not boring. Away from the possibility of bumping into his relatives. Not too taxing for his leg. Food is a plus."

One thing he admired about Ladd and Anna was that they liked a challenge. They were both competitive too. Anna ran half marathons, and both of them had happily crushed Elliott at many a video game. As he'd hoped, they took his question as a test, a new puzzle to be solved.

"Cost?" Ladd asked after a few moments of thought.

"Moderate." Elliott wasn't rolling in dough and didn't want to seem as if he was showing off. The excursion to Columbia had been pretty inexpensive.

"Timeline?"

"I'm picking him up at noon Thursday. We need to be home that night."

Ladd tapped his chin, and Anna sipped her tea. "Any allergies, aversions, et cetera?" she asked.

"Not that I know of. He's easygoing. He's sweet. He really likes to eat, but he's a little embarrassed about it."

Everyone was silent for several minutes, but Elliott could see the wheels turning in Ladd's and Anna's heads. At one point Ladd opened his mouth as if to say something but then stopped and shook his head. "Stairs," he muttered. Elliott didn't ask for clarification.

Anna set her mug decisively on the coffee table. "Got it. Sacramento."

Elliott hadn't expected that. "Um . . . do you think he needs a tour of the capitol?"

"Nope. Old Sac. You can regale him with more history. Take a ride on one of those riverboat tours. Watch him pig out on mini donuts and candy samples—or have a nice meal at one of those restaurants on the water."

Ladd seemed enthusiastic about the plan. "Train museum! That place is cool."

It was a pretty good idea. It met all his guidelines and was quirky without being too weird. He stood, walked to the couch, and took Anna's hand. With a deep bow, he kissed the back of it. "Thank you, Lady Anna. Once again, you're perfection."

"Hey, what about me?" Ladd exclaimed.

Elliott took his hand, kissed it, and was rewarded by Ladd's overly dramatic eye roll.

Sacramento it was.

Before Elliott could spend time with Simon, he had to survive the phone interview with NSU. He was grateful it was scheduled for early in the day. As it was, he'd slept fitfully and awakened before dawn, then he went for a quick run that did little to soothe his nerves. He'd had no appetite for breakfast. By a few minutes before eight, he was pacing the floor—phone in hand—trying to calm himself.

"You can do this," he said, hoping a pep talk might help. "You're smart. You're a good scholar and a good instructor. You've done your homework on this department. It's just a little telephone conversation."

Right.

His phone rang at exactly one minute past the hour. "Hi, Elliott. This is Ginny. I'm sitting here with Berta and Greg, the other members of the search committee."

From his online research, Elliott knew that Berta was a full professor and the director of the Central European Center. Greg was junior faculty, a specialist in the history of medicine—which sounded interesting, although Elliott knew little about it. "Good morning," Elliott said.

They made a few minutes of small talk. Apparently a cold snap was predicted for Nebraska, but this week had been unseasonably warm.

Soon they got into the meat of the interview, with the committee asking a series of questions about his research interests, teaching philosophy, and views on mentoring students. It was hard to judge his impact when Elliott couldn't see their reactions, but he felt as if he answered well, neither droning on nor responding too abruptly. Berta seemed especially interested in some of what he had to say; she asked a few follow-ups about his specific publication plans and about what classes he'd be most likely to teach.

While the interview proceeded, Elliott walked slowly around his living room. Movement seemed more soothing than sitting.

Having apparently exhausted their rote list of queries, Ginny finally asked, "Is there anything else you'd like us to know about you?"

He almost said no, but that would be pointless. So he took a deep breath. "Yes, there is. I don't know if you've done any background research on me. If you have, you've discovered I was embroiled in a scandal in my last tenure-track position. I was eventually cleared of all wrongdoing, but the record is still out there."

A brief pause ensued. He imagined the committee members exchanging glances. "Would you like to tell us about it?" Ginny asked.

"Sure. When I was in grad school, I began an affair with my dissertation advisor. He later became a dean at a different institution, and I was hired into the history department there. Nobody knew about us. Then he got caught stealing money from the college and our relationship became public knowledge. I didn't know he was stealing." Elliott sighed. "He's in prison. I was exonerated and got a settlement from the university."

More silence, longer this time. "Can I tell you something else?" he asked.

Ginny answered. "Of course."

"I was stupid to get involved and stay involved with him, and I shouldn't have gone along with keeping our relationship a secret. But none of that reflects on my suitability for your department. You can read my journal articles and my teaching evaluations—those speak for themselves. I earned my degree and my faculty position, and until John got caught, I kept my job because I was good at it, not because he acted on my behalf."

"We appreciate your candor," Ginny said. "It sounds as if you were in a difficult position."

"I was. And I take responsibility for putting myself there. I'm hoping you'll judge me on my work and not on that mistake."

"We all make mistakes." That was Greg. "God knows I have—as my first two wives would be more than happy to tell you."

Heartened, Elliott chanced a small chuckle. "I think that's one thing being a historian teaches us: everyone screws up. Sometimes on a much bigger scale than I did. The Habsburgs come to mind, for instance."

"You will not be declaring yourself emperor of Mexico?" Berta asked.

"I don't plan on it, no. And if I've been warned that the Black Hand wants to assassinate me, I won't ride around town in an open car."

All three members of the search committee laughed. Good. At least he could produce in-jokes for historians.

Ginny spoke next. "Elliott, we were wondering why you left your previous position for adjunct positions in California. I'm glad you explained. How do you feel about picking up and moving again?"

"Well, I grew up in Modesto and I've never visited Nebraska. But I'm geographically adaptable. I've always spent most of my time on my studies or work, and I don't need a lot of excitement. Actually, Modesto is kind of the Nebraska of California. Our major industries are ag related, and we're surrounded by cattle ranches and orchards. So it wouldn't be as big an adjustment for me as you might assume." He hoped that was true—he was trying to be honest.

Of course, he didn't mention that moving would mean leaving Simon behind. Walking away from the man he was falling in love with. Shit. Falling in love with?

"Elliott?" Ginny prompted.

"I'm sorry—you faded out there for a moment." Thank God bad cell reception was always a handy excuse. "Could you repeat the question?"

"We just wanted to know if you had additional questions for us."

For once, damn it, go for broke. "Could you tell me whether you're honestly still considering me for the position after what I told you?"

"Yes," Ginny responded promptly. "We are. We have several more candidates to interview, and then we'll be inviting three finalists to campus. Probably early in the new year, since the holidays and end of the semester are almost upon us. But nothing you've said today rules you out as a candidate."

Elliott was very thankful they couldn't see him just then—his entire body shuddered with relief at her words. "Thank you."

"Thank you for talking to us today."

There was a brief round of goodbyes before the call ended. For a long time afterward, Elliott remained rooted in place, the warm phone clutched in one hand. That hadn't been so awful. He at least had the impression that Ginny meant what she'd said. If he didn't get an invitation for a campus visit, it would be because other candidates impressed the committee more or were a better fit for their needs, not because of the thing with John.

But, fuck, what about the realization that had raised its fuzzy little head in the midst of the phone call? Falling in love with Simon. Was that even possible at this early point, or was Elliott fooling himself due to lust and loneliness? If it *was* true, what the hell was he supposed to do about it?

It was too much to consider.

Elliott sat in front of his laptop and went straight to Amazon. In short order, he'd added a dozen books to his shopping cart. But they were for the library, not for him. In fact, they were all children's books, some of them for younger readers like the astronomy-loving Girl Scout and some aimed more at teenagers. Those didn't count as additions to his book hoard, right?

He placed his order, closed the laptop, and headed for the bedroom to change back into sweats. He could get in another mile or two of running before settling down to grade exams.

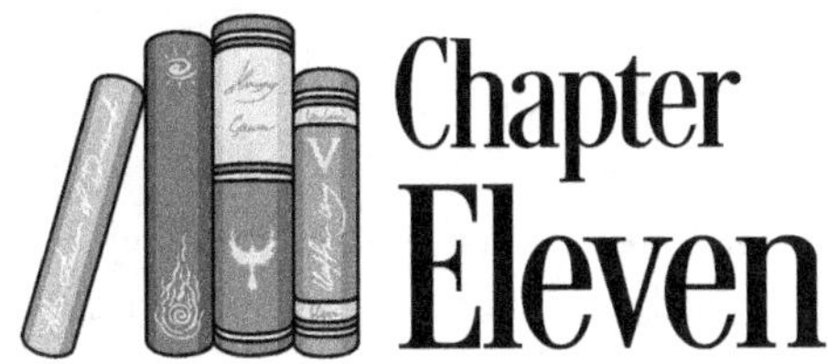

Chapter
Eleven

While Elliott piloted his car on the freeway, Simon sat in the passenger seat, munching on donuts, looking more handsome than ever in a leather jacket and red sweater, and grinning as he told stories from his days as a cop. That alone was enough to distract Elliott from his driving. But Simon smelled good too, damn it, like shampoo and something a bit spicy, and he kept putting his hand on Elliott's thigh.

"If you keep doing that, I'm going to run us off the road," Elliott warned. "You see those cows over there? We're going to land right in the middle of them."

"I'm not even touching you anywhere interesting," Simon protested.

"I disagree. It's *very* interesting."

When Simon laughed, it was amazing that the entire car didn't shake. "Okay. I'll try to be more boring." But even though he took his hand away, he couldn't help looking delicious. Elliott tried to keep his gaze trained faithfully on the highway.

"I have to admit something," Elliott said as they drove through Lodi.

"Yeah?"

"Today's outing wasn't my idea. I had to solicit suggestions from Ladd and Anna." The semi he was passing wandered over the line, forcing Elliott to swerve left to avoid being run over. It was the third time during this drive he'd nearly been run off the road. Apparently everyone was taking the lane markings as suggestions rather than requirements.

"Good evasive maneuver," Simon commented placidly.

"I bet being a cop made you a really good driver."

"They spent a good chunk of time on it in the academy, yeah. Comes in handy in civilian life too. I'll tell you, there are times I wish I were still able to turn on the lights and sirens and write a nice fat ticket for some asshole."

Elliott gave him a quick glance. "Did anyone ever talk you out of a ticket?"

"Once. Guy was driving his wife to the hospital—she was in labor. Now and then a young woman would try to flirt her way out of a citation, but I was immune." He put his hand back on Elliott's leg, and Elliott decided not to complain.

Simon didn't figure out where they were going until Elliott pulled into the parking garage at Old Sacramento. But then Simon seemed delighted, which was a relief. "Really? Here? Awesome!"

"Anna gets credit for the idea, remember."

"I hope I can meet her soon to thank her."

Shit. Elliott had been so focused on avoiding Simon's family that he hadn't thought about introducing Simon to his own. Not that Ladd and Anna would have any problems with Simon, but they'd never met any of Elliott's lovers. They hadn't even known about John, other than a few sketchy bits Elliott had given them in order to allay some of his guilt. Well, he'd consider the issue at another time.

Elliott had put some thought into planning the day. He took them to the Railroad Museum first, where they spent a couple of hours meandering. Neither of them knew much about trains, but Simon was like a big kid, exclaiming over the exhibits and tromping happily through the train cars on display. Several elderly men volunteered at the museum, and Simon stopped to talk with every one of them, listening eagerly to their explanations and stories.

After the museum, Elliott took them for ice cream. He didn't especially want any but he suspected Simon did, and he didn't want to make Simon feel self-conscious about snacking alone. The next stop was another museum, this one dedicated to Sacramento's history. Simon gazed at a large antique photo of people canoeing down city streets. "Wow. They kinda had an issue with flooding, didn't they?"

"Water's weird around here. Always too much or too little. If we were visiting on a weekend, we could do the underground tours."

Simon turned to look at him, his teeth shining white in his wide smile. "What are those?"

"They jacked up the buildings in the 1860s to avoid more floods. Street level is now actually a story higher than it used to be. But lately they've done some excavating in what used to be the ground floors, and they've learned all sorts of interesting things about the early days of the city. Like there used to be this bordello— Shit. I'm sorry. I'll stop lecturing."

But Simon grasped Elliott's shoulder and stared at him, eyes shining with emotion and intensity. "I don't want you to stop lecturing. It's interesting stuff, and I like when you do it. I like it a lot."

"I guess . . . you like learning, huh?"

"Sure. But it's not just that. El, when you talk about this stuff, it's like you become more fully you. You forget that you think you're a snail, and you become a star instead."

Blushing, Elliott ignored propriety, leaned forward, and gave Simon a quick kiss on the lips. Making out was probably not a visitor activity the museum encouraged, but no docents rushed up to expel them.

Touring two museums wasn't all Elliott had planned for the day. "Your knee holding up okay?" he asked after they'd returned to the street.

"Yeah, I'm good. What's next?"

"More food." Elliott took them to a candy store with a huge variety of treats displayed in barrels. Sampling was allowed—encouraged even—and they both munched on saltwater taffy as Simon filled a basket, which Elliott insisted on paying for. Then, with Simon clutching a large paper bag of sugary goodness, they walked down to the river.

"We're going on a boat?" Again, Simon seemed as enthusiastic as a small boy.

"Just for an hour."

"Not a three-hour tour?" Of course, Simon sang the last three words.

"Nope." Elliott glanced up at the sky—a few clouds, but mostly blue. "I don't think the weather will start getting rough."

They hummed the *Gilligan's Island* theme song as they boarded.

Simon insisted on climbing to the boat's upper level, even though the stairway gave him trouble. Once they were up there, Simon took a seat and stretched out his bad leg. "This thing's such a pain in the ass." He poked near his knee. He didn't sound depressed about it, just irritated. "I wish I could keep up with you."

Elliott took the seat next to him. "You're doing fine. And I'm happy to slow down a little if it means spending time with you. I'm in no hurry."

The boat chugged its way upriver, the captain explaining the sights over a loudspeaker. They went under a railroad bridge just as a train was going over, which was fun, and they spied several species of birds in the water and onshore. Somewhere near the confluence of the American and Sacramento Rivers, Simon interlaced his fingers with Elliott's, and that was how they completed their little journey—hand in hand. The water was green and placid, the sky darkened as the sun set, and life's cares seemed far away.

As they were disembarking, Simon got into a conversation with a young woman who worked for the tour company. Elliott stood patiently nearby, listening as the employee divulged her plans to get a criminal justice degree and Simon shared a little career advice.

"Sorry," Simon said when he and Elliott were walking away.

"Like I said, I'm in no hurry. Besides, I like watching you talk to strangers like that. You're good at it. Maybe I'll pick up a few pointers."

With Simon working his way carefully along the boardwalk, Elliott led them a short distance to one of the restaurants hanging on the edge of the river. Reservations weren't needed on a Thursday evening, and he and Simon scored a good table by a window. They ordered two glasses of wine and appetizers and then sat gazing at each other across the table. Simon looked tired; all the walking had evidently been hard on him. But he smiled as if Elliott was the most wonderful thing he'd ever seen.

"I'm going to have to top this for our next date." He feigned an aggrieved sigh.

"I don't think we're having a date-planning competition."

"Sure we are."

Elliott sat back comfortably in his chair. "We'd better not. A dating arms race could get ugly quickly. Escalation."

"Sure. Private jets to Paris. Snorkeling in Bora Bora. Chocolate fountains."

"I thought those were for parties."

"They are," Simon said, grinning. "Two of my cousins had them at their wedding receptions. But I think a private one might be fun too." He waggled his eyebrows and licked his lips, giving Elliott some suspicion of where Simon imagined that chocolate going.

Elliott cleared his throat and shifted in his chair. "I might be able to afford the chocolate fountains, but the rest are a little out of my budget, I'm afraid."

"Mine too. Nobody ever got rich living off disability."

Crap. And here Elliott was, throwing money around. "Hey, we don't have to—"

"It's fine." Simon waved a hand dismissively. "My house? It belongs to my parents. They moved out not long after I got my job. They said they wanted someplace smaller, but I think really they meant it for me and my future bride." He made a wry face.

"If they find out there's not going to be a bride, do you end up homeless?"

"Don't look so worried, El. I won't have to set up a tent along Dry Creek." Then Simon abruptly steered the conversation elsewhere, asking about an oddly shaped building across the river.

They spoke of easier matters and enjoyed their meals, and with a candle flickering on the table and a few boats sailing by outside, lights twinkling, the setting couldn't have been more romantic. Water had an interesting effect on the psyche, Elliott thought, as he recalled his recent impromptu trip to the coast. Gazing at bodies of water somehow calmed the soul. Maybe he should install a little pond in his yard.

Lingering over dessert—and a second glass of wine for Simon— they clasped hands across the table. "I like dating," Simon announced.

"Me too."

"This wasn't a future I saw for myself—even just a couple of years ago. It wasn't something I thought I could have."

"Could you have been out as a police officer?"

After a moment to think, Simon shrugged. "Dunno. People's views have changed, but it's still the Valley, and cops are still cops. Most of 'em are fine, but I worked with a couple guys who still weren't ready to accept women in the department, let alone queers. Universities are different, huh?"

"Mostly. Let's face it, there are assholes everywhere. But I never hid that I was gay, and nobody gave me grief over it." Which made John's insistence on remaining in the closet even more aggravating.

Silence fell, but after a minute or two, Simon squeezed Elliott's hand. "What's worrying you?"

"What makes you think I'm worried?"

"You get a line. Here." Simon reached across and lightly touched the spot between Elliott's eyebrows.

Elliott wasn't sure which unsettled him more—the lightning zap of skin-to-skin contact or the realization that Simon could already read his expressions so well. "I had a job interview," he blurted.

"Hey! That's great! Congratulations!"

"It was just a phone interview," Elliott responded, shaking his head. "Doesn't mean anything. They probably talked to six or seven other candidates."

"None of whom was as impressive as you."

"Well, I'm not so sure." With his free hand, Elliott rolled the edge of his napkin between his fingers. He couldn't look at Simon. Couldn't even look out the window, because somehow he felt that the river was judging him. *Water under the bridge.*

"What?" Simon asked.

Shit. Had he said that out loud? "I was just thinking about our little cruise. It was fun sailing under Tower Bridge."

"Yeah, it was, but that's not what put the worry line on your forehead, Prof."

Maybe dating someone with professional experience in investigations wasn't such a great idea—it certainly made secrecy more difficult.

"The interview was for a university in Nebraska."

Simon's smile dissolved. "Oh."

The waiter approaching their table must have registered the seriousness of their conversation and instead stopped three tables away and meticulously straightened the silverware.

"If they offer you the job, will you go?" asked Simon.

"It's . . . not so simple. They have to do campus interviews first. Then there's usually this gauntlet of deans and provosts and people like that, and there's always one person in the department who hates your guts because they see you as a threat, and then there are negotiations over salary and the number of years until tenure and—"

"Will you go?"

Fuck. Elliott was finally brave enough to look Simon in the eyes. "I don't know."

"Nebraska."

"Yeah. And it's a little town too, not even Omaha or Lincoln."

Simon let go of Elliott's hand. He picked up his empty wineglass, put it down, then found a crumb of key lime pie and put it into his mouth. "Nebraska is a long way from here."

"Fourteen hundred miles or so." He had the urge to fidget too, but managed not to.

"A long way."

Elliott wished Simon's usual chattiness would return. "A long way," he agreed. His mouth felt dry. Then, relenting under silence, he spoke again. "Academic jobs . . . you can't be picky about where you end up. Ladd, he's a high school teacher. He could do that in any town in California. Anna's an escrow officer, so ditto for her. But me, not so much. You have to follow the job."

"To Nebraska."

"Yes! To Nebraska. To fucking Timbuktu if that's where the offer comes from. The market's bad enough anyway, but they're not exactly fighting over a guy who left his last job tainted by a scandal." Elliott puffed out a lungful of air, more irritated with himself and life in general than with Simon.

"You can't just keep doing what you're doing? That's still teaching, right? And you can continue to do research."

"It's not the same."

"Okay." To Elliott's surprise, Simon reached over and grabbed his hand again. "I can't move to Podunk, Nebraska."

"I figured."

"I mean, not that we're ready to settle down with the picket fence or anything. Christ, we haven't done more than kiss. But . . . Jesus."

He chewed on his lip. Then he gave Elliott a sad smile. "I guess I can't bitch about this, seeing as I won't even tell Mom and Dad about us."

"That's different."

"It's . . . complications. Barriers. Either way."

"I probably won't get this job in any case," Elliott offered.

"But eventually you'll get one somewhere. And likely it won't be here."

"Yeah."

They stayed like that for a while, not saying anything, until the waiter worked up the courage to come to the table. "Anything else I can get you guys?" he asked.

"Just the bill, thanks," said Elliott.

But Simon flashed a grin. "And a magic wand that will solve all our problems."

The waiter chuckled. "If I had one of those, I'd keep it for myself. Maybe my wife and I would stop arguing over how to parent our five-year-old."

"I'm not sure that's the same magic wand," said Simon.

"Sure it is. One wand fits all. Fixes every relationship crisis with a single swoop."

On the way back to the car, Elliott and Simon paused to lean against a railing and look at the Delta King, a former ferryboat now serving as a floating hotel. "Wouldn't you be lonely in Nebraska?" asked Simon.

Elliott wanted to tell the truth. *I've always been lonely. I think I always will be. The only times that shadow recedes is when I'm with you.* "Yes," he said instead.

Simon drew close until they were pressed together side by side, and his heat seeped through to conquer a chill Elliott hadn't realized he felt. Simon wrapped his arm around Elliott's shoulders. Comfortable. Comforting. Smelling of food and wine, of cologne, of museums and the river and leather.

"What do you want to do?" asked Elliott quietly. "About us."

"Wave that wand. But since we can't, I guess . . . just take it as it comes."

"Yeah?"

"If we get only a few weeks together, let's make them a good few weeks."

Elliott leaned against him and sighed. "Okay."

On the way home, Elliott put on one of the playlists he listened to while writing. Old stuff by the bands his parents had bought on vinyl. The Beatles. The Stones. The Who. Familiar songs he'd been hearing since he'd slept in a crib, somehow made fresher because Simon was listening with him.

"I like this one," said Simon when the Moody Blues came on. "It's sad, though. And is it knights with a *k* or without?"

Elliott had to consider that. "Without, I think. With a *k* they wear armor, not white satin."

"Not when they sleep. That would be really uncomfortable."

"When they sleep, then they're night knights?"

"And their loved ones tuck them in, read them a bedtime story, and then say, 'Night-night, night knight.'"

The silliness of the conversation made it all the more wonderful.

Although it wasn't especially late, Simon was yawning by the time Elliott pulled into his driveway. As before, they sat in the idling car, not saying a word. When Simon leaned closer, Elliott expected a kiss. Instead, he felt the warmth of Simon's whisper against his ear. "Come inside."

# Chapter Twelve

Elliott entered Simon's house with a certain degree of trepidation and was surprised to discover it was actually clean and neat. The furniture—formal and fairly ornate—didn't suit Simon at all, but it was carefully arranged and debris-free. The carpet was dusty rose, and most of the upholstery involved patterns in creams and sea greens, often accented by carved and gilded woodwork. The pale-yellow walls were mostly bare, although there were a few framed prints of ancient carvings.

"Lamassu," Elliott said.

"What?"

Elliott pointed at a depiction of a winged bull with a bearded human head. "Fifth or sixth century BCE, I think. My knowledge of Assyrian history is a little sketchy."

Simon stepped closer. "You think I invited you here to show you my etchings, huh?"

"That's kind of a dated reference. Nowadays shouldn't it be to watch Netflix and chill?"

"I'm dating a historian."

Simon moved so close they were nearly touching. He didn't quite loom, and Elliott could easily have backed away, but still Elliott was viscerally reminded of how big Simon was and how powerful, despite the knee. This wasn't a frightening realization, although it made Elliott feel a bit weak in the knees himself.

"Your house isn't a toxic waste dump." He sounded evasive even to his own ears. And scared, like a virginal nineteen-year-old.

Undeterred, Simon let his cane drop and enveloped him in an embrace. "I made sure it was clean," he rumbled into Elliott's ear. "In case you came over."

For him. Simon had cleaned his house for *him.* "You didn't have to do that."

Simon took a step back, which was a disappointment. "My mom has been after me about it forever. I finally told her to have her way with vacuum and dust rag."

"Did you tell her why?"

"Ha—no. Maybe if I did, it'd soften her up a little. Convince her you're a good influence on me. But can we please not talk about my mom? It kinda kills the mood."

Elliott's mood was not killed. He was fairly certain a bomb could drop in the next room—a big kitchen he glimpsed through the doorway—and the desire racing through him wouldn't be reduced one bit by the explosion. He'd never felt this needy or this . . . *heated* about anyone.

With a noise surprisingly akin to a growl, Elliott closed the space between them and grasped Simon's hair, pulling him in for a kiss. And he didn't stop there, pushing relentlessly as he backed Simon into a wall—easing the stress on Simon's bad leg—and then pressed his full weight into Simon, finally feeling the whole of that body supporting him.

Since they hadn't yet taken off their jackets, their mouths remained in contact while their arms ended up in a confusing tangle, with hands tugging at collars and sleeves. When the jackets were in heaps at their feet, they attacked shirt buttons. So many goddamn buttons, each one of them a barrier to skin.

Once the shirts came off, though, they got distracted. Simon's broad chest bore a coating of black hair almost as luxurious as his beard. A thick line of hair led down his belly and disappeared under the waistband of his jeans. Elliott moved his mouth to one of Simon's erect nipples, and sucked and nibbled gently while threading his fingers through that wonderfully soft pelt.

A choked noise escaping his throat, Simon *thunk*ed his head against the wall. His hands held Elliott's shoulders firmly, not for support and certainly not to push him away, but Elliott still felt deliciously in control. He worked that little nubbin of flesh mercilessly and paused only to lavish attention on its twin.

Simon emitted an entire symphony of moans, whimpers, and expletives, gliding his hands down Elliott's back and then under Elliott's waistband. Those wide, hot palms and broad fingers on his ass intensified Elliott's need to taste Simon's body; he positioned his mouth on the taut lines of Simon's neck and softly bit.

"Bed." Simon's voice was deeper than ever and as hoarse as if he'd been shouting. He pulled his hands out of Elliott's pants. "Please?"

Elliott didn't need to be asked twice. He followed Simon across the living room—stopping twice to kiss—then down a short hall and into a bedroom. With the lights out, he couldn't see many details, but then he wasn't especially interested right then in critiquing Simon's décor. What he wanted, and what he got, was to be maneuvered against the bed, to be pushed back against the mattress, and to have Simon lie full-length on top of him.

Simon lifted himself onto his elbows. "I'm not too heavy, am I?"

"Jesus, Si. You're not that huge, and I'm not a delicate flower."

"Yeah, okay." With a single finger, Simon lightly traced Elliott's eyebrows and then his lips. "Remember, I'm kinda new to this. I've mostly done . . . you know. Gropey stuff. Quick. Not, well, making love." His voice had dropped to a whisper, and even in the semidark, Elliott could see that Simon's eyes were big and soft.

Elliott answered back just as quietly. "We can do whatever you want. I'm all yours."

"What about what you want?"

"I want to make you feel good."

A tiny noise escaped Simon's lips, somewhere between a sigh and an almost-sob, and then he collapsed fully onto Elliott and nuzzled at his neck, at his cheek, at that sensitive patch of skin beneath his ear. Apparently it was his turn to explore Elliott's upper half, which he did thoroughly, using mouth and fingers, until there was nothing left of Elliott but a writhing, arching puddle of want.

"El, can I—"

"Yes! God, yes."

Simon's chuckle did wonderful things to Elliott's body. "You don't even know what I was going to ask."

"Whatever it is, the answer is yes."

Simon went very still and looked down into Elliott's face. "That's a lot of trust."

"I trust you."

"Even after what John did?"

Elliott gently tugged Simon's hair. "You are not John." He said it lightly, but he meant it. Even as the words left him, he experienced an odd weightlessness—despite the two hundred fifty or so pounds of man on top of him. Although his future contained only uncertainty, this was the first time in years he truly believed that he might have good prospects. That the mess with John hadn't ruined him after all.

"What do you want to do with me?" he asked, tugging again.

"I want to be in you."

"I-I'd like that too."

Simon was clumsy as he rolled off Elliott, but Elliott didn't judge. His own system was overloading, his nerves far more interested in conveying the sensations of sex than worrying about what Elliott did with his limbs. Or with his lungs, which seemed to be working raggedly. Simon's house wasn't especially warm, but Elliott felt as if he might spontaneously combust.

Swearing under his breath, Simon sat on the edge of the mattress and fussed with his knee brace. Elliott took advantage of the opportunity to kneel behind him and play with the wide expanse of back and shoulders—those of a god hefting the world or conquering a minotaur barehanded. While Simon tried to remove the brace, Elliott laid kisses on his nape, on the points of his scapulas, and down the knobs of his spine.

"You were right," said Simon.

"About what?"

"In the car. When you said touching everywhere was interesting."

Elliott leaned over his shoulder and whispered in his ear. "True. But we can do better than this."

"We can."

Although he'd never been one of those men who could skim off his shoes, jeans, and underwear in a seductive fashion, Elliott didn't feel self-conscious about it now, not when Simon had to struggle with his leg. Once they were both naked, Elliott stood at the bedside, torn between turning on the light—the better to see Simon—or foregoing that in favor of simply jumping on him. Simon made the decision by grabbing Elliott's arm and tugging him closer, until Elliott ended up straddling his lap.

They were both hard, and although Elliott hadn't had the chance for a good look at Simon's cock, it seemed proportionate to the rest of him. At the moment, however, what was more important was all the glorious skin against skin, Simon's strong thighs beneath his own, Simon squeezing Elliott's ass and tracing his mouth wetly over Elliott's jawline.

"Fuck." That was Elliott, squirming on Simon's lap, thrusting forward for the friction against Simon's belly and then back into the grip on his cheeks. "Jesus fuck." Because apparently all he had left were blasphemies.

After a few minutes of that—during which their cocks became slick and Elliott skated perilously close to the edge of climax—Simon grunted, held Elliott tight, and in a single powerful move, scooted them around. Now Simon lay flat and full-length along the mattress, and if Elliott couldn't see well, he could damn well touch and taste.

He started with collarbones, then sternum. Simon tensed a bit when Elliott got to his stomach, but Elliott tried to wordlessly convince him that there was nothing unbeautiful about that softness layered over muscle. Soon Simon relaxed, splaying his legs and allowing his arms to rest at his sides. Elliott tickled the point of his hip, the lovely crease between leg and torso, the furred roundness of his balls.

As Simon gasped, Elliott moved southward. God, he could love Simon for his thighs alone—heavy with muscle and covered with more hair. The thighs of a classical hero.

Simon made a distressed noise when Elliott reached his bad knee, and Elliott froze. "Did I hurt you?"

"No. It's just— It's a big fucking mess. Scars."

"Do you think I can only lo—only want you if you're perfect? There is nothing desirable about perfection."

"Is that some famous saying?"

Elliott laughed and then blew gently along Simon's leg. "No, just me. It's true, though. I want the you I have right here, not some idealized, sanitized version. Scars. An extra pound or two.

Complicated family issues." He set a featherlight kiss on Simon's knee before scooting back up so they were again face-to-face.

"I've seen gay porn," Simon said. "Maybe a lot of it. None of those guys look like me."

"Or me either."

"But you're—"

"Here with you, now. There's no other place I'd rather be or any other person I'd rather be with."

They made out for a time after that, just a lot of kissing and stroking, with gasps and groans from both of them. Simon eventually fumbled a little tube of lubricant out of his bedside table. "I bought this yesterday. After my mom finished cleaning."

"Extra points for being prepared."

Simon was slightly hesitant and clumsy with what came next, but his slicked finger felt amazingly good inside Elliott. So much so, in fact, that Elliott made an embarrassingly needy whine and had to silently recite the outcome of the 1878 Congress of Berlin. "Moving along," he finally said through gritted teeth.

Simon laughed as he tenderly pushed Elliott off and accessed the nightstand again, this time producing a wrapped condom. Elliott reached for it, intending to roll it sensually over Simon's cock, but Simon moved it out of reach. "I think it's best if you don't touch my dick right now. Boom."

"Boom?"

"Boom." Simon made an appropriate sound effect to emphasize his point.

After Simon had the rubber on, Elliott was on his back with a pillow under his ass, and Simon was sliding home so slowly Elliott wanted to scream. He grabbed Simon's ass and tried to urge him in more deeply, but Elliott's angle was poor and Simon was strong. "This doesn't hurt your knee?" Elliott asked.

"A little. I'll be okay."

"I can move—"

"I want to look at your face."

And although the room was quite dark, Elliott knew what he meant. There was just enough light for him to make out the white of Simon's teeth and the glint of his eyes. Enough to remind him that this wasn't some anonymous trick he'd arranged over a phone app. Wasn't John, who fucked like a rabbit—fast and without much real attention to Elliott.

"Oh God," Simon said. It sounded like a prayer.

They moved together, finding a slow, deep rhythm that pleased them both, punctuating thrusts with kisses and fingertip strokes. Elliott's cock was caught between them, and he couldn't get at it, but Simon's abdomen provided enough friction. Added to that was the sensation of being filled, of opening himself to a man who had quickly come to mean a great deal to him.

Simon came first, crying out as his movements became erratic. He didn't forget about Elliott, however. He squeezed his hand between them, gripped Elliott's shaft, and continued to thrust until Elliott climaxed too.

"You okay?" Simon asked after Elliott shuddered and went still.

"Fireworks. Earth moved."

Laughing, Simon leaned in for a kiss.

After a few moments, Simon limped to the bathroom and returned with damp washcloths. After they cleaned up, a slight awkwardness fell between them. If this had been anyone but Simon, Elliott would have quickly gotten dressed and left. Even with John, visits to each other's home had been fast and furtive. John had rules about that as well—no parking too close, in case someone recognized the car. No coming or going during times when people were out on the streets and might possibly see them. No spending the night.

But now, Simon clasped Elliott's hand. "Sleep over?"

"You want that?"

"God, yes."

So they settled into bed together, and it was amazing how quickly they found a mutually agreeable position—on their sides with Simon spooning Elliott from behind, his arm wrapped around Elliott's middle. Not a position that allowed for squirming, but Elliott didn't move around much in his sleep, and this was supremely warm and comfortable.

Simon kissed Elliott's nape and then a shoulder. "Whatever happens? This is so worth it."

Elliott totally agreed.

Chapter
Thirteen

They didn't awaken to morning-after awkwardness. In fact, they remained happily in bed for a long time, joking and whispering and fooling around as the sunlight bathed them through gaps in the curtains. This lovemaking wasn't needy and goal-directed like the night before but was playful instead. Still, they stroked each other to completion, gasping their climaxes with lips pressed to the other's skin.

"I should let you get going with your day." Elliott splayed across the mattress with his head nestled on Simon's shoulder.

"I have that PT appointment later. I have time to make you breakfast, though."

It was tempting, but Elliott had work to catch up on, and some superstitious part of him worried that if he spent too long with Simon, something would go wrong. They'd have a terrible fight. Simon would discover something despicable about him. Simon's parents would suddenly show up at the door, possibly right as Simon and Elliott were going at it atop the oversized and fairly ugly coffee table.

"Thanks. But I have to go."

"When can I see you next? Shit. That sounded stalkery and desperate."

"No, it sounded sweet. Tomorrow?" Also possibly desperate.

Simon squeezed him gently. "Yeah. I'll make some plans."

"Remember, we agreed to suspend the dating arms race. We could just hang out. Watch a movie or something."

Simon considered this. "Tell you what: I'll get takeout from the Pita Palace and bring it to your place for dinner. If you don't mind. I like your furniture better."

"Your parents chose yours?"

"Yeah," Simon said with a small laugh. "Could you tell? The bedroom's all mine, though."

That made Elliott curious to see more of it. He peeled himself away from Simon and the bed and, conscious of Simon's steady gaze on his naked body, prowled around the room. The furniture was clearly different from that in the living room. A platform bed, probably from Ikea, a plain but serviceable dresser with matching nightstands, sage-green walls and a beige carpet. No bookshelves, but Elliott smiled when he recognized two of his own books beside the bed. The room held little in the way of ornamentation, although there was a formal photo of a younger, unbearded Simon in a police uniform, receiving some kind of certificate.

"Boring, huh?" Simon lay on his back, his head pillowed on crossed arms. He'd kicked the blankets off so Elliott saw the entirety of him. And although his knee was knotted with scars, he was breathtaking.

"You don't spend a lot of time thinking about decorating. That's okay."

"It's not that. I think . . . I guess I'm afraid if I do much, it'll magically signal to my parents that I'm gay. This feels safer."

"Hmm." Elliott leaned back against the dresser. "I'm gay—"

"I noticed."

"—and you've seen my place. Someone who broke in might be horrified by my book addiction, but I don't think they'd jump to conclusions about my sexuality."

"I know. But still."

What was it like to keep such an essential part of yourself so locked away? It must be exhausting. "Do you get tired of policing yourself?" Elliott asked.

The answer came on a sigh. "Yeah."

They walked to the front door and stood for a minute or two, enjoying an embrace. Elliott couldn't explain why, but somehow he felt stronger wrapped in those big arms than when he stood alone.

It was a short drive home through the chilly morning, and although blue sky stretched overhead, gray clouds loomed to the west. Sometimes he missed the eternal gloominess of the Pacific Northwest sky, so he was glad to see the potential for an overcast day. Besides, unpleasant weather was always a good excuse to curl up with a book and a big mug of tea. And he'd much rather run when it was cold than scorching hot.

Today, though, he decided to take a day off from running. He'd spend a little time with weights instead, then grade papers and have soup and a sandwich for dinner. And he'd think about how lovely his night with Simon had been.

When Elliott pulled into the driveway, however, he saw that the rainbow flag was missing. At first he thought it might have fallen over, but when he got out of the car and went to investigate, the flag was gone, pole and all. Great. He knew that people sometimes stole lawn decorations from his neighborhood; the previous year, one family's large carved wooden bear was taken from near their front door. Elliott had always assumed the culprits were teenagers. If so, he hoped some kid was enjoying his stolen pride.

While he was outside, Elliott checked the library—and swore. When he'd left the previous day to pick up Simon, the shelves had been crammed full. Now they bore nothing but an old newspaper and a flyer for yard services.

He hoped the teenagers were at least reading the books and not throwing them away.

Of course, he had no problem restocking. The children's books had arrived the previous morning, so he put those out, together with an assortment of gay history texts and several novels. That cheered him up. Even better, when he went inside and got on the laptop, he didn't order more books as replacements. After all, it wasn't as if he was in danger of running out anytime soon. However, he did order a new rainbow flag, this one bigger than the first and with a few purple cartoon hearts emblazoned on the stripes.

Since he was already online, he fielded student emails. This one wanted to take the class for credit/no credit instead of a grade, and that one, who'd already missed about half the work, wanted to withdraw from the course completely. Another one inquired about the possibility of extra credit. God, if they were this bad now, what would they be like when the end of the semester drew closer?

After twenty minutes with his weights and a quick shower—he was sorry to wash away the remains of his night with Simon—Elliott ate a light brunch. He spent some time staring out the living room window. The clouds had arrived, but an occasional person still came by on foot or bicycle. Three of them stopped at his library, each choosing one book and leaving another. He loved watching that. One older lady with a tiny fluffy dog must have spent ten minutes examining the options, taking each volume out and reading the back before making her decision. It was hard to tell from inside the house, but Elliott thought she took a book about the history of gay men and women in New York City.

What he should have done next—what he'd originally planned to do—was work on an article he'd begun some months before about Tito's efforts as a leader of the Non-Aligned Movement. But all those Serbo-Croatian words seemed to squiggle before his eyes, and he suddenly found himself completely disinterested in the topic. "I don't care about the Declaration of Brijuni," he said out loud. Let someone else dig around in those documents.

As Elliott sat in front of his laptop and closed his eyes, he didn't see a stout Slavic man in a military uniform. Instead, he saw a tall, bearded man with dark hair and a bright smile. He wore a dark nineteenth-century suit—well-worn and not fancy—with a wide-brimmed hat. He held a pickax and shovel. Another man stood next to him, lighter complected, slightly shorter and considerably more slender, dressed similarly but with a book in one hand. The closeness of their bodies and the angles of their stances suggested they were more than just acquaintances or business partners. A dirt road ran beneath their boots, while a white clapboard bungalow stood behind them, its wide porch holding a pair of rocking chairs.

"What would it have been like?" he mused out loud. Those same streets he and Simon had walked in Sacramento and Columbia—what if they'd walked them a hundred fifty years earlier? Even today, well into the twenty-first century, finding and maintaining a loving relationship was a struggle. Could they have managed it back then?

Abandoning Tito to his fate—a long life into his late eighties and an important place in history—Elliott began to delve into works about homosexuality during the gold rush.

At least at first glance, he couldn't find much. But he knew something was out there. After all, gay people hadn't magically burst into fabulous existence a few decades before Elliott was born. When Walt Whitman published *Leaves of Grass* in 1855, Columbia was at its peak and critics back East were spreading rumors about Whitman's sexual orientation. So people knew about gay men back then and even wrote occasionally on the topic. The hard part was unearthing those little nuggets of truth from the bedrock of history. He was going to have to do some prospecting of his own.

Again, Elliott found his entire academic trajectory shifting, but this time it was his own choice. He smiled as he worked.

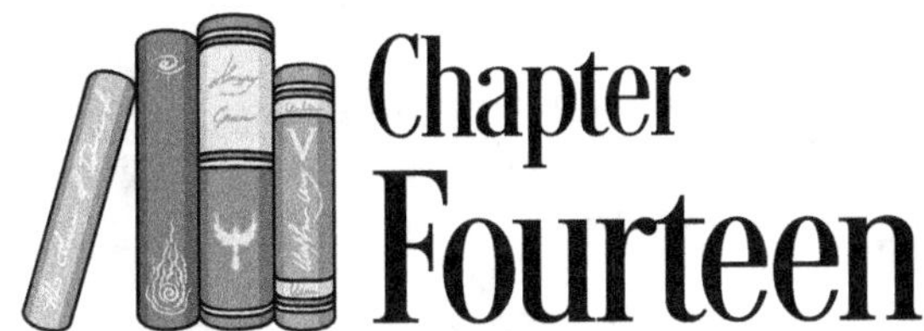

Chapter Fourteen

Elliott ended up working well past midnight, a rarity for him. And he'd forgotten to eat, so when he finally stood up from his laptop to stretch his cramped muscles, he was ravenous. He ate canned soup and a sandwich while hovering over the kitchen counter. He stumbled to bed and fell asleep almost immediately, haunted by fragmented dreams he couldn't quite remember in the morning.

When he checked his phone, Elliott discovered a series of texts from Simon, most of them sent after he'd gone to bed the night before. Nothing urgent. Just sweet little comments about things they'd seen in Sacramento and ideas for movies they could watch together. The final text made Elliott grin.

Text STOP if these messages are getting too stalkery. Usual messaging fees will apply.

Elliott sent a reply:

Don't stop. Not stalkery. Any movie is good as long as you're here. His pesky autocorrect tried to change *stalkery* to *stalkers*.

Under still-overcast skies, Elliott took a long run and then settled to work in front of the living room window. Melanie the Girl Scout came by with her mother and, judging from the look of delight on the girl's face, was thrilled to discover the recently added volumes of Magic Tree House and Captain Underpants. She waved toward the house and, although he wasn't sure whether she could see him through the window, he waved in return.

He was just settling back into reading an article when his phone buzzed with a new text.

Don't kill me.

Shit. Elliott swallowed bitter disappointment. *We can reschedule,* he wrote back. He didn't think Simon would give a flimsy excuse and ditch him; something must have come up.

I'm still coming over. With dinner. And a surprise.

Elliott let out a relieved breath. *Then why would I want to kill you? Wait till you see the surprise.*

Well. That wasn't infuriatingly intriguing, was it? Elliott sent a few more messages, trying to get Simon to explain, but Simon only answered with smiley-face emojis. Elliott finally texted a teeny-tiny skull, but Simon just sent back a police car emoji and then went silent.

"Tease," Elliott grumbled. But even though he was annoyed and apprehensive, he was also amused. And even a little bit pleased, because nobody had ever bothered to taunt him this way before. It was nice. It made him feel like he was a member of the in-crowd, even if it was only a crowd of two.

Elliott was in the bedroom later, double-checking his stash of rubbers and lube just in case things grew hot and heavy with Simon. He really, really hoped he'd be needing them. When the doorbell rang five minutes early, Elliott hurried to the door.

"Hey, Si, so what did you—"

Simon stood on the porch, a smile stretching from ear to ear, and he carried a large paper bag in one hand. It was fragrant with the scent of spices and grilled meat. In his other hand was a nylon leash . . . attached to a large dog. The beast had short reddish fur, floppy ears, and a big grin.

"I had to go to Target today," Simon said.

"Okay."

"And there's a pet-supply store a couple doors down, so I went in there."

Elliott remained in the doorway. "You don't need pet supplies." He'd seen the entire downstairs of Simon's house, which didn't even contain a goldfish. "Unless you're trying to bribe the alleged wildlife on your second floor."

"Nope. They can fend for themselves." Simon shrugged. "I just like to look around in there sometimes. It's fun."

"Okay," Elliott repeated.

"And it's Saturday, so they were having a pet adoption event."

"And you adopted a dog."

Simon's smile was blinding. "Nope. You did. Can we come in? My leg's gonna give."

What else could Elliott do? He stepped aside.

As soon as Simon entered, he let go of the leash and hobbled over to the coffee table to set down the bag. The dog, however, went straight to Elliott and leaned against his legs, clearly expecting to be petted. Elliott discovered it had very soft ears.

"Um, Simon?"

"Hang on. I'm gonna grab plates and stuff, okay?" Not waiting for an answer, Simon went into the kitchen and clattered around in the cupboards and drawers while Elliott rubbed the top of the dog's head. Simon soon returned with dishes and cutlery, which he set beside the food.

"Simon?" Yes, Elliott sounded plaintive.

"I've got her stuff in my truck—I couldn't carry it all. We can get it after we eat."

"Stuff?"

"Dog dishes, a comfy collar for when you run, a brush, a bag of kibble, a big-ass dog bed. And a bunch of toys. The Humane Society gives you a bag of toys when you adopt."

It was a lot of words, and Elliott's brain got caught on the earlier bit. "When we run?"

"Yeah! The adoption guy said she's mostly Rhodesian ridgeback. See that line of backward hair along her spine? Isn't that cool? This breed is especially suited for long runs in hot weather. There's probably a couple other breeds mixed in there too, but that shouldn't matter. The guy said she loves to run."

"But . . . a dog." Despite his confusion and protests, Elliott hadn't stopped stroking her. She was leaning most of her weight against him and seemed in no mood to do anything else.

"They had cats too. But you can't run with a cat, of course. The guy said she gets along with 'em, so you're good if you want a cat too."

"Too?"

"In addition to the dog." As if that were completely obvious. Then he started removing foam containers from the bag and spooning food onto dishes. The dog sniffed the air with interest but didn't move away from Elliott.

"Why did you bring me a dog?"

Simon looked up from a container of hummus. "She needed a home. Look at her! She's the sweetest thing on four legs. The guy said she'd been up for adoption for six months because everyone wants puppies and little dogs—she's four, by the way—and you could tell that she really needed to settle down with someone. I can't take her because I can't give her the exercise she needs." He pointed with a fork. "But you can."

Elliott needed to sit down. He walked to the couch, and the dog followed so closely that he nearly tripped on her. As soon he sat, she collapsed onto the floor and rested her chin on his feet, amber-colored eyes trained on his face.

"I don't need a dog," Elliott said.

Simon handed him a plate heaped with food. "Of course you do. You're lonely, right? Now you never have to be by yourself. She'll follow you into the bathroom if you let her. But she'll never complain or demand possession of the remote control or run up your credit card bills. And she sure as hell won't try to hide you from her family or coworkers."

"Simon—"

"She won't. She will love you unconditionally. I think she's already falling for you."

"I think that's because I'm holding a plate full of beef kebab."

Simon laughed. "As is the case with many humans, the route to a dog's heart is often through her stomach." He ate a big spoonful of seasoned rice.

Taken completely off guard, Elliott didn't know how to manage this argument. The food did smell delicious, however, so he balanced the plate on his lap and began to eat. When he accidentally dropped a bit of meat, the dog gobbled it immediately and then returned her chin to his feet.

"Shouldn't feed her at the table," Simon fake-pontificated. "Bad habit."

"We're not at the table."

"Ah. Okay, then." He tossed her a bit of bread, which she caught in midair.

After a couple of minutes, Simon continued. "There are other reasons you need a dog. You keep yourself holed up in here too much."

"I run almost every day."

"Yeah, but do you interact with anyone while you do it? Nope—didn't think so."

"I interacted with you," Elliott pointed out.

"Barely. I was standing there with lust in my heart, and you just kept on jogging. But with this dog, you'll go out, and people will want to pet her. She'll want that too—the guy said she's a social butterfly. Loves everyone. Um, that might slow you down a little when you run, actually, but she'll be worth it. Maybe you'll even take her to the dog park so she can hang with the canine crowd. You'll end up talking to actual live human beings. She can drag you out of that snail shell you were talking about."

Although his words were light, the earnestness in Simon's tone was real, as was the warmth in his eyes. He had honestly taken this course of action with Elliott's best interests in mind.

"A dog," said Elliott, as if that made a difference.

"A dog." Simon leaned in closer and his smile disappeared. "She'll be there for you, El. If I fuck things up with you. If you move to Nebraska. If . . . whatever. If you really don't want her, I'll take her as soon as my leg's healed. Or I'll take her now, as long as you can exercise her. But I think you should keep her."

Elliott looked down at her hopeful face. Her brows were slightly wrinkled and her gaze steady, as if she were trying to communicate with him telepathically. Probably she was just hoping he'd drop more food. Elliott sighed, resigned. "What's her name?"

Simon whooped in triumph.

Her name was Ishtar. At least that was what Simon claimed. Elliott was fairly certain she hadn't been called that until Simon signed the adoption papers, but she answered to it, wagging her long tail and giving a doggy grin when Simon tried it out.

"So you just happened to find a dog named after a Mesopotamian sex goddess?" Elliott asked skeptically.

"Don't worry. She's spayed."

"Great."

But the truth was, now that the shock had receded, Elliott was finding her intriguing, if not entirely welcome. She'd been patient while they ate, watching with sad eyes but not actively begging, and when Elliott offered her a morsel, she took it delicately from his fingers. After the humans ate, Elliott brought her things in from Simon's truck—with a token protest—and she downed her own dinner in his kitchen without making a mess. Then she'd walked to the back door as confidently as if she'd lived there for years, waited politely until Elliott let her out, and made a beeline for the lawn portion of his fenced backyard.

"Housebroken," Simon pointed out, rather unnecessarily.

Elliott scowled.

Now he and Simon were cuddled on the couch while Ishtar sprawled on her bed nearby. Sometimes she woke up long enough to glance at them and wag her tail before promptly falling back asleep.

"She's comfortable here," said Simon as the end credits ran for *O Brother, Where Art Thou?* Elliott had chosen the movie and Simon hadn't complained, possibly because he'd realized he was in no position to protest.

"I'm not sure I want a dog."

"Why not? Give me one good reason why you shouldn't have one."

Well, that was a poser. Objectively, Elliott's lifestyle was perfect for her—he owned his own house, he was home almost all the time, and he exercised religiously. She appeared well-mannered. And although money was a little tight, he could afford her food and vet bills.

It's a responsibility. He couldn't say that out loud. It would make him sound like a spoiled child. But it was at least the shadow of the truth. He'd taken care of himself but never anyone else. What if he fucked it up as badly as he'd fucked up his life?

"What if I want to spend time at your place?" Elliott finally asked.

Simon scoffed. "Bring her with. I may even pay more attention to her than to you. I told you—I'd have adopted her in a second if it wasn't for my leg."

Unless Elliott wanted to manufacture an allergy, he was out of excuses. As if on cue, Ishtar stood, stretched extravagantly, and wandered closer. She poked her head into their laps, smiling when they petted her, and then she sighed happily and lay down at their feet.

"If she's so great, how come nobody else wants her?"

"I told you—she's big and a little older. The guy told me her original owners moved and left her behind. Which totally sucks. It must have broken her heart to lose her family."

And somehow, those words were the deciding factor. Here was Simon, pressed up against Elliott, big and warm and comfortable, but with his injured leg sticking out as a reminder that his life had not gone as planned. Even if his knee healed completely, his future was uncertain, and he was stuck between denying his identity and alienating his parents. Elliott could do little to help Simon's situation—but he could do something for Ishtar.

"On a trial basis," Elliott said.

Simon's smile was wide. "Sure."

Feeling slightly peevish, Elliott chose a documentary next. It was about the Klondike Gold Rush, which came almost fifty years later than the California version, but Elliott was in the mood. As it turned out, Simon grew interested too, so much so that they paused the movie several times so he could ask questions or they could chat about a detail. Ishtar dozed through the whole thing, thumping her tail on the ground whenever Elliott stroked her flank with his bare toes.

"She'll probably need obedience lessons," Simon said after the documentary ended. "I think she knows a couple of basics, but that's it. The guy recommended a place."

"He was a very helpful guy," Elliott replied sourly.

"Yes, yes he was. He also suggested agility."

"What?"

"You know. Where dogs jump through hoops and do teeter-totters and stuff."

Elliott understood the words, but that was about it. "Why would I want to do that? Does Ishtar have dreams of joining the circus?"

"You'll have to ask her about career aspirations. But the guy said she'd enjoy it—she's smart, and it would give her a challenge. It might be fun for you too."

"Is this part of your general scheme to socialize me?"

"Maybe," Simon replied with an impish grin.

Elliott looked down at the remote control in his hands. "Another movie?"

"It's getting late."

"Oh. If you have to—"

"Another movie and a sleepover?" That came with an eyebrow waggle. "And do you have popcorn?"

"Yeah." Elliott leaned over to plant a kiss on Simon's temple.

Apparently Ishtar had learned about popcorn during her past life, because as soon as the noises began, she charged into the kitchen to stare hopefully at the microwave. Elliott filled a big bowl and grabbed a pair of beers from the fridge, and Ishtar followed him back into the living room, prancing as if she were in a parade.

"Can dogs eat this stuff?" Elliott asked as he plopped down beside Simon. Shit. He was going to have to learn all about canine care. He didn't have a clue. Well, he could certainly find some guides on Amazon.

"Sure." Simon gave her a piece, which she gobbled. "You never had a dog?"

"No. Ladd's childhood allergies, remember? You?"

"We had a couple when I was a kid. Little foo-foo things that my dad got for my mom. They were kind of yappy, but they were fun to play with."

They settled in comfortably again, Elliott nestled into the crook of Simon's arm and the popcorn bowl on his lap, Ishtar with her chin resting on the couch cushion. She was probably drooling on the upholstery, but surprisingly, Elliott didn't much care. He felt too good, hunkered down at home with, apparently, almost everything he'd ever wanted. Even the knowledge that none of it would last forever didn't kill the joy.

This time Simon got to pick what they watched. He chose something with space aliens and explosions; if there was a plot, Elliott was too drowsy to find it. It didn't matter anyway, because he was content to simply listen to Simon's heartbeat and the gentle rhythm of Ishtar's breathing.

"Halloween's Wednesday," said Simon during a lull in the laser-beam zapping.

Elliott had been just enough out of it that he needed a moment to parse the non sequitur. "Yeah."

"Do you do anything to celebrate?"

"I gave up trick-or-treating a couple decades ago."

Simon tickled Elliott's shoulder. "Decorations? Candy? Or are you one of those grouchy old people who hides indoors with the lights off?"

The first year he'd lived here, Elliott had done just that. But he'd felt guilty about it. Their neighborhood tended to celebrate the holiday with gusto, which meant the only houses on the block not currently sporting giant spiders or leering jack-o'-lanterns were his and Mike Burgess's. In fact, people actually bussed their kids into the neighborhood by the minivan load, lured by visions of full-sized candy bars. Elliott hadn't minded the visitors. Last year, he'd given out monster stickers and ghost erasers, and even the teenagers had been polite. Most of them put a lot of effort into costumes too.

"I have some little things to give out," he said. "Bookmarks and stuff."

Simon chuckled. "I hit up my old department. I've got a whole lot of plastic police badges and also a bunch of whistles and water bottles."

"Water bottles?"

"Official police department water bottles," Simon replied in an officious voice. "They have safety messages on them. Kids seem to like 'em."

"And dentists approve."

"Yeah. Also, one of my cousin's sons has a zillion food allergies, so Halloween sucks for him. Everyone else is pigging out on chocolate, and he's stuck trying to pretend he doesn't care that he's munching on apple slices. I figure there's probably a lot of kids in his shoes, and I want them to enjoy Halloween too."

Jesus. The core of kindness in this man was so solid and pure that Elliott was almost frightened by it. Elliott certainly didn't deserve it. He wasn't a bad man, and he avoided harming others, but he'd spent his life mostly absorbed with his own wants and needs. He certainly didn't go around worrying about homeless dogs or children with food allergies. Even Elliott's neighborhood library was self-serving in a way: a method to reduce his clutter and diminish the guilt about his book hoarding.

"Want to do the thing together?" Simon asked, interrupting Elliott's thoughts.

Elliott blinked. "Sure. There's lube and—"

Simon laughed so enthusiastically he woke the dog and nearly spilled the remaining popcorn. "No! No! I mean, yeah, I want to do that too. Soon. But I was talking about Halloween. How about if I come over and we hand out treats together? It could be fun." His expression was a little like Ishtar's when she was hoping for food.

"What if one of your relatives sees us?"

Without even hesitating, Simon shook his head. "Let them. But it's unlikely, actually. None of them live around here, and my Aunt Soso does this big party thing for the kids every year, which keeps them pretty busy. She thinks it saves them from razor blades in apples, and it doesn't matter how many times I tell her that's an urban myth. Besides . . ." He paused and scrunched up his face as if the rest was difficult to spit out.

"What?"

"It's a baby step for me. I don't know how much longer I get to have you, but while I do, I hate hiding. Maybe I'm not ready yet for Thanksgiving or Christmas together—you know, the big guns of holidays. Nobody spends those with a casual fling. But we can start with Halloween, yeah?"

Apparently something inside of Elliott had melted this evening. He wasn't sure whether dinner had been the catalyst or the unexpected yet somehow welcome gift of Ishtar. Whatever the cause, Elliott felt pliant and gooey, like a piece of taffy laid out in the sun. He leaned his head against Simon's shoulder.

"Halloween together would be nice."

Chapter
Fifteen

When they went to bed that night, Simon and Elliott were both sleepy. Ishtar must have been exhausted too—she watched them walk down the hallway without even raising her head from her bed. "I hope she doesn't eat the house while we're sleeping," Elliott said as he closed the bedroom door.

Simon was too busy nuzzling him to respond with more than a hum. Pretty soon Elliott didn't care what the dog was doing; he was intent on admiring Simon's naked body in the soft light of the bedside lamp.

"You really don't care about this?" Simon grasped and jiggled the bit of fat at his stomach.

"I thought we were clear. I *like* this." Elliott smoothed his palm over the body part in question. "It's sexy. You're sexy. You'd be attractive if you lost twenty pounds or gained a hundred." He meant that. Sure, Simon's good looks and solid physique had initially caught his attention. But now that Elliott knew him, he'd never look at him and see anything but beauty.

They kept the light on while they explored each other's body. This wasn't like the ravenous fumblings of their first time—it was slow, languorous, and even a bit playful. Rather educational too, as Simon discovered Elliott's ticklish spots and Elliott learned that Simon liked the gentle scrape of teeth across sensitive body parts.

Simon's leg was a small impediment, restricting him from a few positions he clearly wanted to be in, but they improvised. Really, Simon sitting propped against pillows, kneading Elliott's ass while Elliott knelt in front of him and received an excellent blowjob— neither of them was going to complain about that. And neither grumbled as they lay on their sides, Simon rocking inside Elliott with luxurious and excruciating slowness.

Elliott came first, pleasure washing through him warm and deep. Simon kissed his nape and thrust a few more times before reaching his own climax with a long, shaky sigh.

After they cleaned up a bit, Elliott opened the bedroom door, and Ishtar came into the room just before he switched off the light. She wagged her tail, turned in a circle a few times, and curled up near his side of the bed.

"You'll have to get a dog bed for in here too," Simon said sleepily.

"She's going to take over my life, isn't she?"

"She and I both will."

That was a surprisingly agreeable thought.

Simon had to leave fairly early Sunday morning—it was his family get-together day, when his parents stayed home from work and cooked for him instead. He told Elliott that they'd watch football if it was on, or his father might find a soccer game instead. His parents would fill him in on the latest gossip and the restaurant goings-on, and they'd interrogate him about his recovery and future career plans.

"We kind of argue a lot," he admitted. "Especially if we get started on politics. But it's friendly arguing."

They shared a long kiss at the front door, Simon spent a moment petting Ishtar, and then he walked to his truck. He'd never brought in his cane the night before, and without it his limp was worse.

Ishtar wasn't too upset over Simon's departure, but after she made a visit to the backyard, she was clearly eager for some excitement. She found the pile of toys Simon had brought and dropped a stuffed squeaky duck at Elliott's feet. He looked down at her. "How about a run instead?"

He put on his sweats and shoes and attached the leash to her collar. Even though she seemed a bit confused while he stretched and warmed up, she caught on as soon as he started to jog. It had been ages since Elliott had run with a partner, and as it turned out, Ishtar made a perfect companion. She loped at his side with her tongue hanging out and her eyes glowing with the perfect joy only dogs seemed to achieve. She had an athletic body and made long, fluid strides. He had the impression she was humoring him—going easy on the poor, slow biped.

They encountered only a few other people, mostly other runners. Elliott had seen most of them before, and usually they'd exchange nods and small smiles as they passed. Today, though, he found that the smiles were wider and aimed at Ishtar. One guy even called out "Nice dog!" as he ran by. Ishtar took the admiration as her due, focusing mainly on her pace. But she came to a skidding halt and nearly dragged Elliott to the ground when they met a young woman strolling with an elderly and somewhat stout beagle.

"Sorry," Elliott said as he attempted to pull Ishtar away.

The beagle person didn't seem alarmed. "It's fine. She's friendly." Sure enough, Ishtar and the other dog were sniffing each other, tails wagging wildly.

"I just adopted her," Elliott said apologetically through his panting. "We need obedience lessons."

The woman was ruffling Ishtar's ears. "Aw, she's sweet. I bet she just needs a few behavior tips."

A lot like her owner, Elliott thought. "We'll learn together."

"Have you taken her to the dog park?"

"Not yet."

"There's a nice one at Enslen Park. Ruby's getting too old to want to hang out there, but I bet your dog would have a blast."

"Thanks. I'll check it out."

They chatted a few minutes more about vets and pet-supply stores. The woman inquired about Ishtar's name and breed. Elliott petted Ruby who, he learned, had arthritis and a thunderstorm phobia.

Having been thoroughly greeted, Ishtar was willing to continue the run. Elliott waved to the woman and Ruby. He and the woman had no clue about each other's name, but they knew all about the other's dog. That was funny and, in an odd way, sort of sweet.

As Elliott and Ishtar ran, she sometimes looked up at him, tongue lolling and eyes dancing. *Isn't this great?* she seemed to be saying. *Isn't this the best?*

Although she didn't show signs of tiring, he didn't want to overdo it. He wasn't sure how much exercise she'd been having lately, and he feared her paws might get sore. So he stopped a mile sooner than usual and headed back home. When they got inside, she drank a lot of water, collapsed onto her bed, and was soon asleep.

For the next few hours, Elliott did gold-rush-era research. Although he found some materials online, it became clear he would eventually need to dig through original documents. He wondered if Simon might like to come with him to visit archives and libraries in the Bay Area. Simon could wander the campus or city with Ishtar while Elliott worked, and then they could find someplace for an alfresco dinner. That could be fun.

Feeling restless by the afternoon, Elliott decided he needed more supplies for Ishtar. A second bed, maybe some treats, a fancier collar because hers was boring. And a leash for when they ran; he didn't like the handgrip on the one she'd come with.

Ishtar was hesitant about getting into the car. Perhaps she thought Elliott was going to take her back to the rescue people. But eventually, she climbed into the back seat and stretched out, staring at him mournfully. "It's okay," he told her. "We're just shopping."

To avoid any potential for more trauma, he didn't take her to the same store where Simon had adopted her. That turned out to be a good decision, because after the briefest of pauses in the doorway, Ishtar began wagging her tail and dragging him inside. Laughing, he managed to wrangle her to the shopping carts, where he rapidly learned that steering a cart with one wrist attached to a large dog was a difficult task.

As for Ishtar, she was in heaven. She sniffed at the shelves and cocked her head at the tanks full of fish. She picked out two toys—a sort of stick made of tennis ball material and a giant squeaky hedgehog—and a chew thing that claimed to be good for her teeth. In the treats aisle, she looked enthusiastic over whatever Elliott threw into the cart. Like Goldilocks, she tried out a few beds until they found one that fit her just right.

All of this took considerable time because she also insisted on meeting every person and dog she saw. Elliott wasn't sure he could have stopped her, but luckily nobody in the pet store seemed to mind being accosted by a big friendly dog. Everyone oohed and aahed over how nice she was, and while they petted her or watched her interact with their own dogs, they questioned Elliott about her. They treated him like a bona fide hero for adopting her. They gave him lots of unrequested and often conflicting advice. And since Elliott felt he ought to ask about their dogs too—it seemed polite—he learned all about a variety of breeds.

By the time they reached the cash register, Ishtar was still going strong but Elliott was exhausted. "Ooh, what a lover!" said the cute boy behind the counter, which startled Elliott until he realized the cashier was referring to Ishtar. The boy had dimples and pink-and-purple hair. Nobody else was in line, so he came out from behind the counter, knelt in front of Ishtar, and laughed when she rested her chin on his shoulder.

"She's kind of a slut," Elliott said apologetically.

The boy answered in a high-pitched, singsongy tone usually reserved for babies. "No! She's just a great big sweetheart! Yes, she is!"

Judging from her expression, Ishtar agreed.

Eventually the cashier moved back to his post and began to ring up the purchases. His eyebrows rose when he got to her new collar, which featured glittery gold unicorns prancing atop rainbow stripes. "Looks like she'll be ready for Pride next summer!"

"I can picture her leading a parade."

"Will you be marching with her?" The boy batted his eyelashes shamelessly, which made Elliott roll his eyes. This kid was what? Twenty? Twenty-one?

"Maybe my boyfriend and I will both march with her." And that was a fabrication, because he and Simon hadn't put a label on whatever they were to each other. It was close, though, wasn't it? The idea made Elliott feel almost melty again.

Looking slightly disappointed, the cashier finished ringing up and Elliott tried not to flinch at the total. Then the boy reached over the counter to give Ishtar some cookies. She licked his hand after she gobbled them.

It was a challenge to fit Ishtar and her new possessions into Elliott's compact car. Too bad he didn't have Simon's truck. At least this time Ishtar hopped right in, then gazed at him with adoration and curiosity, perhaps wondering what adventure he'd planned next.

"Home," he told her as he pulled out of the parking lot. "Dinner and work. Mmm, maybe a walk too."

She recognized at least one of those words, and her tail thumped loudly against the seat.

"I've heard that dogs are a great way to pick up dates. I guess it's true. I should have adopted you a long time ago. After John, though. That asshole didn't like animals in the house. 'Not hygienic,' he said. Well, I bet you're a lot more hygienic than whoever's sharing John's cell right now." Every now and then, Elliott got some satisfaction from picturing his ex in prison. This was one of those times.

After unloading the car at home, Elliott checked the library. A couple of the children's books had disappeared, but they'd been replaced by new ones. A young adult novel by Gregory Maguire was gone, and some kind of teenage vampire romance had taken its place. The little box's popularity made him happy.

Elliott ate Pita Palace leftovers, giving Ishtar a few bits even though she'd just eaten a bowl of perfectly good dog kibble. "You have some things in common with Simon, you know. He's really friendly with everyone, and he likes to eat. You both also have a lot of hair. Hmm. Wonder if he likes his ears rubbed." And that led his thoughts all sorts of nice places.

Later, he was still so preoccupied with the images in his head that he ended up sitting in front of his laptop without reading a word. Until his phone buzzed, startling him.

Miss you.

Two short words—only seven letters, one space, and a period—and Elliott almost broke down and cried. *Thinking of you,* he texted back.

I'm sitting here with parents, watching TV. Don't get me worked up. ;-)

After considering and rejecting the idea of sending his very first sext, Elliott sent instead: *Had a good day with Ish. We ran & shopped. Good dog.*

Told you so.

Wow. Elliott hadn't realized it was possible to sound so smug via text. Still, he had to give credit where it was due. *I peopled a lot more than usual today, thanks to Ish. Didn't die.*

Dog's way better than a snail shell, huh?

Infinitely.

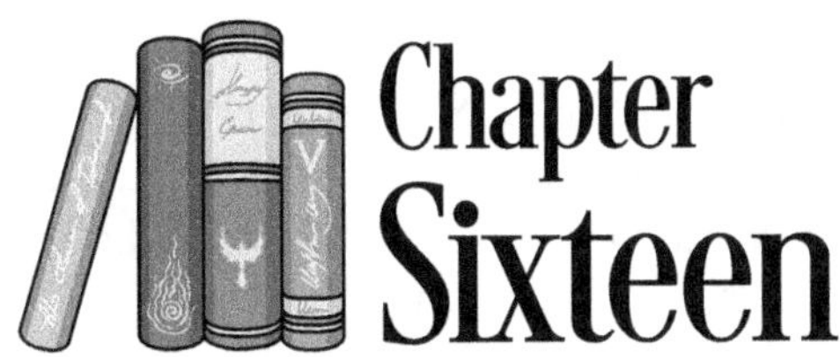# Chapter Sixteen

"You guys want to come over for dinner tonight?"

There was a lengthy pause at the other end of the line. "Are you okay?" Anna's voice was hushed, as if she were speaking to someone who might keel over any second.

"I'm fine. But I never have you over. Besides, I have a small surprise."

"Surprise?"

"It's not severed heads, I promise. You'll like it."

She laughed. "Okay, okay. We'd love to. What can we bring?"

"Dessert."

It was an unusually warm Monday in late October, so Elliott thought he'd grill some steaks. The grill itself had been a birthday gift from Anna and Ladd, but he rarely used it. Didn't seem worth the fuss when it was just him. Today, though, he was in the mood. He went to the store and bought a salad trio: potato, macaroni, and green. He picked up steaks, a bottle of merlot, and because he couldn't resist, yet another package of dog treats.

"Sucker," he muttered as he tossed them into the cart.

Student papers had been due the night before, and of course most of them were submitted in the minutes before midnight. After putting away the groceries, Elliott slogged through the submissions patiently, correcting horrible writing and informing select writers that, no, California did not join the Union in the sixteenth century and the first European visitors were not from Germany. He paused a few times to let Ishtar into the backyard or to rub her belly. In between her bouts of exercise, she seemed inclined to nap. It was funny what good company a sleeping dog made.

Elliott and Simon texted a few times. Simon checked on his protégé and complained about his physiotherapist, who he claimed could have had a promising career doing wet work for the CIA. Elliott shared some of his students' more egregious manglings of the English language.

Midafternoon, Elliott and Ishtar went for a walk. Due to the warm October weather, a lot of people were out and about, which pleased Ishtar immensely. She liked everyone but was especially drawn to children. When a young boy, maybe two or three years old, came running over, Ishtar dropped to her belly so he could pet her. When he tried to climb on her back, his mother peeled him off, which seemed to disappoint both child and dog. The only thing Ishtar didn't like, it turned out, was lawn sprinklers. She gave them a wide berth. Maybe she disapproved of such flagrant disregard of the city's watering restrictions.

When the doorbell rang shortly before six, Ishtar sprang to her feet and barked energetically, ruining much of Elliott's surprise before he even answered the door. Still, Ladd and Anna gaped at her once they were inside, Ladd holding a carton of ice cream over his head like an offering to a sky god.

"A dog!" he said.

"Ishtar," said Elliott, as if that explained everything. He took the carton and waved them further inside. Ladd remained near the entryway, looking dubious, but Anna sat down on the carpet and almost immediately had most of Ishtar in her lap. They both seemed thrilled.

"You got a dog," said Ladd. Very slowly, sounding unsure.

"Simon got her for me. I was pissed off for about three seconds because I didn't think I wanted a pet, but look. How could I not fall in love?" Proving Elliott's point, Ishtar licked Anna's chin.

Elliott hurried off to stick the ice cream in the freezer. By the time he returned, Ladd was on the floor beside Anna, and Ishtar was stretched out between them. It looked like an awkward position, yet Ishtar showed no intention of moving.

"She's friendly," Elliott said. Which was slightly obvious.

At their prompting, he told them Ishtar's story. He was starting to think he should just write down her biography and hand out copies, complete with her paw print as a signature. Anna and Ladd made sympathetic noises over the sad parts, and Ishtar played it up, begging for more petting as consolation.

Eventually, though, Ladd looked over at Elliott. "How serious are you and this guy? I mean, a dog—it's not an engagement ring, but it's not a box of chocolates either."

"I don't know. I . . . like him. A lot. He likes me. But we have complications."

"He still hasn't told the parents, huh?"

"No. And I'm still job hunting, so . . ."

Seemingly content to leave it at that, Ladd shrugged. "Need some help with dinner?"

"Nah. I'll just go throw the steaks on."

His attempt at grilling wasn't a complete success. The meat ended up a little too charred on the outside and too raw in the middle. But it tasted good anyway, especially when eaten outdoors. It was nice to sit in the backyard, chewing on steak, using the patio furniture he usually neglected, and watching Ishtar streak around in the growing darkness. Anna talked about some aggravations at work; Ladd and Elliott exchanged horror stories from teaching.

"We should get a dog," Anna said when Ishtar dropped a soggy ball at Elliott's feet. Elliott tossed it across the lawn, sending her racing at full speed. "You outgrew your allergies, Ladd."

"Yeah, I did. But with both of us gone all day? That won't work very well."

"We could get a teeny tiny dog, and I'll take her to work in my purse. Or we can get a breed that lies around all day."

"The legendary Couch Potato Hound?"

"Yes."

She dropped the subject after that, but her expression remained so speculative that Elliott suspected Ishtar might soon have a canine cousin. And why not? Ishtar would be pleased, and Elliott wouldn't mind a bit of family expansion, regardless of species.

Family. Every time he thought the word, he remembered that Simon was faced with losing his. It wasn't fair.

"What's wrong, El?" That was Ladd, his voice low and concerned.

"Nothing. Just internally railing against injustice."

"Ugh. Well, good luck with that. You've got yourself a really nice roommate, at least." Ladd grinned. "Never thought you'd end up living with a girl."

"I never thought I'd end up living with anyone." Elliott snorted. "Ishtar's a lot more forgiving than a human would be."

Anna had been chasing a last bit of macaroni salad around her plate. "Ishtar. Wasn't that a movie?"

Elliott nodded. He'd heard of it but had never seen it. He'd googled the film the previous day. "Dustin Hoffman and Warren Beatty. It bombed."

"Oh. Too bad. Well, this Ishtar's a winner for sure."

They went inside for ice cream and tea. Ladd and Anna had to wake up early for work, but they showered Ishtar with adoration before they left.

"I'd like to meet Simon some time," said Ladd. "He sounds like a catch."

Elliott gave a wry smile. "That's part of my worry. I was never any good at playing ball."

There was something unsettling about Tuesday. Maybe it was the weather. The barometric pressure had dropped suddenly, bringing colder temperatures and threatening clouds. Ishtar seemed slightly restless too, even after a long run. She had trouble getting comfortable on her bed, and even once she was settled, she kept getting up to wander over and rest her chin in Elliott's lap.

"Already having adoptee's remorse?" he asked, although he knew that wasn't the case. She fit into the household as if she'd been there for years, and she rarely wanted to leave his side. Maybe she was just picking up on his unease, the weird feeling that something might jump out of the shadows and bite him.

So perhaps he could be excused for startling wildly when his phone rang as he was sitting down to lunch. He recognized the area code as Nebraska.

"Hello?"

"Hi! Elliott Thompson? This is Ginny Holmes from NSU."

It was fortunate he had water nearby, because his throat went desert dry. "Hi, Ginny."

"I'm calling because we'd like to bring you to campus for an interview. Assuming you're still interested in us, of course."

"That's great! I'm definitely interested." He hoped he was striking the right balance between enthusiasm and nonchalance, but his heart was beating so furiously he was sure she could hear it.

"Great! Our bureaucratic wheels spin slowly here, and by the time we get all the approvals, we'll be hitting the holidays. So we'd like to bring you out when spring semester begins. The week of January fourteenth?"

Nebraska in January. He was going to have to buy suitable winter wear. "That sounds great."

They chatted for a few minutes about the details of his visit, then sidetracked into a short discussion about weather. Apparently they were expecting a Halloween blizzard, which was unusual for them but not unprecedented. Ginny laughed when she learned that children in Modesto were moaning about the next day's rain forecast. "I suppose you don't get much weather there," she said.

"Only if you count baking heat in summer as weather."

"Oh, we get hot too," she said cheerfully. "But we like to pair it with high humidity!"

By the time he hung up, Elliott discovered his appetite had fled, and his stomach was apparently under the impression it was on board a ship during a hurricane. He wrapped up his sandwich and salad and put them in the fridge, then leaned back against the counter and looked solemnly at Ishtar. "I don't know how I feel about this."

She wagged her tail as if encouraging him to continue.

"You know, when I was finishing up grad school, I got several phone interviews and three campus interviews. Three. Two of those schools ended up offering me a job. John only worked at one of them, but he liked to take credit anyway. He said his glowing recommendations got me in. But I think I got the offers because I'm a good scholar and a good instructor."

Ishtar meandered over to him, then plopped down on top of his feet. She was a good listener.

"So the people at NSU know about the scandal—and know I'm gay—and want to meet me. That's good. I think I can impress them." With some difficulty, he pulled his feet from under Ishtar, then slid down the base cabinets until he was sitting next to her. He buried his face in her neck. "Do I *want* to impress them?" he whispered into her fur.

She didn't answer, which was only fair considering he didn't know either. Ever since leaving his last job, he'd been dreaming of a new tenure-track appointment the way some people dreamed of winning the lottery. Metaphorically speaking, he'd continued buying his tickets, week after week. But now that the shining prize was possibly within reach, he wasn't even sure he wanted it anymore. He'd read about people who won a jackpot and ended up miserable due to lives suddenly complicated by bloodsucking relatives, opportunistic friends, and brazen strangers. Winning wasn't always the best result in the long run.

And in his case, there was Simon. Whom he'd known only a short time, and whom Elliott might very well lose even if he stayed in Modesto. But, God, even the thought of that loss sent his heart into a panicked rhythm. What if Simon was the real prize and that job in Nebraska—or anywhere else for that matter—was nothing but fool's gold?

"Life is hard," Elliott whined to Ishtar. "Why can't I be a dog?"

Except she had led a difficult life too, abandoned by her family and left for months without anyone to love her. He wrapped his arms around her neck; she licked his ear before settling her chin on his shoulder.

That evening, Elliott took Ishtar for a walk and accidentally on purpose ended up at Simon's house. But a Ford sedan was parked in his driveway, so Elliott kept going. He felt like a dirty secret, which wasn't a sensation he wanted to relive. He knew it wasn't Simon's fault, not really, and Simon had certainly been honest about his situation from the beginning. But still it made Elliott a little angry, and then he was angry at himself for being angry at Simon.

He and Ishtar ran the few blocks home.

Chapter
Seventeen

Although the sky was dark on Halloween morning, rain hadn't yet begun to fall. Elliott and Ishtar had a long run first thing. He'd been checking her paws after exercise. They looked fine, and she showed no signs of discomfort or distress, so he assumed she was good for distance running. In fact, she seemed thrilled with it and even a little disappointed when they returned home. She settled in for a nap while Elliott showered and ate breakfast.

Now she was on the front porch. Elliott had rigged a tether using a support column, a bungee cord, and one of her leashes, so she had a little room to roam but couldn't run off. She watched with mild interest while he weeded the front garden for what he hoped might be the last time until spring. Hey, there was an advantage to Nebraska! Unlike California, nothing grew during the winter, so no yard work. Of course, the snow shoveling and ice scraping probably counterbalanced the benefit.

Having conquered the weeds, Elliott fetched his new garden flag, which had arrived the previous day. He hadn't realized it when he ordered, but the purple hearts atop the rainbow stripes were glittery. Even better. He assembled the metal hanger, drove it into the ground, and was in the middle of attaching the flag when Ishtar stood and began to bark.

Elliott turned around. "Oh. Hi, Mike."

Mike Burgess continued to stomp up the walkway without returning the greeting. "The city requires dogs to be on leashes," he said.

"Which she is, as you can plainly see. And I don't think the ordinance applies when the dog is on private property. Which she also is."

That took a bit of the wind from Mike's sails, but only for a moment. "The city limits you to two dogs."

"And Ishtar, who may be quite large, still only counts as one. So we're good."

Mike's face was sour and pinched. Elliott wanted to warn him that if he wasn't careful, it would freeze like that. Hell, maybe it already had. Elliott had never seen him look happy.

Ishtar, uncharacteristically, wasn't wagging her tail and looking desperate for attention. In fact, she was eyeing Mike rather like Elliott eyed door-to-door religious nuts who tried to convince him he was on the road to hell. Yet Mike continued to stand there with his hands at his sides and his mouth pursed up like an asshole.

"Can I help you with something?" Elliott finally asked with only a hint of irritation. Okay, maybe more than a hint.

"That sign—"

"It's a flag. We've been through this. Somebody stole the other one, so I got a new one. I like it. It's in *my* front yard."

"But the CC&Rs—"

"Fuck the CC&Rs." Elliott ignored Mike's shocked reaction. He had enough big shit going on in his life without worrying about this little shit. He brushed some soil from his hands and took a step closer to Mike. "Seriously, what is your problem? I'm a good neighbor. This house was a dump when I bought it, but I fixed it up, and it's really nice now. I don't have loud parties. I don't have kids who ride dirt bikes up and down the street or leave their toys in the middle of the sidewalk. I don't have a zillion cars that I leave parked all over the place. I bring in my garbage bins promptly, I keep my lawn mowed, and I always pick up those stupid free newspapers and recycle them before they become a soggy mess. So what the hell is your problem with me? Is it because I'm gay?"

"It has nothing to do with that!" Mike snapped. "You people are always bringing that up as an excuse."

Oh, this was good. Elliott couldn't remember the last time he'd confronted anyone. His skin was comfortably flushed, and he had to work to keep his hands from balling into fists. But he kept his voice low and even. "Then what is it, Mike?"

Mike opened and closed his mouth, clearly at a loss. "You skirt the rules," he finally said. "We have rules for a reason."

"We certainly do. In fact, written laws are almost as old as civilization. But the CC&Rs aren't exactly the Code of Hammurabi, inscribed in stone. And you, my friend, are not Hammurabi. So even if I was skirting the rules—which I'm not—why do you give a shit? How does it affect you? Do you have nothing better to do than get in a tizzy over rainbow flags?"

As Elliott talked, Mike had backed up a step or two. But now he stopped and snarled, and for a moment, Elliott was dead sure the guy was going to clock him. To his surprise, that didn't frighten him. In fact, a tiny atavistic part of him *hoped* Mike would punch him, because then Elliott could punch back, and for the first time since the skirmish with Richie Pyle in eleventh grade, he'd end up in a bona fide fight. And it would feel good! Elliott might not be as big as Simon, but he worked out—and judging by Mike's physique, Mike did not. Elliott could probably beat the shit out of him, which would be gloriously cathartic.

And okay, yes, would probably land him in jail.

But maybe Simon had pals who worked there.

It was slightly disappointing but probably for the best when Mike backed away. From the safety of the street, he faced Elliott again, hands on hips. "You'd better not violate the CC&Rs!" he yelled. "And you'd better keep control of that dog!"

Elliott just snorted and waved him away.

Simon arrived an hour before dark. He bent in the entryway to adore Ishtar, then stood and grinned at Elliott. "Need your help." He jerked his head toward his truck in the driveway.

And yes he did, because he'd brought several cardboard boxes full of police-themed items to give to trick-or-treaters, along with an enormous tray of homemade baklava his mother had instructed him to share with the parents. "She and Dad have to work tonight, so she's missing out. Usually she goes to Aunt Soso's party and has a blast with all the little kids."

"She wants grandchildren, huh?" Elliott took the tray, leaving Simon with his cane and a paper grocery bag.

"Yeah. She knits things, El. Some of them she gives away to relatives, but I'm pretty sure she has a stash tucked away for my offspring."

Back in the house, Ishtar danced around them happily, making passage difficult. While Simon took his bag into the kitchen, Elliott looked for somewhere to stash the baklava out of Ishtar's reach. He ended up balancing it on some books atop one of the shorter bookcases, and even then he wasn't sure it was safe. Luckily, Ishtar was too distracted by Simon to notice. Elliott didn't blame her—he'd choose Simon over pastries too.

"Dinner!" Simon called from the kitchen.

Simon had set out plates and cutlery, which made Elliott feel warm and fuzzy. Not just because it was pleasant to have someone taking care of him a little, but because it meant Simon felt comfortable in Elliott's house.

"It's kind of early for dinner, isn't it?" asked Elliott.

"Yeah. But as soon as it gets dark, the kids arrive. No time to eat then." Simon looked as excited about the holiday as any child. It was adorable, and it made Elliott want to drag him into the bedroom then and there. But duty called.

Tonight they feasted on pho and bánh mì from a Vietnamese takeout place downtown. Elliott enjoyed the food, but he was distracted by watching Simon eat noodles. That mouth.

"If we get hungry again later, we can always order a pizza or something," Simon said as they were cleaning up.

"Or I have ice cream in the freezer."

Simon waggled his eyebrows. "And chocolate sauce? Whipped cream?"

"No. Sorry."

"Shame." Simon's expression suggested it wasn't frozen dairy products he was thinking about.

It took some time to set up all the giveaways, and the entryway ended up stuffed with boxes. "We'd better get a lot of kids," Elliott said.

"We will."

And Simon was right. The first of them arrived even before dusk, babies and toddlers dressed as flowers and ladybugs and superheroes, each of them goggling in wonder. Elliott couldn't blame them. From a little-kid perspective, it was a weird holiday. You put on funny clothes and went tromping around the neighborhood at night, ringing the doorbells of complete strangers. Elliott didn't know how impressed the little ones were with the stuff he and Simon were giving out, but the parents seemed pleased with the bookmarks and water bottles and things. And the baklava—that was a hit.

Ishtar remained on a leash, wagging her tail eagerly, and whenever a parent gave permission, Simon or Elliott—whoever held the leash's other end—let her move forward to greet the children. She licked their faces, making them giggle, and cheerfully withstood their clumsy pats.

Everyone left the house smiling.

The real deluge began shortly after dark. Sometimes the crowds were so thick and heavy that Elliott and Simon didn't even bother closing the front door. They just stood there, waiting for the next gaggle of kids to come up the walk.

It was maybe among the fifth or sixth group of children that a tween boy dressed as a pirate exclaimed, "You're the book guys!"

"Just him," Simon said.

The boy turned to Elliott. "That library thing is cool! Did you see I put a book in there the other day?"

Elliott smiled at him. "What was it about?"

"Reptiles. I love reptiles. I'm going to be a herpetologist."

"That's great! I did see your book. I think somebody else has already borrowed it."

The boy beamed at that and gave his friend—a boy in firefighter garb—a high five.

Several more people complimented the library that night. A couple of adults even showed up with books to hand over, and despite the call of candy and the street's darkness, quite a few people paused to look the library over. Melanie came by with both of her parents, and her mother handed Elliott a gift bag with black cats and ghosts on it.

"What's this?" he asked.

"For you. To thank you for bringing a mini library to our neighborhood."

The bag contained a bottle of wine and a package of Snausages.

"Wow," said Simon when they had a brief break. "Your books are a hit. Did you expect this?"

Elliott felt a little dazed, actually. "No. I just wanted to get rid of some books."

"Seems to me you've gotten a whole lot in return."

Elliott nodded. Neither of them meant the wine.

As the night went on, the crowds began to thin and the visitors became older. The teenagers came in big groups without parental accompaniment. Elliott was afraid they'd be disappointed at the lack of candy, but they loved the goodies he and Simon gave out, and they spent a lot of time petting Ishtar. She had obviously decided that this was the best day ever and undoubtedly believed all these weirdly attired people were coming just to admire her.

It was almost nine and only a few stragglers remained when a pair of boys came to the door. It was hard to tell under all the makeup, but they were probably in their midteens. One of them wore Dorothy's blue gingham dress with matching bows in his pigtails, and he carried a wicker basket containing a tiny stuffed dog. The other was dressed in a blonde wig and spangly leotard. Lady Gaga, Elliott guessed, but he wasn't sure. The boys held hands.

"Are you gay cops?" asked Dorothy when Simon gave them water bottles and badges.

"I used to be." Simon pointed to his knee.

"I never was," Elliott added. "Gay college professor. Way less cool."

But the boys were polite to him too, and then Lady Gaga announced they'd both been reading Elliott's books. "Together," Lady Gaga said in the most suggestive tone a sixteen-year-old could muster. Great. Elliott just hoped they were reading the parts about safe sex.

Simon shook his head when they walked away. "God, they're so confident in who they are."

"Maybe because it's Halloween."

"Maybe. But I never would have put on a dress when I was in high school, not even as a costume. I would have felt . . . too naked like that."

Elliott gave Simon's ass a quick grope. "What about a kilt?"

"I'm Assyrian, not Scottish."

"Okay, how about a tunic, then?"

Simon pulled him close. "How about nothing at all?" he rumbled.

Almost as if cued by a beneficent god, rain began to splatter the sidewalk.

"I hope those boys get home before their makeup and outfits are ruined," said Simon, which made Elliott kiss his cheek before closing and locking the door.

They ended up close together on the couch, each with a bowl of baklava and ice cream plus a glass of Melanie's wine. Exhausted after her door-greeter job, Ishtar lay stretched on her bed, snoring softly. Sometimes her paws twitched. Elliott liked to think she was dreaming about chasing a squirrel-sized Mike Burgess. In the spirit of the holiday, Elliott had put on *Psycho*, but they weren't paying much attention to the movie. Instead, they snuggled a little and talked about trivial matters. Rain pattered against the window in brief gusts.

Midway through his second glass of wine, Elliott finally found his courage. "Nebraska State called. They're flying me out for an interview."

Simon's expression, usually so open and cheerful, closed up at once. Then he forced a smile. "That's great, Prof. Congratu—"

"Don't."

"What?"

"I don't know how I feel about it, and I sure as hell don't want you to fake being happy over it."

Simon relaxed a bit. "I *am* happy for you. I mean, in a way. Aren't you? Isn't this exactly what you've been wanting?"

"It was, yes. Now . . . I'm not so sure."

With a groan that had more to do with emotional turmoil than tiredness, Elliott stood and collected the empty ice cream bowls.

Ishtar lifted her head as he passed, but she must have decided licking the dishes wasn't worth the effort, and she went back to sleep. He left the bowls in the kitchen sink, along with the detritus from dinner, and returned to the living room. But he didn't sit down.

"Ish and I walked by your house last night."

"Why didn't you stop by?"

"Someone was there."

Simon stared blankly for a moment before frowning. "It was my parents. Shit! You didn't think I had a guy over, did you? I know we haven't talked about being exclusive, but I have no intention of seeing anyone else while we're together, okay? I'm not— That's not me."

Actually, the possibility that the Ford belonged to a hookup hadn't even crossed Elliott's mind. He didn't know if that was because he was oblivious or because he trusted Simon. "I assumed it was your parents."

"Oh." Simon shrank back against the couch cushions. "Okay. They stop by once in a while. They bring me leftovers from the Palace so I don't starve to death. And yeah, I know, clingy much. I don't really mind, though."

"There's nothing wrong with wanting to spend time with your family."

"Next time, you can text beforehand if you want. Save you the trip."

Elliott wanted to pace but didn't. He drained his wineglass instead. "It's not that. I was, literally, in the neighborhood. It's just . . . I hated having to slink on by."

It wasn't easy for Simon to get off the couch, but he did, and ignoring his cane, he hobbled over to gently grasp Elliott's shoulders. "I'm so sorry. You deserve much better."

"So do you!" Elliott wrapped his arms around Simon's middle and sighed when Simon did the same. They leaned against each other, Elliott bearing a bit of Simon's weight. And that was nice until Ishtar apparently decided it was group-hug time, ambled over, reared up on her hind legs, and joined them. She nearly knocked Simon onto his ass but didn't look the least bit repentant.

They ended up taking the party to the couch—more stable that way. Elliott sat almost in Simon's lap while Ishtar returned to her bed with a satisfied grunt.

"Something's gotta give here, doesn't it?" Simon nuzzled Elliott's hair.

"Yeah. Jesus, Si, I really don't want you to damage your relationship with your parents. But I can't—"

"I know. And I can't ask it of you. And if I'm just going to string you along like this, I also can't ask you to give up the job in Nebraska."

"It's just an interview," Elliott muttered, but he knew what Simon meant.

Simon ignored the comment. "You and I, we're stuck in this half-life. In limbo. Between careers. Between, well, loves I guess. It's a fairly comfy place. With you in it, anyway. We haven't known each other long, but we, we feel . . . matched."

"Yeah."

"When I was a kid, I went through a Lego phase. Did you do Legos?"

With a smile, Elliott nodded. "Yeah. Ladd and I used to build things together. He'd make these wild vehicles and my specialty was mansions."

"I think I still have mine, somewhere in the wilds of my second floor."

Absurd as it seemed, Elliott could picture himself sitting with Simon, like a pair of kids, constructing things. Maybe Simon was imagining the same scene, because he chuckled and kissed Elliott's head before saying, "You can look for them next time you're over, if you're feeling brave. But do you remember how satisfying it was when you snapped that last brick into place and your creation was perfect? That's how I feel about us."

Elliott totally understood the analogy; he felt that way himself. But still he frowned. "Ladd used to wreck everything as soon as it was finished."

"Perfection can't last. Do you think we can keep it together for at least a little longer?"

Despite his melancholy, Elliott smiled. "We can put us on the top shelf in the closet. It's where I hid things from Ladd."

"The closet. Great."

They were quiet for a time, Simon absently rubbing Elliott's chest through his T-shirt, and Elliott, with closed eyes, leaning back into the warmth and comfort as if he were a cat. He suddenly laughed with a small note of bitterness. "We're not fighting."

"No. Is that bad?"

"John and I used to bicker all the time. Not yelling, but nasty squabbling. Over stupid things too, not heart-wrenching matters like losing family or moving away. More like whether we should order pizza or Chinese. Which hotel we should stay at during a conference. Which journal I should submit a manuscript to." Even at the time, he'd realized the hostility over what to watch on TV was truly displaced from the real issue, which was their dysfunctional relationship. But knowing that hadn't helped.

"Sounds stressful," Simon said. "I hate fighting."

"Says the cop."

"*Ex*-cop. Anyway, when I did my job right, I settled confrontations instead of engaging in them."

"Or you got shot." Elliott rubbed the thigh of Simon's bad leg.

"That's when I did my job wrong."

"You're alive. But anyway, life with John *was* stressful." So much so that after John had been sent to jail, and even while Elliott was still under suspicion for colluding with him, one of the many emotions flooding through Elliott had been relief. No more arguments with John.

"I'm sorry," said Simon.

"My own damn fault. But you and I haven't bickered at all."

"We have handled our situation like grown-ups."

"It's nice. Really nice."

Simon answered with a kiss, which was fortunate because Elliott's eyes felt prickly, and he might otherwise have cried. He didn't even know why. Everything, maybe. A gestalt weep.

The kiss escalated into mutual petting, but that fizzled out as they melted into couch-bound lassitude. They could always move to the bed later—right now, simply snuggling was wonderful in itself.

"Speaking of adulting," Simon began through a yawn, "I think I know what I want to be when I grow up."

"Yeah?"

"I want to be a park ranger."

Elliott wasn't sure what he'd expected, but it hadn't been that. "Park ranger?"

"Yes! Like the ones we talked to in Columbia. Doesn't that seem like a cool thing to do? It's law enforcement, only less with the meth dealers and more with giving directions to hikers."

Elliott pictured Simon in the green-and-khaki uniform. "You'd look good in the hat."

"That's the important thing, of course." Simon tickled Elliott's belly before continuing. "I did a little research. Park rangers are sworn peace officers, which means I already have most of the training I'd need. I'd have to do some special park-operations academy stuff, but that lasts less than two months. Plus, I could do some of it on the job, and I could qualify as a supervisor."

Although Simon sounded cheerful and enthusiastic, Elliott had to ask, "What about your leg?"

"Yeah, still a small problem. But I talked to my PT, and he thinks that if we work hard, maybe in six months I could be in good enough shape to pass the physical agility test."

"Could you stick around here? Or would you end up on top of Mount San Jacinto or something?"

Simon squeezed him. "Here. Central Valley district includes a bunch of parks—including Columbia."

"You're picturing yourself swaggering down Main Street like Wyatt Earp, aren't you?"

"No." Another tickle. "More like Cleavon Little."

Elliott attempted to sing Lili von Shtupp's "I'm Tired" song, then fondled Simon's crotch and cried, "It's twue! It's twue!"

Simon responded by tickling him in earnest until they landed in a tangled pile on the floor with Ishtar joining the fun. Elliott laughed so hard he was in serious danger of pissing his pants.

"I think I've had too much drama lately." He leaned his head back onto the seat of the couch. He was still giggling a little.

"That's because you're not an Odisho. We're all about the drama. Like the current main episode, which involves Ashur's sister, Miri."

"The pregnant one?"

"Yep. She's nineteen, and the father's some guy—not Assyrian, even—she slept with once after a party. She's talking about putting the kid up for adoption. Cue a whole lot of yelling." Although he shook his head, he appeared more fond than annoyed. Then he shifted his legs. "And I don't think I can stand up."

Elliott rose and gave him a hand. They persuaded Ishtar to visit the backyard one last time, and even though it wasn't yet midnight, they headed to bed. Before they got there, Elliott stopped Simon. "I'm glad you've decided to be a ranger."

"Yeah? Why?"

"Your face lit up as soon as you mentioned it."

Simon kissed him so thoroughly they almost didn't make it to the bedroom.

Chapter Eighteen

By his best approximation—and assuming a fairly broad definition of sex—Elliott had had sex with John somewhere around four hundred times. Which was a lot when you came to think about it, especially when both partners were busy and unable to spend much time together. Some of the sex had been good—very good even— but most had been . . . mediocre. And of course, over time they'd fallen into familiar patterns, so their encounters were like ordering from a menu: *one from column A, one from column B, and if you're lucky, a dessert from column C.*

Elliott and Simon hadn't been together nearly long enough to slide into bedroom ennui. Like explorers newly landed on a mysterious continent, they were still discovering each other's body—and that was a wonderful adventure indeed. They were learning how to make each other gasp and writhe, how to bring each other to the point where begging turned to wordless cries, how to tease and soothe and delight.

So the sex was hot. But almost as good was what came afterward— the tender kisses and murmured words, the restful times while curled in an embrace. Elliott had never had any of that with John, and he had come to realize what a poverty that had been.

Now on Halloween night, Simon and Elliott climbed into bed and spent a long time stroking and fondling, interrupted occasionally by whispers.

"I'm glad you don't wax," Elliott said, petting the sleek hair on Simon's chest.

"You have a thing for bears, huh?"

"Hey, you're the one who wants to be a park ranger."

"You got a pic-a-nic basket?" Snorting at his own dumb joke, Simon caressed Elliott's balls. Elliott might have objected to the humor except, well, Simon was caressing his balls. And that felt damned good.

Elliott rolled onto his back and splayed his legs, encouraging easier access. Taking the hint, Simon continued what he was doing as he tipped onto his side to mouth Elliott's chest, which in its natural state was almost hairless. For a time, Elliott enjoyed simply lying there, luxuriating in Simon's wandering fingers and clever tongue, shivering slightly at the scrape of Simon's beard over his skin. Simon smelled of baklava and wine, and he hummed a bit as he worked Elliott's body. When they were in bed together, it seemed as if Elliott temporarily acquired more senses, and all of them were nearly overwhelmed with the corporeality, the actuality of Simon.

"Hey, El?" Simon's quiet voice rumbled through the sensory noise in Elliott's head. "Would you like to top tonight?"

Oh yes, Elliott would.

Getting Simon ready was a reward in itself. After arranging him facedown, Elliott had an excellent excuse to lavish attention on Simon's round, firm ass. Dark hair grew there too, but more sparsely than on his chest, and these hairs were finer. Beneath that was soft skin and strong muscle, and Simon's cleft invited Elliott's fingers and tongue.

He waited until Simon was gasping—almost growling with need—before rolling a condom onto himself. In consideration of the injured knee, they'd propped Simon's hips with a pillow, but still, before beginning a slow side home, Elliott licked his nape and whispered in his ear. "Doing okay? Leg's all right?"

Simon reached behind himself awkwardly, attempting to urge Elliott's hips forward. "Yes! Don't stop."

Elliott didn't stop, but he did take his time, relishing every additional centimeter of enveloping heat. Due to the pillow, he couldn't reach Simon's cock, which was a shame. Not that Simon seemed to mind—he was pushing backward into Elliott's thrusts, moaning encouragement the entire time. Some of what he said was not in English, but that was okay because Elliott suspected a smattering of Serbo-Croatian words fell from his own mouth as he approached his climax.

When Elliott came, his eyes were squeezed shut, but still he saw sparkles. It felt as if his entire body burst into tiny particles, only to come back together slightly better than before.

He realized he was still plunging into Simon's pliant body, but a heartbeat or two later, Simon called out loud enough to make Ishtar bark from the living room.

Then Elliott was laughing too hard to do much but roll off Simon and be gathered into Simon's arms. "Good?" Elliott asked.

"Yeah. Um, you'll need to wash that pillowcase."

That sent them into more laughter.

After they'd calmed and done a minimal cleanup, Elliott let Ishtar in. Her loud grunt as she collapsed onto her bed said she didn't approve of their nighttime shenanigans.

"Some sex goddess," Elliott muttered.

"Huh?"

"Nothing."

Simon sucked briefly on Elliott's earlobe. "Happy Halloween."

One thing Elliott knew for sure—whatever happened between them, his memories of Simon would haunt him in a wonderful way.

Rain persisted over the next several days. Not a deluge, but drizzles and showers. Elliott couldn't get much running in, which made both him and Ishtar restless. It turned out Ishtar hated rain as much as she hated sprinklers, and she seemed to hold Elliott personally responsible for the bad weather. He'd let her out into the backyard, and she'd stand in the doorway, gazing up at him reproachfully. Then she'd hurry to the front door, only to look disappointed when she learned it was raining there too.

The good news was that the little library held up well despite the moisture. Elliott checked carefully each day, and the books remained dry. The titles rotated at an even busier rate than before, maybe because the weather caused people to spend more time reading indoors. The other good news was that despite his stress levels, Elliott did not buy any new books. He spent time working on his classes and spelunking the internet for sources on homosexuality during the gold rush.

He even put those pieces together by developing an impromptu lesson plan on the subject and offering his California history students extra credit for writing an essay. This was the time of year when they were eager to bolster their grades, so he was confident some of them would take him up on the offer.

Elliott also made some progress on Ishtar, signing her up for an obedience class that would begin in January. Well, he signed them both up. Ishtar was a bright girl who grasped things quickly; Elliott suspected the class would mostly involve him learning how to communicate effectively with her.

"It'll be like learning another language," he told her. "I wonder if it's as hard as Croatian?"

Ishtar didn't have an answer. She was too busy licking peanut butter out of a large rubber toy that looked disturbingly like an extremely uncomfortable butt plug.

Simon was putting in extra effort with his PT and had even bought a treadmill so he could walk no matter the weather. Now that he'd decided on a career path, he was serious about rehabilitating his leg. He came over to Elliott's house almost every night, and they'd have dinner together, watch TV, and usually enjoy a sleepover. It was the most domestic arrangement Elliott had ever experienced, and it was wonderful in spite of the uncertain future hanging over their heads.

Exactly two weeks after Halloween, on the first really chilly night of the year, Simon brought dinner from the grocery store—rotisserie chicken, a bagged salad, a deli salad made with green beans, and a couple of rolls.

"Where's the cane?" Elliott asked as he set the table.

Simon beamed. "Semiretired. I'm going to get a folding one to have handy just in case, but I should mostly be able to manage without one."

Elliott set down the silverware and gave him a celebratory kiss. "You know, once you have full use of that leg, we can get more adventurous in bed. More positions."

"You're bored with me already?" Simon's tone was joking, but his eyes betrayed a hint of insecurity.

"I am not. We could never have sex again, and I'd still be endlessly fascinated with you. But I hope we *do* have sex again, because you knock my socks off."

Simon pulled him close and palmed his ass. "Socks off, huh?"

"And everything else."

So they temporarily abandoned the meal to go work up an appetite in bed. When they came back to the kitchen, Elliott had to reheat the chicken, but it was totally worth it.

After they sat down and started filling their plates, Elliott noticed that Simon took smaller portions than usual. "Feeling okay?" he asked. "Do you want the other drumstick?"

"I feel dandy, and I don't want more food. I'm trying to drop a few pounds." He grimaced.

"Why? You look great. I mean, you'd look great no matter what, but—"

"I know you think I'm sexy, El." He rubbed his belly as he spoke. "The problem is that extra weight isn't good for my stupid knee. And it won't help me pass the physical agility tests either." He snagged a piece of breast meat with his fork.

"Okay, that makes sense. A long as you know I'd lo— Shit." His throat tightened with the enormity of what he'd almost said, and he laid his fork on the table.

Simon chewed and swallowed carefully, all the while keeping his gaze locked on Elliott's face. When his mouth was empty, he stroked his beard a few times, and his voice was deep and quiet when he spoke. "That was a big word that almost slipped out."

"Not really. One syllable. Four letters." Elliott's laugh sounded slightly hysterical.

"Unconstitutionality is a really *long* word, but it's not nearly as big as what you almost said."

Nodding, Elliott conceded the point.

Simon reached across the table to take Elliott's hand. "I really want to hear you say that word. I really want to say it back. But I know I haven't earned it."

"Me either."

They avoided the subject for the remainder of the meal. As they put away the leftovers, Simon "accidentally" dropped a bit of chicken for Ishtar. Elliott washed the dishes while Simon dried and put them away. They ended up on the couch in their usual spots, and while Elliott was startled to realize they *had* usual spots, he was also comforted.

Simon took possession of the remote control and put on a cop show, mostly because he enjoyed making fun of them. Fictional police work, he said, had little to do with the reality of the job.

"Thanksgiving plans?" he asked during a commercial.

"Nothing big. Ladd and Anna order one of those grocery store meals. I bring wine. Do you spend it with just your parents or the whole clan?"

"Whole clan. But it's complicated because the location is a point of family contention. Mom and Dad like to host, which Dad thinks should be his right because he's the oldest. But his next-oldest brother has six kids and a zillion grandkids and thinks superior procreation gives *him* hosting rights."

As usual, a tale about Simon's family made Elliott smile, even if there was a sad edge to it. "Is that Ashur and Miri's father?"

"Nope, that would be brother number three. But due to a disaster he caused at Pita Palace long ago—stuff caught on fire—nobody trusts him anywhere near a kitchen. So it's just Dad and Uncle Isaac fighting over it, which is just as well."

Elliott snuggled closer against him. "And how is this resolved?"

"By doubling the agony. Mom and Dad host on Thanksgiving proper, and then even though we all have leftovers, we go to Uncle Isaac's the next night for another meal. And even more leftovers."

"Wow."

"Yeah. And as if all the eating wasn't exhausting enough, there's the drama. Thanksgiving comes in third on the family-crisis scale, after Christmas and Easter. Somebody always ends up not speaking to somebody else for at least a week."

Elliott squirmed around to see Simon's face. "I bet you're never any of those somebodies."

"No." Simon's sigh was long and loud. "I try not to get in the middle of it."

"Sounds wise."

Simon slammed his hand against the arm of the couch, "Damn it, you and I should be spending the holiday together!" He left unspoken the rest of that complaint—that they might *never* have a Thanksgiving together. Next year, Elliott might be freezing his ass off in Nebraska. Or Simon might have decided that continuing their relationship was too risky.

"You could come over to Ladd and Anna's with me. Anna's dying to meet you anyway."

"Except I can't. I can't get out of the family thing. And I'd love to invite you, but—"

"I know."

And there went another conversational topic into the dead zone.

Despite Simon's warmth, Elliott felt chilly. He walked to the bedroom and pulled a gray microfleece throw from the closet. Soon he'd need his down comforter too, especially for the nights he slept alone.

After returning to the couch and the crook of Simon's arm, Elliott spread the blanket over their laps. "That's cozy," Simon commented after a few minutes.

"Hmm."

"I was thinking about something."

"Hmm?" Simon was gently stroking Elliott's arm—just a light whisper of his fingertips—and between that, dinner, and sex, Elliott was too drowsy to say much else.

"I'll make a good salary as a ranger supervisor."

"That's good."

"And if I stopped being chickenshit about coming out to my parents, you and I could move in together. Your place or mine. That would save a lot on expenses. So if you weren't earning a huge amount with the online or part-time stuff, no big deal."

This thought had crossed Elliott's mind too—more than once. If it weren't for their respective issues, keeping separate residences a few blocks apart would be absurd, especially given that Simon usually spent the night anyway. Elliott would love to share a bed with Simon every night, wake up to him every morning, just . . . have him around.

"It's not only the money," he said.

"If you're freaked about not contributing absolutely equally to the mortgage and stuff, don't be. We'd be partners, and that means we each contribute what we can."

Elliott lifted Simon's hand and kissed the back of it. "Socialism. I could deal with that. I was referring to my job situation, though. There's nothing wrong with teaching online or at community colleges, but it's not what I've worked toward. I'm . . . Shit. A scholar?"

"You can't be a scholar without the fancy university? It seems to me like you can write your books no matter who you work for. Maybe even better if you can control your own schedule."

"That's not how it's done." Elliott shifted uncomfortably.

"Seems to me you should do stuff because you want to do it, because it makes you happy. Don't let somebody tell you how it should be done."

Mulling over those words, Elliott remained silent. Why *did* he so badly want an academic job at a research institution? Simon was right; he could write anywhere. While community college students were different from students at a four-year university, teaching them could be equally rewarding. He'd just always assumed he'd be a university professor—that's what everyone he went to grad school with had assumed. John had certainly nurtured that expectation, giving him long lectures about the quality of various institutions and the need to aim high.

What was the payoff? If Elliott went to Nebraska State—hell, if he went to fucking Harvard—what would he get in the end? A scholarly reputation among the few dozen people who gave a crap. Maybe an award or two to hang in his office, a small grant now and then to fund his travel. A research assistant to do grunt work. Nice enough things. But were they nicer than the embrace that currently enfolded him? The embrace that might or might not last?

He had no answers to any of that. Time to bury this conversation as well.

Chapter
Nineteen

On the Tuesday before Thanksgiving, Elliott wondered why he'd chosen to give exams so close to the end of the term. He had a zillion of them to grade, yet finals were in only three weeks. No doubt the students were cursing him too. While they at least had the comfort of knowing that the current tests would help them prepare for finals, however, Elliott had no such consolation. His brain was numb, and his eyes were sore and gritty from staring for so many hours at the computer screen.

Luckily the rain had stopped, and the cool weather was perfect for exercising. He and Ishtar had already taken a long morning run, but by midafternoon he decided it was time for a walk. Ishtar sensed good things as soon as Elliott got up from the laptop and stretched. Tail wagging, she trotted beside him as he fetched his shoes and coat.

"Do you need a coat too?" he asked as he snapped the leash onto her collar. It wasn't an issue when they ran—the exercise was enough to keep them both warm. But her fur was short and not especially thick, and didn't some of her ancestors come from a pretty balmy part of Africa? By now he'd read some books on dog care, but they'd been silent as to whether a ridgeback mix needed winter outwear in the Central Valley.

"Guess I'll just have to keep a close eye on you," he told her. She seemed okay with that.

Most of the people they encountered on their walk knew them— well, knew Ishtar anyway. They stopped to pet her and chat with Elliott for a minute or two about the weather or the holidays. One of Ishtar's biggest fans, a retired woman with carefully styled hair and a pink-and-gold track suit, pulled a dog biscuit from her pocket.

"Do you mind?" she asked Elliott.

"Nope."

Ishtar took the treat with her usual care—then gobbled it in two bites.

"Were you carrying that just for her?" asked Elliott.

"Yes, I was. I was hoping I'd see you two today. She's a very good girl, and I thought she deserved a little reward."

Elliott chuckled at Ishtar, who was nosing hopefully at the woman's pocket, looking for more. "She thinks so too."

"I'm off to San Diego tomorrow to spend a week with my daughter and her family. I'm looking forward to a little vacation, but not the travel part. How about you?"

"Staying home."

"Well you two enjoy!" She patted Ishtar once more before continuing on her way.

Ishtar smiled up at Elliott. *Look. That lady loves me. She gave me a cookie!*

"I should start a fan club for you. We could have patches and pins and a monthly newsletter." Judging from her expression, she was fully on board.

Usually Elliott checked the library when he returned from his walks. But today when he turned onto his street, he saw a familiar pickup in the driveway. Ignoring the library for the time being, he headed for the porch, where Simon was leaning back against the door. Elliott let go of Ishtar's leash—she was dragging him along anyway—and she raced to Simon and threw herself on him as if she hadn't seen him that very morning. Laughing, Simon rubbed her ears with both hands.

"If you pet her like that, it only rewards her for jumping on you and she'll keep doing it." Elliott had been reading a bit about dog training.

Ignoring Elliott completely, Simon went nose to nose with Ishtar and informed her that she was the bestest wittle doggy in the world. She agreed.

"God, I knew who'd be the strict parent," Elliott said without thinking—then realized what had just escaped his mouth. Simon raised his eyebrows but didn't say anything, which was a blessing.

Eventually Ishtar put all four paws back on the ground, and Elliott pushed past them so he could open the door. Ishtar paused just long enough to allow Elliott to remove her leash, before racing for her water bowl. Meanwhile, Simon paused to pick up a large plastic bag with the Target logo. Something rattled inside.

"What's that?" asked Elliott.

"Peace offering."

That brought Elliott up short. "For what?"

"Oh, you'll find out." With that dire warning, Simon came into the house. He put the bag on the couch but remained standing, doing something on his phone. While Elliott stood in the entryway, watching with curiosity and dread, Ishtar came back into the living room, sniffed the bag, then huffed with disappointment and headed for her bed. Okay. So it wasn't anything she considered edible.

"Simon—"

"Go change. I'll wait."

Elliott looked down at himself. He'd already toed off his shoes, so he was wearing jeans, a sweater, and socks. "Change into what?"

"Comfy clothes."

Nagging at Simon wouldn't get him to spill the beans any quicker, so Elliott frowned and obeyed. In the bedroom, he pulled on a pair of green flannel lounging pants—ugly, but soft and warm—a gift from his parents the previous Christmas. He switched to a sweatshirt with slightly frayed hems and the Fresno Bulldogs logo on the front, a souvenir from Ladd's college days. Elliott kept his socks on.

As soon as he returned to the living room, music began to play from his Bluetooth speaker. "Um . . . what's that?"

"Nat King Cole. 'Unforgettable.'"

"I know the song. But why is it on?"

Simon waved his phone. "I made a playlist. It's part of the peace offering." Before Elliott could ask again why a peace offering was needed, Simon picked up the bag and held it out. "Look."

Elliott reached carefully, as if the bag hid a rattlesnake, coiled and ready to strike. But he opened it and peeked. "Legos?"

"It's Trevi Fountain." Simon looked nervous. "I thought maybe we could do it together later. If you're still speaking to me, that is. But it's architecture and historical, right? So I figured you might like this one. But if you hate it, I can exchange it for one that's Star Wars or Scooby-Doo or something. Or, you know, I could just forget the entire stupid idea." He bit his lip.

After pulling the box out, Elliott dropped the bag onto the couch. He turned the set over in his hands, examining the pictures and descriptions. "This is pretty cool, actually."

"Yeah?"

"Yeah."

Elliott set the box on the couch before stepping closer and cupping Simon's cheeks with his palms. "Now you want to tell me why I'm supposed to be angry?" He was calm about it, figuring Simon wouldn't make a playlist and want to assemble plastic bricks if he was about to break up with Elliott. And Simon hadn't showed up with any additional homeless pets.

"I did something stupid. Maybe a little brave, but definitely a lot stupid."

"What?"

Simon took a deep breath. Instead of answering right away, he backed off a bit and leaned against the armchair. His limp had noticeably improved over the past weeks, but his leg still bothered him when he was tired. Or, apparently, stressed. He stroked his beard a few times, a habit Elliott found endearing. Then Simon sighed again. "My mom called this morning. She and Dad stopped by the house last night after they closed the restaurant—leftover delivery—and I wasn't there."

"You were here."

"Yep. Apparently this is the second time that's happened lately. Mom wanted to know where I was. Jesus, that sounds wrong. She wasn't policing my social life or anything. She was just curious. I've told you—my family thrives on gossip."

"Okay." Elliott sat down and put the box on his lap. He'd forgotten the distinct sound of a new set of Legos: a promising noise with plenty of positive associations.

"I told her I was out with a friend."

"Which was true," Elliott pointed out.

"Technically, yes. It *felt* like lying, though. Just like every Sunday when I sit down with them and they ask about my week. Everything

I say is absolutely accurate. But I leave out the most important thing. The *only* important thing. You. That's not being fair to anyone."

"Including yourself."

Simon shook his head as if that didn't matter. "So here's where I get to the stupid part. I told her I've been hanging out with a neighbor . . . and . . ."

Elliott tucked his hands under his thighs. Otherwise he would have been tempted to leap up and shake Simon's shoulders until Simon finally came clean. But since Elliott had waited out many a nervous student who was trying to get enough courage to admit to a spectacular mistake, he could certainly exercise patience now.

Maybe Simon had hoped Elliott would make his confession for him, or at least engage in a round of Twenty Questions. When neither of those things happened, he scrunched his face. "I asked her if I could invite you for Thanksgiving."

Whatever Elliott might have guessed was going to come out of Simon's mouth, it hadn't been that. "Thanksgiving?"

"Yeah. I know you have plans with Ladd and Anna, but the family thing is really an all-day extravaganza anyway, so you can come by whenever." His confidence visibly waned, and he finished in a tiny voice. "If you want."

"Did you tell your mom who I am? I mean, that I'm not just your platonic buddy?"

Simon shook his head slowly. "No. Maybe she suspects? It's hard to tell over the phone."

"People don't often invite platonic buddies to family holidays."

"I never have." Simon finally let go of the armchair and returned to the couch. He pushed the bag into the corner so he could sit close to Elliott. "You're not pissed off?"

"I don't think a dinner invitation is much cause for ire."

"Dinner with my family. With questionable context."

Reminding himself that Simon needed support more than he needed nagging about hiding their relationship, Elliott put his hand on Simon's knee. "Do you intend to spend the meal pretending we're just pals? Because I can try that, but I'm not much of an actor and I can't guarantee—"

"I won't ask you to lie for me!" Simon's voice was loud enough to make Ishtar raise her head. She must have decided all was well—*dumb noisy humans*—and went back to sleep.

Elliott quelled his desire to rejoice. "So you're planning to come out to your parents over the turkey."

Simon huffed. "Not just my parents. The entire Odisho clan. And a good chunk of the Eshoos. Those are my mom's people."

Elliott pictured dozens of Simon's relatives jammed into a house, all of them forgoing their stuffing and yams in favor of staring at him and Simon. That made him shudder, but he kept his hand on Simon's leg and his voice even. "Are you sure this is the best occasion for this?"

"Of course it isn't! It's a shitty time for it. But El—" Simon's voice cracked. He looked down at his hands lying palms-up in his lap. Then he cleared his throat. "You know what's especially stupid? If I were a girl, they'd be *ecstatic* over you. They'd be falling all over themselves to prebook the Assyrian Civic Hall for our reception. Okay, you're not Assyrian, which is a minus point. But you're handsome and nice and fiscally solvent, you like dogs, and you're a PhD genius guy. So a million plus points."

"If only I didn't have this inconvenient penis," Elliott muttered.

Smiling a bit, Simon reached over to pat the organ in question. "I find it pretty convenient myself."

"Me too."

They simply sat there. Then a new song came on—something by Ella Fitzgerald, Elliott thought—and Simon laughed and stood. He held his hand out to Elliott. "Can I have this dance?"

"I don't dance."

"Why not?"

"I suck at it."

Simon bent and grabbed Elliott's hand. "Nobody here to see but me and Ishtar, and she's asleep."

Elliott allowed himself to be towed to the open space where the builder had imagined a large formal dining table. He felt horribly stiff and awkward as Simon wrapped his arms around him. "C'mon, El. Hold me too."

"But I don't know—"

"We'll start like it's a hug. I know you know how to do that."

It seemed like a reasonable expectation, so Elliott obeyed, planting the flat of his palms beneath Simon's shoulder blades and leaning against him.

"Good," Simon crooned. "Now close your eyes. That'll make it easier." Then he began, ever so gently, to sway their upper bodies to the music while their feet remained still.

Elliott let Simon move them. He rested his forehead in the crook of Simon's neck and felt the strong pulse, smelled the now-familiar odors of Simon's shampoo and soap. He barely noticed when Simon shuffled them a step to one side, then the other, and soon they were truly dancing. It was a rudimentary dance to be sure, but who cared? It felt good. Simon felt good. Elliott gradually smoothed his hands down the lines of Simon's back until they settled just below the waistband of Simon's jeans, right where the swell of his ass began. Perfect.

Ella finished singing, and Sinatra began—another slow tune, so Simon didn't alter their dance.

"You're perfectly fine at this," Simon murmured, then kissed Elliott's head.

"You're doing all the work."

"I'm happy to lead."

"Mmm. I think I like this."

Simon gave him a brief squeeze. "Good. I used to love to dance. When I was a kid, sometimes it felt like we went to a wedding or other event every weekend. I'd spend the whole time on the dance floor—well, when I wasn't eating, anyway. At some level, I knew girls weren't floating my boat, but they were perfectly cool as dance partners."

"Why did you stop?"

"When I got older, my parents tried pairing me up with every girl I danced with. It got too . . . complicated. Difficult. So I just stopped." Simon chuckled. "When I got out of the operating room and the orthopedic surgeon came to check on me, the very first thing I asked was whether I'd be able to dance again. I was pretty doped up."

"What did the surgeon say?"

"She was cautiously optimistic. Hmm. I oughtta send her a note, let her know it worked out."

Elliott didn't know how many songs they danced through. For a short time, he lost himself completely in Simon's arms, feeling Simon's heart beating against his chest. Later they would make love, they'd have dinner, they'd take a slow walk with Ishtar, they'd build the Trevi Fountain, and then they'd go to bed. They'd talk about Thanksgiving some more. But now—now it was just the music and the primal sweetness of two bodies moving in harmony. That was enough for now. It was even enough to make Elliott feel like Simon's surgeon—cautiously optimistic.

# Chapter Twenty

Although Elliott at first felt relatively sanguine about his holiday plans, by early on Thanksgiving Day, he was ready to crawl out of his skin. He added an extra two miles to their morning run, and although Ishtar didn't get sore or fatigued, she did look somewhat confused about the whole thing. "You don't have to worry about your day," he said through his panting. "Lucky dog. You'll have kibble and a quiet afternoon on your bed."

Way to go—getting envious of his dog.

Having decided one social engagement would be enough for the day, he'd called Ladd and Anna on Wednesday to let them know of the change in plans. "Is it okay if I ditch you guys tomorrow?"

"It's fine," Anna said soothingly. "Actually, I was thinking of inviting Kyle—he's spending the holiday solo—but I was afraid it'd be awkward between you."

Elliott felt guilty that Kyle would have spent Thanksgiving alone just because of him. "I like Kyle," he said weakly.

"Yeah, but he's not Mister Sexy Closeted Ex-Cop who I haven't met yet. I get it."

"Tell you what. If we survive Thanksgiving, how about you guys join us for dinner at my house a week from Friday?"

"Done!"

They wished each other luck, and Elliott hung up feeling thankful for understanding, accepting family members.

Now it was early Thursday afternoon and he was going out of his mind.

He'd consulted Simon about the dress code and learned that slacks and a button-down would be totally acceptable. "Would it help if I wore a dress?" he'd said, then immediately regretted it.

Simon had only laughed. "If that's what you want to do, go ahead. I bet you'd look fetching. It wouldn't help smooth things over, though."

Ishtar had picked up on Elliott's anxiety, and while he paced the house, waiting for Simon, she paced with him. Petting her calmed him a little, but they both jumped when the doorbell rang. At least Elliott didn't join Ishtar's barking.

Simon laughed at the eager greeting he received. "I'm glad to know I'm welcome here!"

"Always." Then Elliott sighed. "At least as long as I'm here too. Hey, what happened to the beard?"

Simon rubbed his clean-shaven jaw. "Do you hate it?"

"No. You were dead sexy before and you still are." Smiling, Elliott reached up to touch. Simon's prominent nose and thick eyebrows were more obvious without the beard, though neither of them detracted from his good looks, and now his strong chin was visible too. "What made you decide to do it?"

"Don't know. I was standing in front of the mirror and just . . . I think it's a metaphorical shave. Coming clean and all that."

While Simon let Ishtar into the backyard one more time, Elliott put on his coat and gathered gifts. He'd consulted Simon on this as well, and they'd agreed that a bottle of wine, a bouquet of flowers, and a box of chocolates were sufficient. "More than," Simon had said, but Elliott wanted to cover all the bases.

They got into Simon's truck, and he started the engine but let it idle in the driveway. "Are you sure you're okay going with me, El?"

"Positive." Sort of a lie, but a white one.

"Things might get . . . loud. Unpleasant. I don't want to put you through that."

"I've been interrogated for a crime I didn't commit. I can withstand hostile Odishos." Elliott squirmed in his seat to face Simon. "If you'd rather I stay home, I will. Maybe it'd be easier on you if I'm not there. But if you want me there, I'm going."

"I don't know what's easier. I want them to see you, though. So you're not some faceless ogre their son has fallen in love with, but a real person. An amazing person. God, I hope they can see that."

Elliott hoped so too, but he was still stuck on another thing Simon had just said. "The big word. That was the big word."

"Yeah." Simon looked at him gravely. "I'm not going to unsay it either. I love you, Elliott. Only reason I'd subject you to my coming out gala. Unless I hated you—then I might drag you along too."

It was the damnedest thing. Elliott wanted to laugh and cry at the same time. He wanted to yell at Simon for foolishly falling in love with him, and he wanted to drag Simon back into the house so they could tear off their clothing and not come up for air until the next day. He wanted to run up and down the street yelling at the top of his lungs: *He loves me!* And he wanted to stay in this quiet moment for the rest of his life. Instead, he did the one thing he really had to do.

"I love you too, Simon."

Simple and true.

They kissed after that, of course, and kissing a beardless Simon was a new sensation, one Elliott was keen to explore. They finally reached a point where they had to either stop kissing or take it inside. With unspoken consent, they decided on Thanksgiving dinner.

But when Simon stopped at a light just a few blocks from Elliott's house, Elliott must have made a noise. "You okay?" asked Simon.

"More or less. What you don't realize is that I'd be nervous as hell even if your relatives were charter members of PFLAG who'd painted their house like a rainbow. Meeting all those people—bad enough. Meeting my boyfriend's people? Uncharted territory."

"I was less scared when I was being shot at," Simon admitted. "But one way or the other, we'll be okay."

Usually Simon totally ignored speed limits—a habit from his cop days, probably. But today he drove as if he were leading a funeral procession. Kids on bicycles could have passed them. No matter how slow he went, however, the few miles were covered too soon. His parents lived in an older ranch house with a well-kept front yard. Three vehicles were squeezed into the driveway and many more lined the street. Simon finally found a parking space two blocks away.

Elliott grabbed the bag holding his gifts, then glanced over at Simon. "Do you want your cane?"

Simon considered the folding version stashed in the footwell. "No. Potential weapon." He grinned, but Elliott wasn't sure he was completely joking.

It was a long two blocks—and yet not nearly long enough.

When they were one house away from their destination, Simon stopped Elliott. "You need to know this. My parents? They're good people. Kind and loving and generous. They're not even raging homophobes. If you and I weren't lovers, they wouldn't care that you're gay, and they'd treat you well."

"I get it."

"They've got hundreds of years of tradition and religion telling them it's wrong for one man to love another. That's a really hard thing to shake. I think they've made an effort to be tolerant." He tried to stroke the beard that wasn't there. "But it's harder when it hits so close to home."

"I get it," Elliott repeated gently. "You love them. I wish this was as easy for you as it was for me, but I'm not going to judge anyone. I just want you to be happy."

Simon stared at him wide-eyed, like an archeologist who'd unearthed a long-lost treasure. "Jesus, you're amazing."

And they walked to the front door.

Simon opened it without knocking, and a wall of sound and smells and sheer volume of humanity hit Elliott so hard he almost stumbled back. Mustering his courage, he followed Simon inside. The door led directly into a living room so packed with people that it was difficult to see anything else. Elliott had a vague impression of fussy old-fashioned furniture, like the stuff in Simon's house, and clusters of photos on the wall. He would have liked to examine those pictures more closely, because some of them probably showed Simon as a child, but suddenly he was face-to-face with a man and woman.

Sargon Odisho looked very much like his son—the same strong features and tall, solid build, even the same soft brown eyes. He was less muscular than Simon, carried extra weight around the middle, and had hair that had thinned and grayed, but there would be no problem identifying him as Simon's father. Nahrina, on the other hand, was quite short and somewhat round, her thick hair dyed red. Ah, but she had Simon's mouth, wide and soft and, Elliott suspected, prone to smiles.

She was smiling now, in fact, and so was Sargon, but it was easy to read caution and concern behind the welcome.

"Mom, Dad, this is Elliott Thompson, my—"

Nahrina interrupted him with a click of her tongue. "Later. Now, please introduce him to everyone. We will get to speak soon." She looked about as eager for that as Elliott felt. Still, she and Sargon thanked him for the gifts—with sincerity, Elliott thought. Then they hurried away, probably into the kitchen.

"So far, so good," Simon mumbled.

Next came an extremely dizzying round of names as Elliott met some of the people in the living room. He felt like an exotic creature transplanted to a new continent, but everyone was polite, many even appearing eager to get to know him. He saw the light of recognition in Ashur's eyes when Simon introduced them, but when Ashur opened his mouth to say something, Simon shook his head, and Ashur just grinned.

The only other name to stick in Elliott's head was that of Ashur's sister, Miri. A very pretty girl who looked young for her age, she was all sparkling eyes over Elliott. "Si, is this—"

"Don't," Simon begged.

She put a hand over her mouth, but her smile was still visible in the crinkle of her eyes. "It's really nice to meet you!" Her palm muffled her words a little.

Elliott found himself liking her immediately, which was unusual for him. Her physical resemblance to Simon was minor, but he sensed she shared his good nature. "I'm happy to meet you too," he said. "Simon's told me good things about you."

She rolled her eyes. "Like I was a dumb-shit and got knocked up?" She patted her stomach, although her pregnancy wasn't yet visible.

"I teach college. Making mistakes is par for the course for my students—and some of their mistakes are much worse. I've had three students get arrested." And his ex-lover too, but he didn't mention John.

"Ooh! You're a professor! That's so cool!" She gave Simon a reproachful tap. "Why didn't you tell me that!" Then she turned to Elliott again. "What do you teach?"

"History."

"Wow! Cool! I'm taking classes now. Just at the junior college, but I'm supposed to transfer next fall." She rubbed her tummy again, and for a moment her smile fell away. But it reappeared quickly.

"I'm in the pre-nursing program. When Simon was in the hospital, I talked to some of his nurses, and they said if I get a BSN degree, it'll be easy for me to get a great job."

Simon put an arm around her shoulders and beamed. "She gets top grades now, but I used to babysit this brat. I know what she's *really* like."

Miri slapped his chest playfully. "And I know what you're really like too." She looked at Elliott and raised her eyebrows meaningfully, clearly conveying more than she said. But she was still smiling, and Simon leaned down to kiss the top of her head.

Then the others in the room had to be introduced, mostly people in their twenties, thirties, and forties, with some teens hanging around the edges—generally staring at their phones—and little kids darting in and out of the crowd. The majority were Assyrian, but not everyone. The assembled spouses represented a variety of ethnicities.

Eventually Simon tapped Elliott's shoulder. "Time for the rest."

"There's more?"

Simon just grinned.

The fragrant kitchen was as packed as the living room, but mostly with older women. A lot of them were engaged in food preparation, while others seemed intent on giving advice. The only man in the midst of the action was Sargon, who was fussing over an enormous turkey. Simon kissed several cheeks as he and Elliott made the rounds. There was some whispering among the women, which Elliott couldn't understand because it was in Assyrian and Simon pretended he didn't hear. His mother stood at the stove, stirring an enormous pot and ignoring them both.

Then Simon took him out into the backyard—a large grassy space with a wooden fence and several leafless trees—where all the older men and some of the children had gathered. The men wore light jackets and sat in patio chairs, smoking, drinking coffee, and talking loudly in Assyrian. "They're not arguing," Simon hastened to explain. "It's just what they do."

"I know."

"Yeah, you've probably seen some of them around town. They hang out at coffee places for hours. That's what they do when they retire. I think their wives shoo them out of the house."

Elliott had seen these men, or people like them, around Modesto. But he'd also encountered them in Sarajevo and Zagreb and Trieste. Only the languages differed.

"Will that be you when you retire?" Elliott asked.

"I won't have a wife to kick me out."

They exchanged a long look.

Then Simon was introducing Elliott again, and while these men were more cautious in their greetings than the younger crowd, they remained polite. When Simon mentioned that Elliott was a history professor, they became animated, and soon Elliott was being given an impromptu lesson on the Assyrian people. He knew very little on the subject and found himself quickly engrossed in the conversation, asking numerous questions and receiving many—often conflicting—replies. Simon stood close by, quiet for once but watching fondly.

Elliott and his new comrades were deep in the middle of debating the pros and cons of the Ottoman Empire when Sargon stepped outside. "The food is ready!" he bellowed.

A small stampede ensued.

Although the house contained a formal dining room, it could hold only a tiny fraction of the assembled crowd. Food covered every inch of the large table and the sideboard, while the kitchen table and counters held the overflow. Everyone gathered as close as they could to the dining room, although Elliott and Simon stayed toward the back of the crowd. Sargon and Nahrina said a few words about how blessed they were to have everyone in their home. Sargon followed with a brief prayer. Then the feasting commenced.

As Simon demonstrated to Elliott, after you took your place in the long line, you eventually reached a small table where you collected a plate, cutlery, and napkin. "Do your parents really own this much tableware?" Elliott asked quietly.

Simon laughed. "They own a restaurant, remember?"

Oh. That made sense.

Nobody could possibly fit all the varieties of food on one plate, so the plan was to take some turkey, then choose among the rest. According to Simon, coming back for a second round—or a third or fourth—was encouraged. And that didn't even include the desserts. The foods themselves ranged from traditional Thanksgiving fare to

Assyrian specialties, with a smattering of other ethnic additions such as tamales, sushi, and ravioli. Elliott had never seen so much food in one place, nor such an interesting combination. He piled his plate almost as high as Simon's.

Smiling, Simon took Elliott down the hall and opened a door to what looked like a spare bedroom. "Perks of being the hosts' kid—I can hide out in here. You want a break while we eat?"

"Please." Elliott hoped he didn't sound too pathetic.

Simon abandoned him, but only long enough to fetch wine and sparkling cider from the kitchen. They sat next to each other on the pink chenille bedspread and dug in.

"You know what this room is for?" Simon asked.

Elliott took a more careful look around. There was a dresser and an empty desk with a chair. A pair of seascapes hung on the white walls, and a navy-blue curtain covered the single window. "Guests?"

"Occasionally, but they've got another room for that. *This* room is so their grandchildren can stay the night sometimes."

The turkey had been delicious, but it suddenly felt dry in Elliott's throat. "Oh."

"Mom keeps saying she'll decorate the room properly when she knows whether she has a granddaughter or grandson. Jesus, El. How am I supposed to deal with that?"

Elliott set his plate on the desk and sat down again, his thigh against Simon's. "I'm sorry. It stinks. But you can't let other people's expectations rule your life." Yeah, he knew it was easier advice to give than to follow. What was that awful old saying? *Those who can't do, teach.*

Simon nodded but still looked miserable.

"Will it help if you explain that you can still have children?"

"Will I?" Simon asked bleakly. "With who?"

Elliott wanted to make a promise to parent with him—hell, he wanted to be a father too—but he couldn't. Not with Nebraska looming. He settled for an inadequate reassurance. "You will."

Shrugging as though it wasn't important, Simon spooned some rice dish into his mouth. "You impressed my uncles," he said after swallowing.

"Are all those old guys your uncles?"

"Uncles, second cousins, old family friends, whatever. They'll happily draft you into their ranks. You could spend the rest of your life arguing history and politics with them."

For some reason, that image made Elliott laugh.

They finished their meal in silence, then Simon looked at him questioningly. "More?"

"I'm good. You go ahead."

"Trying to shrink this, remember?" Simon patted his belly. "Although I'm tempted to eat everything. I'm still really nervous."

"Do you want to leave?"

Simon considered it for a moment before shaking his head. "I need to do this, El, and there's no time like the present. In fact . . ." He stood with his plate in one hand and held out the other to Elliott.

Oddly, Elliott wasn't nervous. Well, that wasn't quite true. He was worried about what might happen and how Simon would be affected. But he wasn't stressing about his own role in the upcoming drama. He'd survived the introductions to the Odisho clan, had even been a hit with the uncles, if Simon was to be believed. All he had to do now was support the man he loved, and damn it, he could do that.

Most of the people in the living room were eating and watching football on TV, so few of them saw Elliott and Simon's arrival. Those that noticed did double takes at their clasped hands, but nobody said anything. Miri, however, made a squealing noise with her hand over her mouth and started to rush toward them. But she stopped and backed off when Simon shook his head and waved his plate toward the kitchen. She gave them a double thumbs-up instead.

Elliott was relieved at their low-key reception, but he also realized that the living room contained the relatively easy younger crowd. The truly tough audience—the more traditional members of the family—lay ahead.

In the kitchen, Sargon and Nahrina were supervising a dishwashing assembly line, although the actual washing and drying was being done by teenagers, who stacked the clean tableware on a wheeled cart. The older ladies were covering filled plates with foil and drinking coffee, nibbling on this and that as they went. The ladies noticed Simon and Elliott right away, and they all went quiet and still as Simon handed the dirty dishes to a gaping teenager.

"Mom, Dad," said Simon in a whisper. Then he repeated it so they could hear him over the noise of the running water. They turned to face him.

As everyone stared, Elliott studied Nahrina's and Sargon's expressions and realized two things. First, they were not astonished to see Simon holding Elliott's hand. And second, they'd been deliberately avoiding Simon this afternoon, most likely because they suspected what was coming.

Nahrina was the first to speak, her voice sounding strained. "Simon, why are you playing these games? We are busy." She knew it wasn't a game.

"Mom, Elliott is my boyfriend."

"These are silly games!"

"He's my boyfriend. We love each other. He makes me so happy." Then, in case his message wasn't already glaringly clear, he added, "I'm gay."

She narrowed her eyes. "This is a stupid joke."

"You know I'm serious." As if to prove his point, he brought their clasped hands to his mouth and kissed the back of Elliott's. "I love him. Just like you love Dad."

One of the teenagers finally thought to turn off the faucet, and relatives started crowding into the kitchen from the living room and backyard. They were all eerily quiet, as if they were an audience at a play. It remained to be seen what kind of play. Tragedy? Farce?

Sargon took two steps closer and pointed a thick finger at Elliott. "You have done this! You have confused our son!"

Before Elliott could respond, Simon placed himself between Elliott and Sargon. "C'mon, Dad. Give me some credit for a mind of my own. I've known for years that I like men."

"But you danced with all the girls."

"Of course I did. If I'd danced with the boys, the entire hall would have fainted in shock. I know you've noticed I'm not dating any women—you guys bring it up now and then. Surely you must have speculated why."

"You have not found the right girl." Voice wavering, Nahrina sounded unconvinced by her own claim. "That is all. I will help you—"

"There *is* no right girl. There is a right man. Elliott."

Sargon scowled more deeply. "He has tricked you. He has . . . seduced you!"

Simon's laugh was bitter enough to hurt. "Seduced me? Really? I wasn't some fainting virgin when I met him. I'd had sex with plenty of men. But Elliott's the one I fell in love with." His grip made Elliott's hand ache, but there was no way Elliott wanted to let go.

At the mention of sex, many of the older ladies made muffled gasps or pressed their hands to their chests. Elliott would have considered Simon's proclamation to be TMI under other circumstances. Yet Simon's parents needed to hear this—and he needed to tell them the unvarnished truth.

After shooting Elliott a quick glance as if to confirm he was all right, Simon spoke again. "Look. None of this changes who I am. Nothing's changed at all—I've always been this way. I love you. I just can't go on any longer lying to you. It hurts worse than my damn knee! Please, please understand."

"This is not how we raised you," said Nahrina tearfully.

Simon's eyes were wet too, and he worked his jaw as he struggled to keep his composure. This time when Simon looked back, Elliott thought he saw a hint of desperation. Hoping he was doing the right thing, he stepped forward to stand beside Simon. "Mrs. Odisho, you did a wonderful job raising Simon. He's an amazing man. He's patient and sweet and funny and smart, and he has the kindest heart I've ever met. He brought me a dog—a rescued dog, of course—so I wouldn't be such a hermit. On our second date, he took me to Columbia because he knew I'd enjoy it. He is a *good* man. The best I know."

By this point, several members of the audience were crying, and Elliott's throat felt thick. But Simon graced him with a broad, beautiful smile that shone with love and gratitude, and someone in the back of the room clapped. Elliott suspected it was Miri.

Even Simon's parents were visibly moved by Elliott's little speech. Yet Sargon rubbed his chin—a shockingly familiar gesture—and Nahrina shook her head slowly. "We cannot have this," she said.

"Mom, I can't be any other way."

"We cannot have this."

God, Elliott had thought he'd known what a breaking heart felt like. He thought he'd experienced it when he learned of John's betrayal. That was nothing, though—a flea bite, a tap on the wrist—compared to the ripping agony he felt now on Simon's behalf. He wanted to howl with pain. He kept silent, however, holding Simon's hand as Simon nodded stiffly.

"I love you, Mom and Dad. Nothing will ever change that. I hope—" He stopped for a deep breath, then turned to Elliott. "We need to go."

It was surely one of the most awkward social situations Elliott had been involved in. Sargon and Nahrina remained as motionless as statues, and dozens of people stared as Elliott and Simon walked toward the front door. The crowd parted for them like the Red Sea for Moses. Elliott briefly considered throwing out a thank-you for the meal but decided it might be interpreted as mockery. Instead, he kept his mouth shut and his hand firmly in Simon's.

During the walk to the truck, Simon limped so badly Elliott wished they'd brought the cane. They'd almost reached their destination when running footsteps sounded behind them. They turned around to discover Miri rushing toward them at top speed.

"Wait!" she called.

Simon waited until, panting, she reached them.

"You shouldn't be running," he scolded.

She rolled her eyes. "The doctor says I'm perfectly healthy and can do all my regular exercises. Anyway, I need to tell you something."

"What?"

Instead of answering, she threw herself onto him in a fierce hug that made him stagger. When she was done with that, she astounded Elliott by bear-hugging him too. "I'm happy for you guys. You seem amazing, Elliott, and Simon deserves some amazing."

"He does," said Elliott quietly.

"And I want you to know that I love you, Simon. Aunt Nahrina and Uncle Sargon will come around if you give them time. They love you way too much to be stubborn about this forever."

Simon managed a smile. "You're just happy because now everybody's going to forget about your drama."

"Yeah, I think your Thanksgiving scene is going to be a top hit for a while. Thanks for that." She tapped his arm playfully. "But I heard that Rachel and her husband are close to separating, so unless they get some successful couples counseling or something, you might drop out of first place soon."

"Great. Thanks for your support, brat. Elliott needs to get home now and feed his dog." Simon bent to hug her, and his was more gentle.

Simon was quiet during the short drive home, but Elliott watched his face betray a range of emotions. In Elliott's driveway, Simon left the engine idling. "I should—"

"Come in, Si. Please." Because one thing Elliott had recently learned was that even the heaviest sorrow became easier to bear with sympathetic companionship.

Simon cut the engine and followed Elliott inside.

Ishtar, of course, was ecstatic to see them, nearly falling on the floor in her eagerness to be petted. They couldn't get past her, and Elliott thought a few of the shadows disappeared from Simon's eyes as he stroked her.

It took some time to care for Ishtar—a trip to the backyard, some food and fresh water, then another trip outside because she always had to shit after she ate. When Elliott returned to the living room, Simon was sitting on the couch, staring at nothing. It hurt Elliott to see such a vibrant, joyful man—the man he loved—reduced to blankness.

"Can I get you anything?" he asked as he sat beside him.

"Think I should eat these feelings away? 'Cause that's what I do." Simon's voice was bitter, and he didn't meet Elliott's eyes.

"If it'll make you feel better to eat something, that's okay." There were a million ways to deal with grief, some of them healthier than others. Overeating and compulsively buying books were probably not the best coping mechanisms, but they were better than binge-drinking, drugs, or violence. Elliott scooted closer.

After several minutes, Simon broke the silence with a sigh. "Can we go for a walk or something?"

"Of course."

Ishtar recognized one of her favorite words and, tail wagging hard enough to create a hazard, ran to the hook where Elliott kept her leashes. He couldn't help but envy her a bit. Wouldn't it be nice if humans could become so easily joyful over something so small?

Simon took his cane, which was a sign of his general distress, but he held Ishtar's leash in his other hand. The three of them walked slowly through the darkness. Whenever Ishtar wanted to sniff at something, Simon and Elliott paused until she was satisfied. Then they moved on. They were four blocks from home when Simon spoke. "I'm sorry."

"For?"

"Doing that to you. I should have—"

Elliott darted in front of him, blocking Simon's path. "Don't. If that was easier with me at your side, then I'm really glad I was there."

Simon almost smiled. "You were great. You were perfect, actually. How can you be so patient?"

"It's an acquired skill. Remind me to show you some of the emails my students send me—then you'll see I've had a lot of practice."

"Yeah?"

Elliott moved out of the way, and they continued strolling. "Yeah. Last semester, one kid demanded a passing grade in the class because he was paying my salary and I needed to be more customer-service oriented. Another one said I was violating her constitutional rights by not offering extra credit."

It was lovely to hear Simon laugh. "Wow. At least in my old job I had the option of arresting people."

"German universities used to have student prisons, back in the day. I've often thought we should consider reinstating that tradition."

When they came to a corner, Elliott thought Simon might turn back, but he continued across the street. Although Elliott shivered in his light jacket, he didn't complain. Simon's stride seemed more animated now, his expression less defeated. Maybe it was because every step was a reminder that whatever adversities life had thrown him, Simon could still keep moving, and that in itself was a triumph.

"Miri seems pretty great," Elliott said after another block.

"She is. She's probably the smartest one of us. I hope the pregnancy doesn't mess up her education too much."

"Will she keep the baby?"

"Don't know. Her mom's been having serious health problems, so her parents can't do childcare. Ashur works two jobs to help support everyone. And their other brother is in the Army. He's stationed in

Texas." Simon stopped while Ishtar investigated a lamppost. "I guess she could go back to school when the kid's older, but that's hard, isn't it?"

Elliott nodded thoughtfully. He'd seen it before. People dropped out due to babies or financial problems or family obligations, and while they intended to return, obstacles always seemed to block their path. Some did manage, of course, but often years later. He had one student this semester who'd told him via email that she was a grandmother. She'd started college fresh out of high school but left during her sophomore year, and now here she was trying again, thirty years later. Would that be Miri?

"You're probably thinking 'No big deal, she's just going to junior college,' right?"

Stricken, Elliott grabbed Simon's arm. "No! Jesus, do I come off as a snob?"

"Not a snob, no. Just . . ."

"Elitist," Elliott said miserably.

"No, I get it. I know a sheriff's deputy in Lassen County. Mountains, trees, a couple of prisons, and not a whole lot else up there. I know another guy who's with the Oakland PD. They're both cops, right? Their jobs are a whole lot different, though. I don't think either of them would be happy if someone made them swap places."

Elliott mulled this over. "Okay, sure. But both jobs are equally important. Your pal in Oakland, he's got gang shootings and robberies and whatever, and the other guy . . . well, I don't know what keeps a cop busy in Lassen County. I'm sure things happen there too, and sometimes people's lives are at stake."

Ishtar took a sudden intense interest in a bush, which made Elliott wonder if a small creature was hiding in there. If so, he hoped it stayed hidden until Ishtar moved on—both for the little creature's sake and for Simon's. If Ishtar took off running, Simon would be no match for her. But although Elliott stayed watchful, he didn't offer to take charge of her leash. He had the impression Simon needed her right now.

As they stood in the darkness with the wind whispering softly, Elliott thought about his students. His current ones, not the ones he'd taught in his tenure-track position. Many of his present students didn't really have the skills to succeed in college. Some were too lazy or immature to put in the required work. Others might have done well, but their time was filled with jobs and family, leaving them little opportunity to study. Yet there were a few like Miri—bright, hard-working, trying their best to improve their lives. They were as talented as anyone he'd taught at more prestigious schools, but finances or other life circumstances meant they were taking online community college courses. He could help those students. Mentor them. Spark their curiosity. Offer them encouragement to do their best. Wasn't that as important as anything he'd accomplish at a fancy university?

"You're cold." Simon interrupted Elliott's thoughts with a gentle elbow nudge. "Why didn't you say something?"

"Because I like walking with you."

"Let's head back. And hey, do you have any hot chocolate mix?"

Chapter Twenty-One

Elliott did not have hot chocolate mix. He had herbal tea, however, a vanilla chamomile mixture received as a sample when he'd ordered something more hard core. He made them each a big mug, and they sat on the couch, Elliott slowly defrosting from the warmth of his drink and the heat of Simon's body. Eventually they turned on the TV, but Elliott's thoughts were elsewhere, and he suspected so were Simon's. Ishtar was fast asleep.

Long after they'd drained their cups, Simon remained quiet. Contemplative. But sometimes he leaned his head on Elliott's shoulder, and that was nice.

"Christmas," Simon said out of the blue.

"What?"

"Christmas. It's in a month."

"True."

Simon didn't respond, so Elliott waited him out. Eventually, he spoke again. "What are your plans, El?"

"Nothing. My parents and Ladd and Anna are going on a cruise to the Bahamas or somewhere. Mom and Dad invited me—even offered to help pay my way."

"You're not going?"

"No. I can't with Ishtar, can I?"

Simon poked him. "I'd dog-sit for you."

Elliott shook his head. "I'll stay here." Really, Ishtar was only an excuse. Back when the rest of the family had been planning the trip, he hadn't even owned her yet. Hadn't met Simon yet either. Sitting around on a boat, stuffing his face at the buffets, and invading islands with a horde of other tourists—none of those things appealed to him.

Besides, having a stateroom to himself would be depressing when everyone else was paired up.

"Aunt Soso hosts a huge party every year. She has a big house in Turlock. The family sort of camps out there all day, talking and eating, but lots of friends stop by and stay for a while. It was great when I pulled a holiday shift, because I'd still get a chance to celebrate with everyone." His normally deep voice became quieter and thinner as he spoke.

"It sounds like a nice celebration."

"It is." Simon rolled the hem of his shirt, which had become untucked at some point in the evening. Then he looked at Elliott. "I don't know what I was expecting today. A fucking miracle?" He snorted.

"You were hoping for acceptance."

"But I knew I wouldn't get it. I *knew*! How could I be so goddamn stupid?"

Elliott was going to tell him there was nothing stupid about hope, that love drove people into all kinds of untenable situations, that Simon's parents were fools for rejecting such a remarkable son. But before he could get a word out, Elliott began to cry. Not noble, silent tears either. No, it was the kind of sobbing that rendered speaking impossible, that immediately made his nose all snotty. His eyes burned and his lungs hurt, and he didn't even know *why*.

Then Simon was hugging him tightly—and he was crying too. They wept and wailed and dripped tears onto each other's shirts, and when Ishtar pressed up to them in concern, they included her in the messy group embrace.

Eventually Elliott regained enough control to shuffle to the bathroom and return with a box of tissues. He and Simon each used several, which did nothing for their puffy eyes or damp shirts.

"Sorry," Elliott said with a sniffle as he resettled next to Simon.

"I haven't cried since my grandma died. That was over ten years ago."

Elliott nodded. He couldn't remember the last time he'd cried. He must have been a kid. He just wasn't the type—except today apparently. "Sorry," he repeated.

"Don't be. I feel a little better. Don't you?"

Although Elliott nodded again, it was a lie. The tears hadn't given him any sense of catharsis, maybe because he knew they didn't solve anything. He was still a moron who'd made poor life choices, and he was still stuck between damned and double-damned when it came to his future. "That was really brave of you today." That, at least, was honest.

"Nah. People come out all the time. Kids even. I saw this one teen on YouTube who—"

"What was scarier? Telling your parents you're gay or getting shot?"

Simon frowned and rubbed where his beard used to be. "Parents," he admitted grudgingly.

"But you did it anyway. That's what courage is—moving forward in the face of fear. I think Mark Twain had a quote about it."

The noise Simon made in response sounded like denial, yet he leaned his head on Elliott's shoulder. "It feels like something's been amputated."

"Then think of yourself as a lizard."

"Not a snail?"

"No, I'm the snail. You're a lizard. Like those cute little guys who live along the greenbelt. They lose their tails, but they grow them back."

After seeming to consider this for a moment, Simon grunted. He grabbed Elliott's hand and guided it to his own hip. "I still have my tail."

"I'm glad. It's a nice one."

"Will you show me how nice you think it is?"

Elliott kissed his cheek. "With great pleasure."

After they made love, Simon remained in Elliott's bed, his solid body cradled in Elliott's arms, and he fell asleep quickly. But Elliott stayed awake, thinking about bravery and hard decisions.

"Want to go for a . . . perambulation?"

They were both naked, and Simon spat a mouthful of toothpaste into the sink and blinked at Elliott. "What?"

"A w-a-l-k? I can't say the word because Ishtar knows it." He turned to look at her hopeful face and rapidly waving tail. "And I think she's learning to spell it."

"She's a smart girl. But no, thanks. I'm going to head home."

"You sure?"

Simon rinsed his mouth, wiped his face with a towel, and ran his fingers through his hair, which did little to tame it. He stroked his cheek where dark bristles had sprouted already. "Yeah. I need . . . I think I need some time alone. Not that I don't love hanging out with you, but it's hard to clear my head when you're near." He palmed Elliott's bare ass.

Although some time apart was probably a good idea, Elliott wasn't enthusiastic. Which was surprising, given that he'd willingly—eagerly, even—spent the majority of his life by himself. Hadn't Simon had to practically force him to interact with other human beings? But that amputation thing Simon had mentioned the night before, that was suddenly a real fear for Elliott too. Shit.

"Okay," Elliott said as neutrally as possible. "Breakfast first?"

"Not hungry."

While Elliott wondered if Simon had ever uttered that phrase before, he tried not to appear surprised. "Okay. I think I'll take Ish for a run, then."

They got dressed—Simon in his clothes from the previous day, Elliott in sweats and running shoes. Neither of them said anything, and Ishtar watched them closely, a worried crease on her forehead.

Simon hesitated at the front door. "I think . . . I maybe shouldn't come over for a while."

All of the oxygen left the room at once, and Elliott made an embarrassing little moan. "Are we breaking up?" he managed to say. He felt like the world's biggest idiot. It wasn't as if he and Simon had sworn eternal oaths to each other—and Elliott was the one planning to leave.

"No." Simon looked mournful. "I don't think so. Not yet, anyway."

"Did I do something to make you angry?" Elliott racked his brain for possibilities but couldn't think of anything especially stupid or damning.

Simon swiped Elliott's cheek with his thumb. "No. Look, you've been honest with me from the beginning, and I can't tell you how much I appreciate that. But now I've alienated almost my entire family, and maybe coming clean was the right thing to do, regardless of whatever happens with you and me. But . . . Fuck." He closed his eyes as if he were in pain. "I can't even say this clearly."

Stomach tied in queasy knots, Elliott waited.

"I guess I am kinda mad at you, only it's not your fault. I know that doesn't make any damn sense."

Feeling as if he'd been punched, Elliott stepped back and crossed his arms. "Then explain. I'm listening."

"We . . . I love you, okay? But we had these two things in our way—my closet and your job. In a way, they sort of balanced each other, right?" He moved his hands, palms up, as if they were parts of a scale, each of them weighing life challenges.

"Okay. But I don't—"

"My closet is gone." Simon's right hand rose while the left dropped. "Your job's still there. I knew every fucking bit of this, so it's my own damned fault, but I still feel . . ." He growled, sounding more frustrated than angry.

"You've made a sacrifice and I haven't."

"No. Yes. I don't know. Damn it, you never pressured me to come out, and you've been clear from day one about your career. I still feel like I'm losing, though. Losing everything, you know?"

The thing was, Elliott understood completely. "I'm losing too," he replied softly.

"Yeah. But you can do something about it. I can't." Simon shook his head. "I know my reasoning is fucked up. It's why I need time to get my head together."

"I don't know where this is coming from. Last night—"

"Last night I wasn't having issues, I know. Then this morning I got out of your bed and I thought 'How many more times?' Like, how many hours do I get with you before it's all *poof*! It just hit me. Like a bullet." He waved vaguely at his knee.

Maybe Elliott could stop this right now if he argued. He could yell. He could point out that if their time together was limited, they ought to make the most of it. He could describe how much Simon was hurting him. He *ought* to make a fuss. If he'd been less of a pushover with John, if he hadn't just sat back and taken whatever was dished out, that mess would have stopped much earlier.

But how would pushing back help now?

"I'll be here," Elliott said. "If you want to talk or anything."

Simon gave him a long, searching look. Then, as if he couldn't bear to leave without something, Simon pulled him close for a long, tender kiss. He gave Ishtar's head a rub and headed out the door.

After a long run followed by a shower, Elliott spent the morning brooding. Several times he caught himself on the brink of ordering books but was able to stop himself each time. Instead, he rearranged some of his existing books and restocked the outdoor library with fresh titles. He went on a cleaning binge. He dug around in a few obscure texts, searching for snippets of information on two men who were buried side by side in the Columbia cemetery and who might possibly have been lovers. They'd both died young, one of them the victim of a shooting.

Midway through the afternoon, as Elliott slumped on the couch with a cup of coffee, Ishtar began to bark. The doorbell rang a moment later. Elliott briefly considered pretending he wasn't home but ended up unlocking the door after all. Anna and Ladd stood there, smiling. Ladd held a paper grocery bag that looked heavy. "Leftovers," he explained as he squeezed past Anna and Ishtar, who were having an enthusiastic reunion in the doorway.

Elliott closed the door. "You didn't have to do that."

"It's not Thanksgiving weekend without turkey-and-stuffing sandwiches. We have way too much to finish off ourselves."

Elliott had eaten little all day and wasn't hungry, but he didn't protest as Ladd took the food into the kitchen.

"Where's Simon?" asked Anna, glancing up from Ishtar.

"Dunno. Home, probably."

That made her examine him more closely. "Something wrong?"

"No."

Ladd came clumping back into the room. "You might as well spit it out now, El, before she drags it screaming out of your guts."

"He doesn't have to tell me anything he doesn't want to." Anna clicked her tongue. "He's not married to me."

Ladd rolled his eyes and muttered something, Anna flipped him off, and Elliott laughed despite his sour mood. God, he was so lucky to have family who cared about him. But of course that thought immediately led to Simon, who was—for the time being, at least—on his own, and suddenly Elliott wanted to talk about it.

"He came out to his entire family yesterday. Like, a cast of thousands. With the notable exception of his pregnant teenaged cousin, not a soul was on his side. So we came back here, and now he's pissed at me because I'm an asshole, and he doesn't even want to be pissed but he can't help it, and I don't blame him, and now I feel like king of the assholes even though I've been upfront with him from the start."

With that out of his system, he stomped over to the armchair and threw himself down with all the melodrama of a fourteen-year-old. Which was appropriate, perhaps, since he seemed to be emotionally stunted.

He had to give Anna and Ladd credit. Instead of making a hasty exit, which is what he would have done in their position, they sat on the couch. They asked him for details. They sympathized. At one point, Ladd even heated a plate of leftovers and insisted Elliott eat them. While their compassion made Elliott feel better, he grieved that Simon was receiving no such comfort and support. Kind, good Simon, who deserved far better from life.

In the end, they didn't give him advice. Maybe there wasn't any to give. But they hugged him and told him they loved him, and Ishtar joined in too, and that helped a bit.

Chapter
Twenty-Two

Elliott's students were not happy. They'd returned from Thanksgiving break to the realization that the semester was almost over, and now they were emailing with tales of woe, pleading for due-date extensions or extra credit, begging him to give them Incompletes or a No Credit instead of an F. He tried to be patient with them, he truly did, but his responses tended toward terse. For once, he was grateful not to face them in person. If they'd been standing in front of him, he would have yelled.

An entire week passed. He ate all the leftovers Ladd and Anna had brought, and he never once saw Simon. Oh, he was tempted. Sometimes he jogged by Simon's house and considered ringing the doorbell on the pretext that Ishtar missed him. Which she did; she was a little mopey actually. Elliott kept running on by.

Miss you, Elliott texted to Simon on Tuesday, followed immediately by *But I'm not stalking you.*

Simon replied right away. *Miss you too. A lot. Still thinking though.*

Got it. Are you okay?

Simon answered with a thumbs-up emoji.

On Thursday night, Simon texted first. *Drove to Columbia today. Don't know why. No fun without you.*

That almost made Elliott cry, which was really dumb. He texted back with Simon's final sentence: *No fun without you.* That was true.

After that, they sent messages to each other a few times a day. Nothing extensive or earthshaking, just reminders of where their hearts were. Elliott sent a few photos of Ishtar. It was all slightly ridiculous since they were only a couple of blocks apart, but sometimes a couple of blocks might as well be a million miles.

Other than that? Elliott ran a lot, even though the weather was cold and sometimes drippy enough that Ishtar refused to go with him. He didn't buy more books.

Business was brisk at the little library. Melanie came by almost every day. He'd catch sight of her in a bright-red jacket as she selected new books and replaced them with some of her own. She always waved at him. Other people came too, ten or twelve every day. They represented a wide range of ages, but what struck Elliott was that every one of them smiled as they walked away with fresh titles clutched under their coats to keep them dry.

On Friday, Elliott was restocking the library when the mail truck pulled up to the community mailbox across the street. Elliott ambled over while the mail carrier was unlocking the big door that provided access to the entire block's incoming mail. "Hi," said Elliott, feeling awkward.

Apparently the mail carrier had no such reservations; his thin face lit up in a broad grin. "Oh, hey! I'm glad I finally get to see you. I've been meaning to tell you how much I love your library idea."

"Well, it really wasn't *my* idea."

"Yeah, I've seen a couple others around town. They're great. Now I know why you need all those Amazon deliveries!"

Elliott laughed politely. He didn't mind that the guy knew of his book addiction, but he wasn't used to being enthused at so cheerfully. "I enjoy keeping it up."

"Hey, would you mind if I borrow a book now and then? I know I don't live here, but—"

"Help yourself."

The mail carrier smiled even wider and waved a handful of envelopes and sales circulars. "Thanks! I'll return 'em, of course."

"No worries. I have plenty." This time, Elliott's smile felt less forced. He was genuinely pleased to know his library's use could expand outside his little circle of neighbors.

"Thanks. Hang on. I've got stuff for you."

While Elliott waited for him to sort the mail, Mike Burgess shot out of his house and marched over at full speed. He didn't bother greeting either Elliott or the mail carrier. "Last week somebody else's mail was in my box!"

Judging from the mail carrier's long-suffering expression, this wasn't the first time he'd heard this complaint. "I'm really sorry to hear that, sir. We try very hard to deliver accurately, but sometimes—"

"It's your job! You guys get paid far too much to stroll around doing a job a trained chimpanzee could get right. Then you stand around lollygagging all day." Burgess gestured angrily at Elliott.

"Lollygagging?" Elliott asked. Who wrote Burgess's script?

While Burgess glared, the mail carrier seemed unperturbed. "I was just complimenting Mr. Thompson on his library, that's all."

"That!" Burgess spat. "It's illegal!"

"What the hell's illegal about it?" demanded Elliott. He didn't add that his maybe-boyfriend, a former cop, was an enthusiastic supporter of the library.

"You're trumpeting your agenda where children can access it." Burgess said *agenda* as if it were a dirty word.

"My agenda is to get people to read, so yeah. I think that's good for kids."

"I mean your other agenda! Which is obscene."

"I think, Mike, you should look up the proper definition of obscene. And if you don't like my books, don't read them. Simple as that."

Although he didn't add to the discussion, the mail carrier looked as if he were enjoying it. He'd angled his body closer to Elliott, perhaps to clarify his loyalty.

Burgess growled. "That filth shouldn't be where children can see it."

"It's not filth, and I think I'll let the kids and parents decide for themselves what's appropriate."

"Appropriate!" Burgess's face had turned red. "You people come in and you act like you deserve special rights, and you wave your politics in everyone's faces all the time. It's disgusting!"

"'You people'? What people are those, Mike? And exactly what special rights do you think I'm demanding?"

Burgess pointed at Elliott's house. "That! Those books and that sign."

"So the First Amendment is a special right?"

Burgess sputtered, but before he managed an answer, the mail carrier addressed him. "I think a person's choice of reading material is his own business." He raised his eyebrows and cast a significant look at Burgess, whose face flushed even more.

"Just . . . do your job!" Burgess shouted. He turned on his heel, marched back to his house, and slammed the door as he went inside.

"He orders some interesting magazines?" Elliott asked.

The mail carrier's smile was back. "I can't divulge. But . . . yes."

"Ew. I don't even want to know."

They chatted for another minute or two while the mail carrier finished sorting. Then he handed a few items to Elliott. "Guess I oughtta quit my lollygagging. Have a good weekend!"

Elliott smiled. "You too. And help yourself to the books."

He was still smiling as he crossed the street and walked up his driveway, shuffling through his mail as he went. But when he got to the final envelope, his stomach clenched. The return address was a prison in Washington.

Chapter Twenty-Three

Dear Elliott—

The handwriting was familiar. Elliott had first seen it scrawled on chalkboards and, in red ink, filling the margins of his exams and papers. Later it had adorned numerous versions of Elliott's dissertation because John Davis didn't believe in using Track Changes. *"Ink is better,"* he used to insist. *"More organic and conducive to thought."*

The letter was written in black ink, not red, and the words crowded closely across the page. The paper itself was somewhat wrinkled, as if John had handled it repeatedly before putting it in the envelope. Or maybe prison officials were to blame—didn't they read outgoing mail?

Elliott sat at the kitchen table with a cup of coffee in front of him and Ishtar near his feet. He could have read the letter in the living room, but that was his space to share with Anna and Ladd and Simon—not with John. The kitchen was better. Maybe somewhere impersonal like a Starbucks would have been best, but his hands were shaking and he didn't trust himself to drive.

"Should just throw the fucking thing away," he said to Ishtar. But he couldn't bring himself to follow through. The pull of words was just too strong.

Dear Elliott—

The arrival of the holiday season has made me introspective and inspired me to reach out. The holidays are a melancholy time in prison. Some of the staff make an attempt, a bit of a nod toward the season, but the food remains awful and the atmosphere gloomy.

I hope you, at least, are enjoying the season. I asked my attorney to find your new address, so I'm aware you've relocated to California. You must appreciate the proximity of your relatives and the comparatively balmy climate, but it's a shame you've retreated so thoroughly. I do hope you're not squandering your potential. You have it in you to become a fine scholar.

Speaking of scholarship, I've been thinking a great deal about my book. Of course, my access to research sources is severely limited here, but I've been able to flesh out my thesis and outline, and that part is going well. When complete, my book will be an excellent contribution to the literature.

My attorney is working now on obtaining my parole, and I expect to be released by early spring. Once my book is published, the royalties will provide an adequate income, and I expect the quality of the work will persuade institutions to overlook my unfortunate history and offer me employment. Until then, however, I will need a place to live and access to academic libraries. This will be your opportunity to obtain the goal for which you've been pestering me for so long—we can finally move in together. You will have to relocate, as I cannot leave Washington while I'm on parole, but I assure you that you'll be better off here.

You should begin investigating positions in Washington at once, if you've not already begun to do so. Even Portland would be acceptable, as it's close enough to the border that we could live in Washington and you could commute. I understand that moving again might be difficult, but you can assist me with my book, and I'll list you as second author. That should offset the inconvenience.

In the meantime, Elliott, do keep up with your own work. If you'd like to send some of it to me, I'd be happy to provide feedback. One thing I can continue to do while I'm stuck in this place is provide mentoring to you.

I look forward to our reunion.

Yours,

J

For a long time, Elliott stared blankly at the letter, the lines of writing blurring before his eyes. He felt disconnected from his own thoughts, noting like a clinical observer that his hands were curled into tight fists and his jaw was clenched hard enough to make the muscles jump. He was breathing rapidly, as if he'd just returned from a long run, yet his skin felt icy.

Rage. This was rage. And the focus wasn't so much on John as on himself. How could he have been such an idiot? How could he have allowed himself to be seduced by such grandiose lies? How could he have pinned his entire life, his future, his *heart* to a narcissistic fuckwad like John Davis?

"I don't deserve Simon," he whispered. He didn't deserve anything. Not his loving family. Not his fancy degrees. Not the potential position in Nebraska or the online jobs he had now. Not the sweet dog who stood beside him, burrowing her head into his stomach.

For a long, cold minute, he seriously considered walking Ishtar over to Simon's house, leaving her there, and then . . . disappearing. Erasing himself. Because continuing onward felt so fucking hard.

But that wouldn't be fair to Ishtar and Simon, and it wouldn't be fair to Anna and Ladd and his parents. They'd blame themselves. While he might have fucked up his life, he wasn't about to ruin theirs too.

Fine then. If he couldn't erase himself, he could at least start with a blank slate. He would move to Nebraska—or somewhere else far away—and begin a new career with people who didn't know him. He would leave Simon to find his own way, because Simon was strong and wonderful and would recover from the loss of his family. Because Simon didn't deserve to be saddled with someone who'd let himself be so easily conned by blatant deceits. Soon enough someone better than Elliott would discover Simon and help him find the life he deserved.

The only things Elliott would take from his old life were Ishtar and his books. Not even all of his books—just the ones he truly needed. He'd give the rest away.

That decided, he dashed off a quick note.

John,

Fuck you.

E

He put the note in an envelope, printed the address, and slapped on a stamp. Then he went to prepare for a run.

Monday was a strange day. Ginny Holmes called from Nebraska State to let him know they'd be contacting him with travel arrangements later that week. He tried to sound enthusiastic about the prospect, but he'd been numb since Friday. Simon texted him twice—once to ask for a book recommendation for Miri and once to warn him that a big storm was forecasted. Elliott answered both, but he felt that the messages between them carried more unsaid meaning than actual words. Too bad he couldn't decipher what Simon meant. A student emailed with an unlikely excuse about having to go to Washington, DC, to meet with her congressman, and when Elliott replied with skepticism, she sent him a phone number for the congressman's staff. Elliott called and the story checked out. So he apologized to the student, granted her an extension, and wished her well.

Shortly after lunchtime, the sky went an odd yellow color. "We'd better run while we can," Elliott told Ishtar, who'd been restless all day. He put on his running gear, but Ishtar—who usually threw herself around the living room in ecstatic celebration when he geared up— hovered near the couch with her tail hanging low.

"It's not raining yet. And even if it does, you won't melt." As he clipped on her leash, he wondered whether pets really could sense earthquakes and, if so, whether that was Ish's problem. Hell, something felt off to him too. Maybe it was simply the drop in barometric pressure.

Although Ishtar wasn't exactly eager, she didn't hesitate to join him when he left the house. He locked the door as usual, tucked the key into the pocket of his jogging pants, and began to run. He didn't take his phone this time. If it did storm, he didn't want to worry about it getting wet. Besides, listening to music would make it harder to maintain an emotional connection with Ishtar, and if her anxiety increased, he wanted to be aware of it.

They took one of his usual routes past the edge of town and out into farmland, where a few cows and goats watched them race by. Since the livestock seemed calm, maybe no calamity was in store— just some rain and perhaps some wind. Hell, Elliott was going to have to endure a lot more than that if he ended up in Nebraska. "Blizzards!" he said breathlessly to Ishtar. "Hailstorms. Tornadoes!" She wasn't impressed.

They reached an old farmhouse he'd always liked. Its white siding needed fresh paint, but he liked the wide front porch and wondered what the owners had done with the attached structure that had once housed a water tower. In late spring, the people who lived there sold cherries for two dollars a bag, usually on the honor system, with the fruit set out on a wooden table near the road. During the summer, their front yard was a veritable jungle of vegetables and bright flowers. Even with the calendar turned to December, a few blooms survived near the front porch and the short row of orange trees near the driveway promised a large harvest very soon.

Elliott would miss that house when he moved. Sure, Nebraska had plenty of farmhouses. So did just about anywhere else he might end up. But none of them would be *this* familiar place with the tire swing hanging from an oak tree and the chipped concrete fountain near the lavender hedge.

Although he often ran farther, today Elliott turned toward home.

He gave in to a bit of weakness and detoured by Simon's house, but he didn't stop. Sometimes Ishtar would tug him toward Simon's door, but today she pulled him down the sidewalk, apparently eager to get home.

They turned the corner onto their street. Elliott was looking down at his feet, idly wondering how many miles they'd taken him over the years and how many miles remained. It seemed odd to realize you could measure out your lifetime one small stride at a time. He didn't look up until they'd nearly reached home—and when he glanced toward his house, he cried out and came to an abrupt stop.

The library was in ruins.

The books were still there, but they'd been ripped to pieces. Paper scraps were now scattered across his lawn like the victims of a terrible war, bleeding words into the damp grass. The library's wooden post was broken near the base, and the stump ended in a ragged edge. The larger part of the post lay on the sidewalk, while the book enclosure was only bits of ruined plywood and cracked plexiglass.

Elliott had dropped Ishtar's leash, but while he stood still as a statue, she remained at his side, whining worriedly.

Elliott steeled himself. All right.

Moving deliberately, he picked up the leash and led Ishtar into the house. He disconnected the leash and hung it on the rack near the door. Then he found his phone and texted a brief message to Simon: *Come get Ish.*

Leaving both Ishtar and the phone in the house and the door unlocked to make it easier on Simon, Elliott strode across the street. A few raindrops fell on him, fat and cold, as he marched up to Mike Burgess's house. Ugly house. Ugly yard. Ugly man. Forgoing the bell, he pounded on the door with his fist.

It took only a few seconds before the door swung open. Burgess stood just inside, cell phone in hand. He wore jeans and a Raiders T-shirt with the logo slightly peeling. "What do you want?"

"You son of a bitch."

Fear flickered in Burgess's muddy brown eyes, and he took a small step backward. "I don't know what you mean."

"You fucking son of a bitch." Voice low and even, hands opening and closing at his sides. "You took a good thing—one of the only good things I've done—and you destroyed it just because you're a small-minded, bigoted piece of shit."

Burgess jutted his chin and tried to shut the door, but Elliott stepped onto the threshold, blocking him. The wind was picking up, sending rain against his back.

"You're trespassing!" Burgess yelled shrilly. "I'm calling the police!" He lifted his phone, but Elliott batted it out of his hand, and it went flying across the entryway and onto the tile floor, where it shattered.

Huh, said an eerily calm voice in Elliott's head. *Too bad we weren't that coordinated when we tried to play high school sports.*

Burgess, on the other hand, wasn't calm at all. His face bright red, he screamed at Elliott. "That's assault! You've assaulted me!"

Elliott answered in a growl. "I haven't done anything yet. I'd like to do to you what you did to my library." He'd never hated before. Never yearned for violence. Never been so sure that the only logical course of action was to begin swinging with his fists and to keep on going until nothing remained but blood and devastation and a cold rain to wash everything away.

Do it, urged the voice. *Our life is fucked anyway. Do it, and go out with a bang. Stop being a goddamn patsy.*

Do it because Burgess fucking deserved it. Because right this moment, he symbolized an entire world full of hatred and rejection, and while Elliott couldn't take on the world, he could at least pound this one abhorrent face. Do it because the worst that could happen was he'd end up in prison—just like John, who Elliott should have abandoned years ago if he'd had the brains and the balls for it.

Do it. Do it.

"Elliott! No!"

Elliott turned slowly and saw Simon's truck stopped crookedly in front of Burgess's house, the engine still rumbling and the driver's door wide open. Simon, squinting against the pelting rain, hurried closer as fast as his bum knee allowed. Elliott was dimly aware of Burgess running more deeply into his house, yelling something incoherent the entire way. But that was of little importance. What mattered was the miracle of Simon's sudden appearance—and the nauseating feeling as Elliott seemed to slip back into his own body.

"What the hell are you doing?" Simon demanded as he wrapped a hand around Elliott's fist and pushed Elliott's hand down.

Oh. Apparently Elliott had been about to punch Burgess.

"He wrecked my library." That sounded almost rational, right? Elliott tried to gesture toward the evidence of the crime, but Simon embraced him, holding him still.

"Shit! El, you can't— What the hell is wrong with you? You can't hit people. You can't— I thought—"

Before Simon could articulate what he'd thought, Burgess came tearing back into the entryway. "I called the cops! I called the cops!"

Elliott remained emotionally disconnected, tethered in place by Simon's strong arms and shivering against Simon's damp shirt. "Good. You can tell them what you did to my library." He didn't bother looking at Burgess while he spoke.

"I didn't do anything!"

It was Simon who responded first. "Then where did you get those scratches on your hands and arms? And the splinters of wood in your hair?"

Burgess's hand flew to his scalp. Sure enough, several long, shallow marks ran along his forearms, and his fingernails looked torn and slightly bloody. He crossed his arms. "I was working in the garage today. He assaulted me!" He jutted his chin toward the wreckage of his phone.

Elliott felt Simon sigh against him. "Fine," Simon said. "We'll let the cops sort it out."

Considering that Burgess had been the one to call the police, he looked less than pleased with that idea.

Simon continued, his tone as pleasant as if he were discussing the weather. "Did you know simple assault is a misdemeanor? Someone like Elliott here, who doesn't have a criminal history, he might have to pay a fine. Maybe get a few months' probation. Which is about what someone would normally get for criminal trespassing. But vandalism can be a felony if there's more than four hundred bucks' worth of damage. And books are expensive, aren't they, El?"

Elliott made an affirmative noise.

"Not only that," Simon continued. "If the offenses were motivated by Elliott's sexual orientation, they're hate crimes. That can get you penalty enhancements. Mmm, maybe as much as three years in prison."

Burgess looked as if he was going to be sick, which was oddly satisfying. But Elliott was shivering in the wind and rain, his hair and clothing sticking to his skin and water running under the collar of his shirt. Simon was equally wet—more so, since he was sheltering Elliott with his bigger body—but he stood straight and seemingly unbothered.

"I didn't . . ." Burgess muttered. He didn't seem to know how to finish the sentence.

A police car came zooming around the corner, sending up spray from a newly formed puddle. The siren was off, but the lights flashed brightly. The car stopped behind Simon's truck, and a man and woman in uniform got out. They both looked profoundly unhappy to be venturing outside in this weather, although their faces brightened when they saw Simon.

"Odisho!" the man called out in a friendly greeting.

"Hey, Calvillo, Babb. We're practically drowning here. Mind if we chat on Elliott's porch?" He pointed across the street.

The cops seemed agreeable, so while the male officer stepped inside Burgess's entryway, the female cop waited for Simon to turn off his truck and shut the door. She followed them across to Elliott's house, where Ishtar barked a few times from inside until Elliott ordered her to be quiet.

"So what's going on?" asked the cop whose name tag said *M. Babb*. She was thirtyish and nearly as tall as Elliott, her blonde hair cut short.

"This is Elliott Thompson," Simon said. "My boyfriend."

Babb's eyebrows rose slightly, but Elliott was even more surprised—both that Simon still considered him his boyfriend and that Simon had acknowledged their relationship so easily. "Are you the one who called, Mr. Thompson?" she asked.

"No. That was Burgess." By now the rain was falling so heavily that it was difficult to see Burgess's house. The street would flood soon—downpours were anathema to hardpan soil—but fortunately the water had never risen high enough to reach any houses.

"Okay. Why don't you tell me what happened?"

Elliott knew her shoulder camera was recording the entire incident. He felt no need to lie or hide the truth, so he told her everything—discovering the destroyed library, texting Simon, confronting Burgess, even slapping away his phone. Simon stood close to him, listening carefully but not speaking. Babb asked whether Elliott and Burgess had experienced any previous run-ins, and Elliott described those as well. She nodded thoughtfully, her expression nonjudgmental.

When Elliott was done, she nodded again. "Aside from the library and its contents, was there any other damage to your property?"

"I had a rainbow flag in my front yard. It's gone." He'd noticed this as they'd approached the porch.

"Okay. You two stay put, all right? I'm gonna go talk to Calvillo."

"We'll be right here," Simon said.

They watched as she ducked her head and shoulders against the deluge and splashed across the street. She knocked on Burgess's door, and a moment later Calvillo emerged. He and Babb ran to their car and sat inside, apparently to discuss the situation.

Simon put his arm around Elliott's shoulders, lending his body warmth.

"He ruined my library," Elliott said in a small voice.

"I'm sorry. He's a shit-bag. But, Jesus, El. You scared the crap out of me with that text."

Elliott wiped water from his face with the back of his hand. "I wanted to make sure Ish was okay in case . . ."

"In case what? What the hell were you doing over there?" Simon waved angrily in the direction of Burgess's house.

"He ruined my library." Even now, the wrecked books were nothing but soaked little heaps of paper and cardboard, and the remains of the library itself were splattered with mud and storm-tossed dead leaves.

"That's worth going to jail over?"

"I don't know. Maybe nothing I do is worth anything."

"Elliott." Simon sounded stern, an echo of what must have been his cop-voice coloring the name.

They didn't say anything for a minute or two. Elliott sighed. "Thanks for coming over right away."

"Of course! I love you, remember?"

"Is your leg okay?"

Simon shook the leg slightly as if testing it. "Yeah, it's fine. But it's my heart you really should be worried about. You nearly gave me a heart attack today."

That was . . . interesting. Simon was a brave man. He'd faced gun-wielding bad guys, irate homophobic neighbors, and a horde of rejecting family members, all with calm and dignity. But what frightened him was believing Elliott might be in danger. Elliott truly didn't deserve him. If such a good man cared about him, though, loved him, didn't that suggest there was something valuable about Elliott? Something of worth?

Babb and Calvillo got out of their car—reluctantly—and hurried back into Burgess's house. They weren't there for long, and when they left, they headed for Elliott's porch.

"Good to see you, man," Calvillo said, patting Simon's shoulder. "How's the knee?"

"Recovering."

"When are you gonna rejoin us?"

"I'm heading to the Parks Department instead. Ranger."

Both cops seemed interested in that, but after a few moments of chatter, Babb steered them back to the matter at hand. "So, Mr. Thompson. Your story and Burgess's are pretty close, although he keeps insisting your library violated some kind of imaginary city codes." She shook her head. "Anyway, he's willing to forget you broke his phone if you forget he damaged your property. That's up to you, of course. We'll arrest him if you really want us to."

Elliott shook his head. "No." All the anger had left him, flames doused by the rainstorm.

"Good choice. Just stay away from him, okay? We've made it very clear that if he even thinks about entering your property without your permission, he's going to find himself bunking in jail."

"*Very* clear," Calvillo added gleefully. He was short but looked as if he spent a lot of time lifting weights.

"Thank you," said Elliott.

And apparently that settled it, because both cops turned their attention back to Simon. "So, um, you guys are a thing, huh?" Calvillo asked.

Simon answered simply. "Yes."

"That's cool."

The smile that spread across Simon's face was enough to warm Elliott's heart. "Do you want to come inside and dry off? Have some coffee, maybe?"

They spent a half hour together, the four of them. Calvillo ended up sitting on the floor with Ishtar mostly in his lap, and he laughed at how she was getting fur all over his uniform. Babb was interested in some of Elliott's books. Both cops got the rundown on Simon's surgeries and rehab, plus his future career plans, and they told him some of the department's recent gossip. They seemed ready to stay all afternoon, but a call to assist at an accident scene came in. So after a round of handshaking and promises to get together later, they left.

"You're still damp," Simon said as soon as they were gone. "I'm gonna park the truck in the driveway. Go change into something dry before you catch a cold."

"Colds are caused by viruses, not by being wet," Elliott said. But he took a quick hot shower and then put on flannel lounging pants and his old Bulldogs sweatshirt. He emerged from the bedroom with a T-shirt and pair of sweats he hoped would fit Simon and found him in the kitchen, heating a can of soup. Ishtar was supervising.

"Sit," said Simon, pointing at a chair.

"Are you talking to me or the dog?"

Simon shot him a look.

So Elliott and Simon had soup and a sandwich, and then they curled up together on the couch and watched the storm rage. The weather was still miserable. The library was still ruined. But in Elliott's warm, dry living room, with his dog at his feet and Simon pressed against him, even a tempest felt survivable.

Chapter Twenty-Four

Simon stayed. They didn't talk about their future or his family or even Mike fucking Burgess and his library-ruining ways. They watched movies and petted the dog and ate popcorn, and then, when the rain had subsided to a drizzle, they climbed into bed. They didn't make love—Elliott didn't have the energy for it. But they held each other all night, and in some ways that was even better.

On Tuesday morning, Simon woke up early and, while Elliott was still meandering blearily around the kitchen, cleaned up the mess in the front yard. When Simon came inside, he kissed Elliott on the cheek and told him to relax. "I'm taking Ishtar for a walk. We'll stop by my house so I can grab a change of clothes."

Ishtar, of course, started dancing as soon as she heard the *w* word, and she pranced out the front door with Simon, not even sparing a glance for the abandoned Elliott.

Actually, Elliott didn't mind staying home. He felt as if he were recovering from an illness—weak and wobbly, his brain unreliable in its focus. Nevertheless, he managed to clean up the breakfast dishes and shower and shave and then grade a few student assignments. Accurately, he hoped. He didn't like looking out the front window at the absence of his library—the jagged stump like a rotten tooth—so he sat in the kitchen and looked out back instead. The sky was steel colored, but the ground had dried.

He was beginning to wonder whether Simon had abandoned him and kidnapped his dog when the two of them returned. Ishtar tracked muddy footprints over the wood floors, but Simon remained in the entryway, smiling. "Get your shoes and coat."

"Why?"

Simon didn't answer. He just stood there with a sneaky, slightly infuriating little grin that somehow felt like a warm embrace. Because of that, Elliott didn't put much effort into his glare, and he obeyed quickly.

Wherever they were going, it involved Ishtar. She got to ride in the back seat of Simon's truck, which clearly made this a red-letter day for her. She lounged across the bench seat happily, sometimes moving forward to poke her nose at Simon's or Elliott's shoulder. "We need to get her a doggy seat belt," said Simon after they'd gone a few blocks. "Safer."

"Is that where we're going? The pet store?" Elliott wouldn't mind that. It would be a fun little outing.

"Nope."

Since Simon was obviously not going to divulge his plans—and he looked damn smug about it too—Elliott changed his conversational tack. "You're growing your beard back." He'd noticed at some point the previous day but hadn't mentioned it.

Simon ran a palm over the stubble. "Yeah. You mind?"

"I like your beard. I like you clean-shaven. I like you any way I can get you."

"Yeah?" Simon glanced away from the road long enough to flash him a smile. "That's a good thing to know."

"You handled that thing yesterday really well. Handled me, I mean. Burgess too."

"That used to be my job. Someone took a shot at me only once, so that's a pretty good track record."

Elliott shuddered. "What if that bullet had hit you somewhere else? What if—"

"What if, what if. Look, if I hadn't been shot, I wouldn't have been walking past your house. I wouldn't have known about your library, and we would've never met. I'd take a bullet a dozen times over if it meant meeting you."

"Hopefully it won't come to that," Elliott muttered. He took Simon's hand in his.

After several minutes of driving, it became clear they were heading for the foothills. "Columbia?" asked Elliott.

"Nope."

The fall had been wet enough that the rolling hills past Oakdale were beginning to turn green. They made a pretty sight beneath the sky, which had lightened to an ashy shade. If Elliott had possessed any artistic talent, he might have painted this landscape. Or hell, sap that he was, he'd paint Simon standing tall and strong with happiness shining from his eyes.

"Babb and Calvillo didn't freak out," said Simon as he rounded a curve. Oak trees grew here, branches now mostly bare, cows standing around their trunks.

"Well, I probably wasn't the scariest bad guy they've ever faced."

Simon poked Elliott's leg. "About me, I mean. About us."

"Did you expect them to?"

"I don't know. Neither of them ever struck me as a bigot, but I guess at some level I sort of expect everyone to reject me. Except you."

"Not everyone will."

"Yeah." Then Simon's expression brightened. "Miri's been texting me a lot. I guess she's been doing covert efforts on my behalf. A lot of our cousins are on my side, she says. She's working on my parents."

"Will she win them over?"

Simon shrugged. "One of those books I borrowed from you had advice on coming out to family. I've known for a long time that I'm gay, but Mom and Dad had to suddenly confront it head-on. I'm supposed to give them time."

"Sounds like good advice." It was consistent with Elliott's own experiences, in fact.

"Probably. Of course, that author doesn't know my parents."

Elliott squeezed Simon's leg. "But your parents seem like fundamentally good people. And they love you."

"Yeah," Simon responded with a sigh.

They reached Jamestown, another former gold rush town that now boasted a few thousand residents and a small main street with historic buildings. But Simon bypassed downtown—apparently antiquing was not on the agenda—and instead turned onto a side street a few blocks away. Elliott laughed when he became aware of their destination. "Railtown?"

Simon pulled the truck into a parking spot in front of the park. "We had fun with the trains in Sacramento, so I thought we could visit these too. It's okay?"

"Sure."

Ishtar also liked the idea. They took turns holding her leash, and she tugged them around the park, sniffing at everything. She was especially taken with some of the greasier chunks of old metal that had once been train parts. Elliott and Simon let her explore freely. They had the place almost to themselves, and the couple of volunteers on site just gave them friendly waves.

"Too bad it's not a weekend," Simon said. "Then we could do a train ride. They even allow dogs—I checked. I wonder if Ish has ever ridden behind a steam locomotive before."

"Seems doubtful."

A while later, they stopped to read a sign about the movies and TV shows that had been filmed at this location. "*High Noon*," Elliott said. "I could go for that. Want to watch it when we get back? Gary Cooper and Grace Kelly."

"The lawman resigns and runs off with his true love. Sure—I'm up for it."

Elliott hadn't thought of it that way.

They sat on a bench near the roundhouse, where Ishtar nosed at anthills before lying down at their feet. She perked her ears whenever a crow called from a tree nearby. Elliott cleared his throat. "You were mad at me. Before Burgess pulled this shit, I mean."

"I don't know if 'mad' is the right word for it. Frustrated?"

"No, you were angry at me, and that was justifiable. I'd made things fall out of balance between us."

Shaking his head, Simon stroked Ishtar's flank with his shoe. "It wasn't really your fault. It was just life. We make choices and sometimes shit happens. I needed some space to remind myself of that, you know?"

"What would you have done if I hadn't texted you yesterday? Would you have stayed away?"

"No." Simon's deep chuckle warmed Elliott. "I'd already *almost* come over about a thousand times."

"But nothing's changed, has it? We're still imbalanced."

"I guess so. But when my stupid knee fucks with my balance, I keep on walking. I might be slower, but I get where I intended to go."

Elliott joined him in petting Ishtar. *Keep on walking.* Sounded simple enough. The real question was where he wanted to end up. Maybe instead of limping along to nowhere, he ought to change the destination.

They spent a couple of hours at Railtown, wandering slowly and chatting aimlessly, until Elliott noticed that Simon's limp was getting more pronounced. "Want me to fetch your cane?" he asked, hoping Simon had thought to bring it.

"How about if we take off and find something to eat instead?"

They drove a few miles farther uphill into Sonora and parked downtown. Since Ishtar was with them, they couldn't eat inside a restaurant, so Elliott and Ishtar sat on a bench outside a burger place while Simon went in to order. Fifteen minutes later, they had a bag full of food. After rejecting the idea of eating in a little city park, they returned to the truck and ate there. The meal was messy and delicious, and Ishtar got more than her share.

After they collected all the napkins and wrappers and shoved them in the bag, Simon hopped out of the truck to throw the bag away in a nearby trash can. He checked his phone and texted someone, it looked like.

"Ready to head back to the valley?" he asked once he was inside.

"Yeah. Thanks, Si. This outing was a good thing."

Simon leaned in close and they kissed, onion breath and all.

As they drove downhill, Elliott felt oddly at peace. What if his life could be like this forever? Spending some time with online classes, a little more time with his books and research, and then hanging out with Simon. Day trips to the mountains or the coast, maybe a long weekend now and then somewhere farther away. That wasn't what he'd dreamed of when he'd been laboring over his dissertation, and it certainly wasn't the existence John used to promise him.

Perhaps this dream was better. It certainly offered a new destination.

They held hands most of the way home, like high school sweethearts or newlyweds, and Simon tuned the radio to NPR because he knew Elliott preferred it to music. Far to the west, on the other side of the valley, the sun was breaking through the clouds, sending beams of light like messages from the heavens. Elliott hadn't made any decisions, yet he felt as drowsy and content as Ishtar, who was fast asleep on the back seat.

An hour or so of light remained as they reached their neighborhood. Elliott hadn't run that day; maybe he'd get in a quick jog before night fell.

Then Simon turned the corner onto Elliott's street, and Elliott's breath caught in his chest.

A crowd covered his front lawn. Anna and Ladd stood there in matching blue jackets, and Kyle was next to them. Miri was there too, and her brother Ashur, along with a gaggle of younger Odishos Elliott recognized from Thanksgiving but couldn't name. Melanie the Girl Scout was there, and her parents, and some of the neighbors who'd frequented the library. Probably close to thirty people in all, and every one of them was smiling and waving.

Right in the middle of the crowd was a new miniature neighborhood library. Only it wasn't actually all that miniature. This one was mounted where the old one had been, but on a much broader base, which was good because the book enclosure was nearly three feet tall and similarly wide. It held three shelves, all of which were stuffed with books. The enclosure looked like a tiny version of Elliott's house, except it was painted in rainbow colors.

When Simon stopped the truck in the driveway, Ishtar woke up and began wagging her tail wildly, almost frantic to greet everyone. Elliott, stunned, just sat. "Simon?" he whispered.

"Surprise."

"But . . . how?"

"It was easy. Just a bit of research, a few texts. Man, these people were so on top of it, you're lucky they didn't build a book skyscraper while we were gone."

"I don't . . ." Elliott swallowed hard. "Why?"

"With a little help, we can rebuild after any disaster. It's called community. These are your people, El. Well, with a few recent recruits from Miri."

"My people?"

Simon squeezed his shoulder. "Yours."

Everyone started clapping as soon as Elliott got out of the truck. He would have felt horribly awkward, except Ishtar started tearing around, demanding pets from everyone and making them laugh. People dragged him over to admire the library, and then everyone wanted to point out which books they'd contributed and explain why. People were happy. Complete strangers talked to each other about books and dogs and how they knew Elliott, and somehow cookies and pizza materialized and the whole crowd was eating. Simon kept close to Elliott's side, holding his hand and beaming.

Community. It was a hell of a lot more beautiful and valuable than tenure and academic acclaim.

"Your people," Simon whispered in Elliott's ear.

Elliott whispered back. "Yours too."

Then he pulled his phone from his pocket and punched in a number. He was shunted to voice mail, which he'd expected.

"Hi, Ginny? This is Elliott Thompson. I want to say how much I appreciate that you were willing to give me a chance. Something's come up, however. Actually, I've fallen in love. So best of luck with your search—but I'll be staying in Modesto."

He ended the call, tucked the phone away, and fell into Simon's fierce embrace.

# Epilogue

"Oh God." Elliott looked around in horror.

Standing behind him, Simon thumped Elliott's shoulder. "I warned you it would be bad. Wildlife, remember?"

"The spiders have built entire civilizations."

"Let's hope their weaponry hasn't evolved yet."

Cleaning out the downstairs of Simon's house had been easy. Several of his older relatives had happily laid claim to the furniture, and it took only a couple of truckloads to transport Simon's clothing and other personal effects to Elliott's closet and drawers—which were now Simon's closet and drawers as well.

But the second floor of Simon's house was another story. One bedroom was a museum to his childhood, with everything from kindergarten artwork to high school yearbooks tucked away in overstuffed, dust-festooned cardboard boxes. His long-lost Legos were undoubtedly in there somewhere. The other bedroom held hideous furniture his parents had saved for the apocalypse, along with boxes containing holiday decorations, table linens, and enough dishware to serve half the county. Spiderwebs stretched everywhere, and Elliott itched just looking at them.

"Can't we walk away and leave all this?" he whined.

"Nope. Can't sell the place until we clear this out."

That statement referred to the first major thaw in Simon's relationship with his extended family, which had occurred the previous month at Aunt Soso's annual Christmas party. Well, the first thaw had actually occurred when Aunt Soso insisted that Simon attend the gathering—with Elliott—and when Simon's parents had shown up knowing he'd be there. They'd greeted Simon stiffly and nodded at

Elliott. Then, at the point in the evening when almost everyone had imbibed a few glasses of holiday cheer and as Elliott and Simon were standing quietly in a corner of the kitchen, Sargon and Nahrina had approached them.

"Miri says you have moved to his house." Nahrina waved a hand toward Elliott.

"Yeah. So if you want your keys back or—"

"We want to sell the house you lived in. No use keeping it now."

Simon's shoulders slumped a little. "Okay. Most of my stuff's out already. I'll get the rest out."

"After the holidays. Nobody buys a house now."

"Okay."

Sargon pointed at Simon. "You take care of selling it. We have no time for that." His stern expression eased a little. "You keep half the money."

"It will help settle your new life," Nahrina added. With that somewhat enigmatic comment, she sailed away, taking Sargon with her.

Since then, Simon had spoken with them briefly a few times, mostly about the contents of the house. Those bits of communication weren't huge progress, but they were something, and Elliott could tell they'd lifted a great deal of Simon's emotional burden.

Now Elliott looked around the room in dread. "How about if we tackle this later? I bet Ishtar wants to go for a run." They'd left her at home, knowing she wouldn't be much help during a cleaning project.

"You guys ran already today. She's fast asleep." Simon gave Elliott's ass a friendly pat. "Shirker."

"You and I could get another kind of exercise instead." Elliott waggled his eyebrows.

"Are you trying to seduce me out of this job?"

"Yes."

"Hmm." Simon dropped the broom and pulled Elliott close, then nibbled on his earlobe. "That may be negotiable."

Elliott entered into negotiations by sliding his hand down the back of Simon's jeans. Before Simon could make a counteroffer, his phone buzzed.

"Damn it," he said.

Elliott disengaged his hand as Simon pulled out the phone.

"Miri," he said with a frown. "She needs to talk to us."

A half hour later, after Simon and Elliott had returned home, Miri's little Honda pulled into the driveway. Elliott greeted her at the front door while Simon held Ishtar's collar in an attempt to moderate her enthusiasm. Simon did a double take when he saw who was with Miri.

"Mom?" he said, his voice slightly choked.

She cast him a stern look over Elliott's shoulder. "We need to talk."

"Is Dad okay?"

Nahrina blew an annoyed puff of air. "He is home, watching television. Football playoffs." Judging from her expression, she wasn't a fan.

She'd never been to their house, so once Ishtar calmed down, Elliott gave her a quick tour while Simon made coffee. She seemed interested in Elliott's gardening books, so he lent her some.

"This library you have, Miri told me about it. Now I see them in your neighbors' yards too."

That made him smile. While his version remained the largest, miniature neighborhood libraries had popped up in several front yards over the past weeks, each uniquely designed. He'd contributed books to several of them. Burgess, of course, hadn't built one, but a For Sale sign had appeared in front of his house, and Elliott had high hopes for a good temperament in his future neighbor. "Yeah. I guess it's kind of a thing now."

"Do you have books in Assyrian?"

"I don't think so."

She nodded as if that settled something. "I will give you some."

"I'd love that."

A few minutes later, they all settled into the living room. Nahrina held her coffee as regally as a queen, but Miri fidgeted and petted Ishtar. Small talk fizzled. Simon looked as if he was running out of patience—a feeling Elliott was beginning to share.

And then at last, Miri scrunched up her face. "So there's this baby thing." She patted her belly, which had begun to grow.

"Baby thing?" Simon asked.

"My baby. Only, jeez, I'm not even twenty, and I really want to keep going to school, and I don't think I'm mature enough to make a good mom. Someday, sure, when I'm, like . . . old. But not now."

Elliott and Simon exchanged a puzzled glance before Simon replied, "We'll support you, whatever you decide, Miri. You know that."

"Good. 'Cause what I've decided is to ask you to be her daddies."

Simon's mouth fell open. It would have been almost comical if Elliott could have managed to breathe.

"What?" Simon squeaked.

"Her daddies. If you want to. I've always known you'd be the world's most awesome dad, Simon, like blue-ribbon award-winning. And Elliott, God, you're spectacular. I can picture you reading to her, teaching her." She sniffled slightly. "You'd both be perfect."

"Her?" was all Simon could say—which was still more than Elliott could manage.

Miri shrugged. "Or him. Whatever."

"But this is your baby."

"You guys would make way better parents than me. I'd be really happy just to be the way-cool aunt, you know?" She chewed her lip. "Not that I want to force you into anything. I know this is, like, huge. But I feel like it's the right way to go." She held both hands clasped against her chest.

Although Simon turned toward him, Elliott remained too stunned to speak. Stunned and . . . excited. His heart was racing. He felt as if he was on the verge of receiving the most wonderful gift ever. And Simon? His eyes *glowed*.

"Mom?" Simon said very quietly, looking at her.

She set her mug down. "You will be a good father. You will both be. It is always best for a child to have two parents. One should be a mother." She shrugged. "This one can have a grandmother instead."

"I . . . I . . ." Simon grabbed Elliott's hand, held it tightly, and finally managed to speak. "El and I have to talk about this. It's a big decision. Huge. It's—"

Elliott stopped him with a gentle stroke of Simon's beard. "Do you want this?"

His lower lip slightly wobbly, Simon nodded.

Elliott had never felt so warm and big and important. Maybe his career wasn't as prestigious as he'd once imagined, but that faded away in favor of what was truly consequential. Love. Family. The very best of new beginnings. "I do too," Elliott said.

There were some tears after that and a lot of hugging, and Nahrina pinched Simon's cheek and then Elliott's, and Ishtar knocked over a stack of books with her tail. Then Miri and Nahrina pulled out phones and began texting the entire clan.

Elliott and Simon held each other tightly.

"Baby books," Simon said. "We'll need to stock up on baby books."

Elliott kissed Simon's cheek. "Let's start with *Goodnight Moon*."

Also by Kim Fielding

Ante Up
Running Blind
Staged
Love Is Heartless
Love Can't Conquer
Rattlesnake
Astounding!
Motel. Pool.
Pilgrimage
The Tin Box
Brute
Venetian Masks
Good Bones
Buried Bones
Bone Dry
Stasis
Flux
Equipoise
Corruption
Clay White
Grown-Up
The Pillar
Housekeeping
Night Shift
Speechless
Guarded
Treasure
The Downs

About The Author

Kim Fielding is the best-selling author of numerous m/m romance novels, novellas, and short stories. Like Kim herself, her work is eclectic, spanning genres such as contemporary, fantasy, paranormal, and historical. Her stories are set in alternate worlds, in fifteenth-century Bosnia, in modern-day Oregon. Her heroes are hipster architect werewolves, housekeepers, maimed giants, and conflicted graduate students. They're usually flawed, they often encounter terrible obstacles, but they always find love.

After having migrated back and forth across the western two-thirds of the United States, Kim calls the boring part of California home. She lives there with her husband, her daughters, and her day job as a university professor, but escapes as often as possible via car, train, plane, or boat. This may explain why her characters often seem to be in transit as well. She dreams of traveling and writing full-time.

Website: kfieldingwrites.com
Facebook: facebook.com/kfieldingwrites
Twitter: @KFieldingWrites
Instagram: instagram.com/kfieldingwrites

www.ingramcontent.com/pod-product-compliance
Lightning Source LLC
Chambersburg PA
CBHW061236210726
48293CB00003B/791